GO THERE.

OTHER TITLES AVAILABLE FROM PUSH

TYRELL

COE BOOTH

SCHOLASTIC INC.

NEW YORK   TORONTO   LONDON   AUCKLAND   SYDNEY
MEXICO CITY   NEW DELHI   HONG KONG   BUENOS AIRES

ISBN 0-439-83879-7

Library of Congress Cataloging-in-Publication Data

Booth, Coe.
  Tyrell / Coe Booth.
     p.   cm.
  Summary: Fifteen-year-old Tyrell, who is living in a Bronx homeless shelter with his spaced-out mother and his younger brother, tries to avoid temptation so he does not end up in jail like his father.
  ISBN 0-439-83879-7 (hardcover)
  [1. Homeless persons—Fiction.   2. Poor—Fiction. 3. African Americans—Fiction.   4. Bronx (New York, N.Y.)—Fiction. I. Title.
  PZ7.B64632Ty 2006
  [Fic]—dc22
                              2005037330

12 11 10 9 8 7 6 5 4 3   7 8 9 10 11/0

Printed in the U.S.A.   23
First printing, October 2006

for daddy

ACKNOWLEDGMENTS

I would like to thank my family: Mom, Lisa, Rashid, Mike, Haadiya, Micayla, Alyssa, Hamza, and Hasan for always supporting me and believing in me; Samantha for reading and *re-reading* everything I've ever written and encouraging me to keep writing anyway; Denise, Tammy, Karen, Mark, Faith, and Sheiba for inspiring me and pushing me to finish this novel; Sarah Weeks for helping me nourish this idea; the writing group at The New School: Caroline, Chris, Emmy, Jenny, Kathryne, Krissi, Lisa, Lisa GW, Melinda, and Randi for being so enthusiastic from the very beginning; my NAACP ACT-SO students for giving me more than I gave them; DJ Pete La Rock for his expertise in everything old-skool; and, of course, David Levithan for giving me the freedom to tell this story my way and for being the best editor I could have asked for.

ONE

When I pick Novisha up from school, she actin' all weird and shit. I mean, she the one that called my cell this morning and told me she needed to talk. Then all the way to her place it's like she wanna say something but don't know how to tell me. So we just walk without saying a whole lot, which is alright 'cause I got a lot on my mind anyway.

Novisha live in the Bronxwood Houses. I don't mind walking her all this way 'cause this place is still like my home even though we moved from here a couple years ago. Back in the day, these eight buildings was my whole world. I used to do some stupid shit 'round here with my boys. But I don't hardly get to hang with them no more. Not like I used to.

Matter of fact, I don't even get to see Novisha everyday no more. Our buildings used to be right 'cross the parking lot from each other. Now I gotta take two trains just to see her.

When we get to her building, I don't really wanna go upstairs 'cause I know her moms don't work on Fridays, and she gonna be

1

there making sure me and Novisha don't do nothing. I mean, her moms is cool and everything. She always cooking stuff for me and sending me home with all kinds of food for my family, but I know she only doing it 'cause she feel sorry for us.

When we get upstairs, not only is her moms there, but her pops is there too. He sitting at the kitchen table eating pork chops and rice like he live there. Like he ain't walk out on them a couple years ago. Novisha moms is cleaning up the kitchen and watching some shopping show on TV. "Hi, Tyrell," she say. "How's everything? Your family hanging in there?"

"Yeah, Ms. Jenkins," I say. "We doing okay. Hi, Mr. Jenkins."

He kinda wave at me, mouth full of food. Asshole. A couple weeks ago I walked Novisha home and we heard him and her moms going at it in the bedroom all loud and shit. Then when he was done he just up and left like that was all he wanted. That and some good food.

"You hungry?" Ms. Jenkins ask me. But before I can even answer, she putting a ton of rice on a plate for me.

"Eat," Novisha tell me. "I wanna change my clothes." She go to this Catholic school and gotta wear this blue uniform with this short plaid skirt. It's so goddamn sexy, but she hate it and can never wait to change outta it.

I'm so hungry I just sit there and eat the pork chop in like two bites, then wolf the rice down like I ain't never ate nothing before. Meanwhile, Ms. Jenkins is just talking on and on 'bout how me and my family need to stay close and keep our faith in God strong while we going through hard times. I nod every couple minutes so she think I'm really listening, but to be honest,

I'm really tired of everyone saying that. Like they know what we going through.

Novisha come outta her bedroom in sweatpants and a T-shirt. No matter what she wear, she still look cute as hell. She got a real pretty face, and even though she only five foot, she got a bangin' little body. And she only fourteen years old.

Novisha tell her moms 'bout some weekend trip she wanna take with her school in March to go look at some Black colleges down south. "Slow down, girl," Ms. Jenkins tell her, pouring the pork chop oil from the frying pan into a old Maxwell House can. "You're only a freshman. You don't have to think about college for a couple of years."

Novisha roll her eyes.

Mr. Jenkins sit back in his chair like he all full and satisfied. "Bonelle," he say to Ms. Jenkins, looking at his watch, "you still want me to fix that VCR in your bedroom? I got a little time before my shift starts."

Me and Novisha look at each other like this guy think he slick.

Ms. Jenkins tell him okay, then they go into the bedroom and close the door.

"Your pops is a real playa," I tell Novisha.

"I don't wanna talk about it," she say. "It's disgusting." We go in her room and lock the door. Another thing I like 'bout Novisha is that she still like a little girl. Her room is all decorated with posters of them little pretty-boy singers, and she still got stuffed animals and shit. Two seconds later she pulling her T-shirt over her head and I'm kissing her and feeling her up. Then she go over to this little tiny statue of St. Mary she got on the shelf over

3

her bed and turn it 'round so it face the wall. She do this every time she 'bout to do some nasty shit, so St. Mary can't see her. I can't help but smile 'cause I never expect nothing on a Friday, so it's a good thing her pops is there to keep her moms busy.

Novisha is still a virgin and she ain't giving it up 'til she married. She don't even let me put my hand in her panties or nothing. But she do like blowing me. I'm the only guy she ever did it to, but she real good at it. She know how to take care of me.

When we done we go back out to the living room so her moms don't know what we just did. They still in the bedroom, but we can't hear nothing this time. So we just chillin', sitting on the couch watching TV, leaning against each other. She got her hands in my hair, rubbing my head. "Your hair's long enough for me to braid now," she say.

"Yeah?"

"C'mon, let me do it now."

"I ain't got time today. Next time, okay?"

"Alright." She go back to rubbing my head, which feel real good.

It's nice just being like this, here in this room. I been coming to this apartment forever, and this living room ain't never changed. That's what I like 'bout it. Ms. Jenkins still got that same big ol' console TV that ain't never worked and the little 19-inch TV on top of it. She got the same couch and chair with the same plastic slipcovers on them, and the same Jesus and Mary paintings covering the water stains on the wall. And everything is real clean like it always is. That's another thing I like 'bout Ms. Jenkins apartment. When I'm here, I could forget I'm in the projects.

Even though me and Novisha is relaxing together, I can tell she still got something on her mind. "What's up with you?" I

4

ask her. "You acting all quiet today. What you wanna talk to me 'bout?"

She shake her head. "Nothing. I just, you know, wanted to see you. And be with you." We kiss. Novisha the first girl I really like kissing. She wear this cherry lip gloss, and her lips always taste all sweet and juicy.

But even while we kissing, I feel like she ain't really into it, so I stop and look at her. She look away.

"C'mon, Novisha," I say. "You the one that always, like, we need to talk and all that. You keeping secrets? 'Cause I got too much on my mind these days and I don't need my girl keeping things from me."

"I'm not keeping anything from you." She take a deep breath. "It's just, well, there's this new guy at school and he's —" She shake her head again. "I don't know why I'm telling you this, but he's always bothering me."

Now I'm mad. "Bothering you how? I don't wanna hafta kick some nigga ass today, but I will."

She sigh. "That's why I didn't wanna tell you. I don't want you acting like some thug who's gonna —"

"What he doing to you?"

"Nothing." She look at me, and she know I don't believe a word she saying. "Okay. He asked me out a few times. But I told him I have a man."

I like it when she call me her man. That kinda calm me down for a second.

"Then last week, I was standing at the candy machine and he comes up and puts his arm around my waist and tells me he's gonna buy me anything I want."

I can feel my blood pumping through my body fast again.

"I told him to get his nasty hands off me, and he did. Then after that I keep finding these notes in my locker, saying he wants to, you know, get with me and stuff. I know it's him. Then yesterday, I'm walking down the hall and I feel someone grab my butt. I turn around and see him just smiling at me like a dog."

I can see that she getting tears in her eyes, and I don't like to see that. I'ma hafta do something to this guy. I can't have some dude thinking he can touch my girl whenever he want.

"You got them letters?" I ask her.

She get up and go to her room, then come back with two letters all folded up. She give them to me. One of them say, "I fantasize about you every night." The other one say, "When are you going to get with me? Let a brother know." My blood feel like it's on fire now.

"There were more, but I threw them away."

"You know where he live at?" She shake her head, but I can tell she lying. "What, you trying to protect this guy?"

"No. I'm trying to protect *you*." She grab my hand. "I don't want you to end up like —" She stop talking and look away. Then she whisper, "I'm sorry, Ty."

I push her away from me and stand up. "I gotta go." I'm outta there before she can say anything else to piss me off. I fly down the hallway and keep punching the down button for the elevator 'til it come. In the elevator, I punch the lobby button over and over 'til my hand hurt.

When I get outside I walk 'round the projects trying to cool myself down. Even though it's real cold, it's still a nice sunny day for the end of January. But the weather ain't helping me none. I wish I knew who this guy is and where he live at. I swear.

I walk 'round some more, buy a loose cigarette from the bodega on the corner, smoke it and feel myself calming down a little. Novisha right. I know she just looking out for me. She don't want me ending up like my pops. In jail. Again.

TWO

I get back to the EAU a little after 6:00. There ain't ever enough room inside for everyone, so as usual there's more people standing out in front of the place than inside. Mothers and children. That's all I see. Moms and they kids. No fathers nowhere.

My seven-year-old brother, Troy, is playing with my basketball out in front of the building, throwing it up against the wall and catching it, acting like it's summer out here. My moms is outside too, leaning against a van, smoking with some other woman. All our stuff is packed up in one tore up black suitcase and two garbage bags on the ground by my moms. I wanna ask her if they found us a place, but I just glare at her and walk by without saying a word. I don't got nothing to say to her no more.

Troy throw the ball against the wall and it fly over his head into the street. He 'bout to go chase after it without even looking to see if cars is coming, and my moms ain't even paying him no mind.

I call Troy and he stop right before he get to the street. Then

I go get the ball myself. He hold up his hands like I'ma throw it to him. "Ain't you too old to be running in the street for a ball?" I ask him.

"I wasn't gonna run in the street," he say with his hands still in the air. "Come on, Ty, gimme the ball!"

"First tell me you ain't gonna run in the street no more."

"I said I wasn't, right?"

I fake a move like I'ma throw him the ball and watch him jump to catch it. Then I laugh and dribble the ball, just to mess with him a little. "Now tell me you ain't gonna take my stuff no more 'less you ask first."

"Okay, okay."

I finally throw him the ball, then I walk back over to my moms. Just as I'm 'bout to ask her for money, she say, "If you hungry, you better get on in there and get yourself something to eat."

"I ain't eating no more of that nasty EAU food," I tell her.

"What you gonna eat then? I ain't got no money for McDonald's, so don't even ask."

"I ate at Novisha house. Real food."

"What, Ms. Jenkins didn't send us nothing this time?"

"Nah. She was busy when I left."

My moms suck her teeth. "Well, tell her I said thanks."

I hate when my moms get that way, always thinking everybody owe her something. "You look for a job?" I ask her.

"You know I went to see your father today."

I just shake my head 'cause I know she ain't never gonna change, no matter what that man do. We ain't never gonna get a apartment of our own 'cause she gotta go to Rikers Island when she need to be looking for a job. Not that she know how to do anything anyway.

"You get the mail?" my moms ask me, even though she know I always do.

I go in my backpack and get the mail for her. "I had to pay for the box. And there's a bill from the storage place that we gotta pay by the first of the month."

My moms flip through the mail. "I don't know how they expect me to pay all these bills when I don't got no job. They just wasting stamps."

She go on and on, talking junk, and I stop listening. 'Cross the street I see a woman and a teenage girl coming down the block. I can tell they coming to the EAU by the size of the duffel bags they carrying, like they got everything they own in there. They look as lost as my family looked two weeks ago when we got here, like they don't got nowhere else to go. Just like us.

The woman go inside while the girl drop her bag on the ground and light up a cigarette outside. She wipe some tears off her face real slick, like she trying to hide the fact that she crying. I go up to her 'cause I feel kinda sorry for her. And 'cause she got a real nice body in tight, tight, *tight* jeans.

"This place ain't all that bad," I tell her.

She shake her head. "You just saying that to make me feel better." She look up at the building, then roll her eyes when she see the big sign over the door: NEW YORK CITY — EMERGENCY ASSISTANCE UNIT. "We actually have to sleep here?" She make a face.

"Nah. The city don't let them keep us here at night. If they don't find us a place, they send us to some cheap-ass motels to sleep. This is Friday, so if they ain't found nothing for us yet, they ain't gonna look again 'til Monday. We gonna be stuck wherever they send us."

10

She offer me some of her cigarette. I tell her no 'cause she look like she really need the whole thing herself. "How long do I have to go through this?" she ask.

"A few days, pro'ly. Then they gonna put y'all in a Tier II shelter. It's kinda like a apartment. I mean, you and your moms can stay there for a while."

"That's my big sister, Reyna. She's my guardian, if you can call her that." She wipe more tears away with her free hand. "You been through this before?"

"Yeah. A couple years ago."

"What's your name?"

"Tyrell."

"I'm Jasmine."

"That's a real nice name," I say 'cause I can't think of nothing really cool to say. She smile a little. She look good. Puerto Rican, I think, 'cause she got that light skin and long dark hair. Her face got some acne and shit, but her body make up for it. I mean, she kinda big, but she got it all in the right places. Straight up, she got them jeans working.

My moms call me over again, interrupting my flow. "Ty, go to the store for me," she say when I get over there. "Get you and your brother some chips or something. And get me a Pepsi and a pack of Juicy Fruit."

"You think you can watch Troy this time?" I ask her. "I mean, he only like ten feet away from you, and you not even watching him. He almost just ran out in the street after a ball."

"He wasn't gonna run out in no street. He ain't stupid."

"Then why you got him in special ed?"

She ignore me. "And get me some of them chocolate donuts with the sprinkles on them." She hand me a five-dollar bill.

11

"Thought you ain't have no money." I walk away before she can tell me another lie.

"If you going to the store, I'll go with you," Jasmine say when I get back over to where she standing. "I need another pack of cigarettes."

"You shouldn't smoke so much. It ain't good for you."

"You don't smoke?" She look like she shocked or something.

"Yeah, I do, but I only buy loose. That don't count."

She laugh and even I gotta laugh at myself. We walk down the block together and, by the time we get to the store, I can tell she like me. She keep talking and talking and laughing at everything I say, even when I say shit that ain't funny. On the way back from the store, she say she hope we get sent to the same motel.

I'm all smooth when I say, "Yeah?"

She smile, and for the first time I see that she got braces on her teeth. Damn. Now I gotta let go of some of them nasty thoughts I was thinking. Shit. Braces can really mess a brotha up!

"Yeah," she say, looking me straight in the eyes. "My sister's going out tonight. We could hang out together."

I look down the block and see that the buses is there already. "Oh, shit."

Jasmine laugh, then she start running down the block like she wanna race or something.

"Slow down," I say, running after her. I'm not in the mood to chase nobody, but I don't got no choice. The girl got a hot body, she nice, and she like me. What the hell else I'm s'posed to do?

THREE

On the bus, Jasmine get all sad, and them tears start running down her face again. The bus they got us on is one of them yellow school bus types. It's all old and broke down. There's 'bout twenty-five people on it, but we ain't all going to the same motel. They gonna make three stops. Two social workers from the EAU is on the bus too. They sitting in the front seat like they always do, talking to each other. They don't never look back. Like they don't even wanna see us or something.

Me and Jasmine is in the back. Last row. I always sit in the back so I can see everyone. All the guys my age is in the back. Most of them is just talking 'bout girls and cracking jokes and shit. Acting like they ain't going through none of this.

The mothers and young kids is sitting in the middle of the bus making the most noise, 'specially with all them kids jumping from seat to seat like they playing some game. Troy doing the same thing them other kids is doing, acting like he ain't got no kinda sense. Most of the babies on the bus is crying.

And the women on the bus is just talking and talking 'bout nothing.

Some woman is telling my moms 'bout how her landlord threw them out just 'cause they couldn't pay the rent, and how she went to a fair hearing, but the judge took the landlord side just 'cause they was both White. Everyone on this bus got some excuse for why they here. None of it is they fault.

Jasmine rest her head on my shoulder like we been friends for years or something and keep crying. My cell ring. I know I seen the number on the caller ID before, but I can't remember who it belong to. The cell keep ringing. I flip it open and answer.

"Ty, it's Dante." Damn. I can't stand that nigga. "Went to see your pops the other day," he say, "and he gave me your cell phone number. Man, I couldn't believe it when he told me y'all was back in the shelter. Why y'all ain't call me?"

I wanna say it's 'cause you say you my pops friend, but the second he out the picture, you try everything you can to get in my moms pants. But I know he just gonna lie and deny everything. Nigga couldn't tell the truth if there was a gun to his head. "We a'ight, Dante," I say, and can't help but look 'round this sorry-ass bus we on, on our way to another nasty motel. We been doing this shit for two weeks now, and I gotta admit, the whole thing getting old. But I ain't 'bout to tell that to Dante. I don't want him thinking we need him or something.

"Well, y'all should of called me before y'all lost the apartment. Me and your pops go way back. Man, I was there when he met your moms."

"I know, Dante."

"And you know I could of helped y'all out with money while your pops is away."

"Yeah, I know, Dante, but —"

"Now your pops told your moms to contact me, but I ain't heard from her."

I don't say nothing.

"Me and your pops talked for a long time, Ty, and he wants me to do what I can to get y'all out of that shelter, you hear me?"

I hear him talking, but I ain't listening to his words. I'm waiting to find out what he really calling me for. Dante ain't never done nothing 'less there was something in it for him. Either he trying to get my moms or he trying to get ahold of my pops equipment. We don't got nothing else.

"So, I was thinking. You know, it don't make no sense for all your pops equipment to just sit there when I can be out there making money with it. And of course I'll give y'all a cut of the money so y'all can get out of that shelter and back into an apartment. So, see, we both win."

I try not to sound mad when I tell him, "I know my pops ain't say you could use his shit."

"Well, not in them words —"

"Look, Dante, I gotta go, a'ight?"

"But, look, Ty, me and you, we got to get together and talk about this, okay?"

"Bye," I say, and flip the cell closed. I knew that nigga was trying something.

I'm 'bout to say something to Jasmine to get her to stop crying, but my cell ring again right away. It's Novisha. "I just wanted to make sure you were okay," she say. Her voice is extra sweet and

15

soft, the way it always is after I get mad. "I don't like when you're upset with me."

"I ain't upset with you," I tell her, trying to keep my voice kinda low so Jasmine won't hear, even though she in her own world right 'bout now. "I just don't like when you keep stuff from me, 'specially when you got some nigga stalking you."

"He's not stalking me, Ty. Anyway, if anything else happens, I'll tell you. I'll even tell the guidance counselor. Okay?"

"Yeah, okay. Just make sure you keep it real with me. I don't like secrets. You know that."

"Yeah, I know. Where are you?"

"On the bus. They taking us to some shelter in Hunts Point."

"Hunts Point? God, that's got to be bad."

"It ain't gonna be good. Look, Novisha, I gotta go. My prepaid is 'bout to run out." It's a lie, but I ain't in the mood to talk 'bout nothing right now. I just want time to think.

Novisha start talking fast now. "Okay, I'll let you go, but I just wanted to remind you about my awards ceremony. It's at my school tomorrow at two. You're still gonna come, right?"

I forgot all 'bout that shit. "Yeah. I'm coming."

"Good. It wouldn't be any fun without you. Oh, and my father gave me fifty dollars before he left — guilt money — so I'm gonna buy you another prepaid card. I wanna make sure I can always talk to my man, no matter where they send you."

"Nah, Novisha, you don't gotta do that. That's your money."

She sigh. "Why don't you ever let people do nice things for you? I love you."

Damn. That make me feel so good, I can't even explain it. "A'ight. But only a twenty-five-dollar card. Take the rest of that

16

money and buy yourself something nice, a'ight? Don't worry 'bout me. I can handle myself. You know that."

"I know, baby," she whisper. "See you tomorrow."

I close the phone. Jasmine is still crying, and she ain't even trying to hide it no more. The girl is a mess. I don't know why, but I put my arm 'round her. "It ain't gonna be so bad," I tell her. "It's only a couple days."

She look all worried and shit. I don't even think she hear a word I say. After a while she ask me, "Who's Novisha? Your girl-friend?"

"Yeah," I say. "She my girl." I think of Novisha cute little face and I wanna smile, but I hold it in. I don't want Jasmine thinking I'm in love or something.

"I should of figured you had a girlfriend. All the good ones do."

I smile. "Who said I'm good?"

"I can tell," she say. "You a good guy."

She get all comfortable on my shoulder and, by the time the bus make the first stop at a motel near the Reservoir, she 'sleep. Just like that. If I move my arm, she gonna wake up, so I just stay still.

While one of the social workers read off the names of the families going to this motel, I look out the window at the scene going on 'cross the street from the motel. In front of a liquor store, two drunk Mexicans is screaming at each other, and all they friends is trying to keep them from fighting. The guy from the store is screaming too, but he got a shovel in his hand and he swinging it 'round, trying to get them to move from his store. People is walking up and down the street like nothing is going on. Like it's just another night in the Bronx.

I shake my head and close my eyes for a second. Then I try to figure out what Jasmine meant when she said I was a good guy. She just met me. How she know what kinda guy I am? I hope she don't think I'm all soft and shit, 'cause that would just make me mad. I don't want people looking at me and thinking that. Not now. Not when I got so much pressure on me.

FOUR

I shoulda knew they was gonna send us to the Bennett Motel. Some niggas I was talking to last week told me 'bout this place. They had me rolling, talking 'bout how Bennett got rats the size of cats and shit. One dude said his room had bullet holes in the walls and bloodstains on the rug. This other guy said the roaches was getting paid to run Bennett, that the roaches signed you in and took you to your room, and that Bennett even hired roaches that would come to your room to kill other roaches. Man, that shit was funny.

But there ain't nothing funny no more. The place look like a bombed-out building from the outside, like something you see in them war movies. Inside it ain't no better. The place stink like old sneakers, probably 'cause there ain't no fresh air in here. That's the first thing I notice.

The next thing I notice is how busted the lobby look with all these old chairs and couches that got holes with stuffing hanging out of them. The floors is dirty and look like they ain't never been mopped. In one corner of the room they got Burger King bags, food wrappers, and soda cans and shit all over the floor. Then they got these plastic flowers on all the tables like that gonna make the place look nice, like that gonna make us feel right at home here. Assholes.

The women line up at the front desk to sign they family in. Jasmine don't say nothing 'cause she probably in as much shock as the rest of us. Even them guys from the bus ain't making no jokes now. 'Bout ten minutes later Reyna come over and tell Jasmine they going to room 207. "C'mon," Jasmine say.

Jasmine give me a little wave and whisper, "Come over later."

I don't say nothing. I just watch her walk away. Damn. Her ass could make a brotha forget his problems for a little while, but I gotta stay focused. Keep my shit together.

The second we get in our room, my moms shake her head. "Ty, can you believe this shit? Why they got us here? I got a seven-year-old *child*!"

I don't say nothing. This whole situation got me so mad I know I gotta keep my mouth closed. I need to keep all this shit inside and wait 'til it all settle back down again.

"How they gonna do us like this?" she ask. "They gonna have *children* sleeping here for three nights? I don't get this."

My moms go on and on, and I just stop listening. I'm tired of the way she act, like everyone s'posed to do everything for her all the time. Even if she don't do nothing. Even when my pops was home, she never did nothing for herself. She just sat 'round expecting him to do everything for her and buy her things. No matter how he got them.

Troy start crying and my moms don't do nothing to help

him, so I go through the garbage bag and find some sweatpants for him to sleep in. Then I tell him to go to the bathroom and get ready for bed. Five seconds later he call me 'cause there's a roach in the sink. I take off my beat up old jacket, then go in there and kill the roach with some toilet paper. While I'm in there, I kill two more I see on the wall. Then when I come out, my moms is on my cell talking to one of her friends.

"That's my phone," I say, and try to snatch it from her.

She push me away. "Get out my face, Ty."

"You using all my minutes. Damn." I sit down on one of the beds, mad. How she gonna go through my jacket and take my shit without asking? I hate that.

Troy come out the bathroom. "Go to bed," I tell him. I don't want him staying up and seeing how jacked up this room really is.

"I wanna watch TV," he say.

"Just go to bed. You can watch TV tomorrow."

He so tired he don't even fight me. He just lay down on the other bed and pull the blanket over him, which is good 'cause a big roach is crawling on the wall right by his bed. I don't kill it 'cause I know it ain't gonna matter. This motel got more problems than just some roaches.

Our room ain't got no bullet holes or blood or nothing like that, but the paint is all dirty and peeling and the rug is all worn out and shit. They got two double beds in this room with blankets but no sheets, and the mattresses is tore up. Bennett is the worst. So far.

My moms use up the last ten minutes on my prepaid and throw my cell on the bed. Then she just turn on me. "What your lazy ass doing?"

"What that s'posed to mean?" Man, I ain't got time for this.

She fold her arms in front of her. "It mean, what you doing for this family? Why ain't you doing something so your mother and brother don't gotta live like this?"

For a second I try to hold it in 'cause I want Troy to sleep, but I can't this time. Before I know it, I'm off the bed, screaming back, "What I'm s'posed to do?"

"You never do nothing. Look at you. You don't go to school 'cause you too damn lazy and ign'ant. And when you do get your Black ass to school, all you do is fight and get in trouble, and I gotta go down there every other day to talk to that goddamn vice principal."

"What else you got to do? Don't talk about lazy. What *you* doing for this family?"

She don't hear me. She just keep on going. "You don't go to school and you don't even work. You damn near sixteen. What kinda man you gonna be? Some lazy-ass nigga?"

I get right in her face now. "What you want? You want me to go out there and sell weed? That what you want?"

She don't back down none. "We wouldn't be at Bennett if you *was* out there, would we?"

Troy start crying again, and my moms move away from me. She start walking 'round the room like she some kinda animal trying to get outta her cage. "Tyrell, you gotta do something. This shit is serious now." She ain't screaming no more, but she look real mad and real scared. "You spend all your time walking around the streets and screwing that little girl, but that don't make you a man, you understand what I'm saying? A man gotta take care of his family."

"Well, what your man doing for his family? You want me to take care of you 'cause your man can't keep his ass outta Rikers. Well, that ain't my problem. That's your problem."

I grab my cell and my jacket, open the door, and I'm gone. I get in the hall and just wanna punch or kick something. I make a fist and rub it into my other hand, but I really wanna put my fist through the wall. I can't calm myself down. I can feel the blood pounding in my brain. I gotta do something. I wanna go somewhere, but I don't got nowhere to go.

FIVE

I walk down the hall. When I get to room 207, I knock on the door. Reyna open it, and all she got on is a towel. "I'm not gone yet," she tell me, folding her arms in front of her and looking at me like there's something wrong with me. She turn to Jasmine. "Tell your boyfriends to come over *after* I leave, okay?"

Jasmine is sitting on the bed watching TV. "Be quiet," she tell her sister. Then she get up and come to the door. "Come in, Tyrell."

I shake my head. "Nah, I just wanna say bye, that's all. I ain't staying in this place."

"Where you going?" she ask, like she worried 'bout me or something.

"I don't know. It don't matter."

Jasmine grab my arm. "You can stay here. My sister is on her way out anyway."

Reyna roll her eyes at me. Then she say, "Yeah, stay. God forbid my sister spend a night alone."

Jasmine glare at her sister. "Shut up. You don't know anything about me."

"I know *everything* about you. You want me to tell him all about you?"

Jasmine seem like she don't wanna get into it with Reyna no more. They stare at each other for a couple more seconds, then Jasmine tell me again to come in.

Reyna smile. "I thought so, *puta*." She laugh and go into the bathroom.

I step inside. The room look just like ours, but they only got one double bed. I take off my jacket, sit down, and try to relax.

"Why you running away?" Jasmine ask. "You and your mother get into a fight or something?"

"Yeah. I'm tired of her. Always making me feel —" I shake my head. I don't wanna get into this with Jasmine. I mean, I don't even hardly know this girl.

"Feel what?" she ask.

"Nah, nothing. I'm just tired."

"Well, lay down and rest."

I do. I just lay there on the bed looking up at the ceiling. I don't know what I'ma do now, but I don't wanna go back to my room just so my moms can start yelling at me again.

Jasmine start flipping through the channels on the TV. "I wish they had cable," she say. She keep flipping, then stop when she get to some Spanish talk show. She watch it for a long time, laughing every couple minutes. I took Spanish in ninth grade and almost passed it, but I can't understand shit they saying. But that's alright 'cause I just wanna chill for a little while.

Reyna come out the bathroom looking kinda hot herself.

She don't look as good as Jasmine do, but she fine. She stand in front of the mirror and do her hair and put on makeup.

"Is he really staying here all night?" she ask Jasmine like I ain't in the room.

"He had a fight with his mother," Jasmine say.

"You don't even know this boy."

"I know. Just let him cool off for a little while, then he's gonna go back to his room."

"Okay," Reyna say. "He'd better not be here when I get back."

"I said he's not staying, right?" Jasmine sound mad now. "Just go already."

The second Reyna leave, Jasmine put the TV on mute, turn off all the lights, then get in bed next to me. "I thought you was gonna make me leave," I say.

"You don't have to. My sister's just trying to be *parental*. But if she really cared about me, she wouldn't leave me here alone like this." She sound like she all hurt or something.

"Where she going?"

Jasmine don't say nothing and I can tell she don't wanna talk no more.

The next thing I know she kissing the side of my face, my neck, and my lips. She stroke my head real slow and gentle. "I'm glad you're here with me," she say. I can see her smiling face in the flickering light from the TV. "I know you got a girl, but can I make you feel better when she's not around?"

I don't say nothing and Jasmine unzip my fly and start to take care of me with her hand. I can tell she a ho, but I'm trying not to judge her 'cause that ain't right. I don't know what her life is like or what she been through. And it ain't none of my business.

"Relax," she whisper.

I take a deep breath and feel all the pressure and anger start to fade away. She working me so good I can't hear my moms voice no more. I can't see the roaches or even smell the odor of Bennett. And I'm falling asleep with a smile on my face.

SIX

When I wake up it's almost 6:00 in the morning and Jasmine is sleeping next to me. It take me a little while to figure out why I'm in bed with her, and when I remember what happened I feel like shit. Why the fuck did I let Jasmine do that to me? What's my problem? I gotta stop letting things like a stupid fight with my moms make me do shit I don't wanna do. I can't mess up what I got with Novisha 'cause that's the only thing I got going for me right now.

I get up outta bed and flip the light switch on the wall. As soon as the lights is on, all I see is, like, hundreds of roaches and shit running 'cross the floor and walls, back to they hiding places. Bennett is nasty, I swear.

Jasmine wake up. "Where you going?" she ask me. The lights is bothering her eyes. "Come back to bed," she say.

"Nah," I tell her. "I wanna go to my room and get my clothes."

"It's too early to wake up your mother and brother. Stay with me. *Please*." She sound all desperate, like she need someone in her bed with her. It probably don't gotta be me, just anybody.

I grab my jacket up off the chair. "I'ma be back," I say, even though I ain't planning on coming back.

I walk down the hall to my room. I hate going back there, but I sure as hell can't stay with Jasmine right now. Not after what happened last night. I knock on my room door hard 'cause I know my moms sleep like the dead, but she don't answer. I knock louder and she still don't answer. Then I kick the door.

"What?" my moms yell. Her voice is all rough and dry. I swear, she need to stop smoking so damn much 'cause she sound like a fucking man.

"It's me."

"What you want?"

Why she gotta act like I'm bothering her or something? Her attitude make me sick sometimes. "I want my clothes, what you think?"

"You shoulda thought of that 'fore you walked your ass outta here."

"I want my shit," I say, and kick the door three more times. Hard.

I hear Troy say, "Mommy, let him in."

"Go back to sleep," my moms tell him. "I ain't got time to deal with his nonsense."

I punch the door a few times, then go back to kicking it. I'm mad as I can get. Who the fuck do she think she is? Fuck her. She probably in there all happy 'cause she got me mad.

I walk away from the door 'cause I don't want her thinking she in control when she not. I don't need them clothes anyway. Shit. She want them so bad, she can keep them for all I care.

I get to Novisha apartment looking and probably smelling as homeless as I am. I'm wearing the same clothes I was wearing yesterday and the same clothes I slept in. I couldn't even take a shower or brush my teeth 'cause I ain't wanna go back to Jasmine room and hafta deal with what happened last night. I don't know how I'm s'posed to go to some awards ceremony like this.

Ms. Jenkins open the door and when she see me I can tell she feel sorry for me, like I'm one of them hungry kids they put on them TV commercials late at night. Novisha come outta her room wearing this short blue nightshirt. If I wasn't so funky I would give her a hug, but I don't even wanna get close right now.

She don't mind though. She wrap her arms 'round me and give me a little squeeze. This the kinda hug she give when her moms is 'round. The good girl hug. "I'm so happy you made it, Ty." She smell so sweet, like that peach bath stuff she like so much.

Ms. Jenkins don't let me say a word though. "Go put some clothes on," she tell Novisha. "You know it's not right to run around like that in front of Tyrell."

Novisha roll her eyes. "I told you, Mom. Tyrell respects me." She smile up at me.

"He's still a boy and you're still a girl. Respect's not gonna change that."

Novisha turn 'round to go back to her room and I try not to look at the back of her legs. "You don't gotta worry, Ms. Jenkins," I say. "You got a good girl there."

"I know *she's* a good girl. I just hope *you're* being a good boy 'cause I trust you. Don't make me regret that."

Since I'm so early, Ms. Jenkins let me take a shower, and she send Novisha downstairs to the Rite Aid to buy me a toothbrush, some new underwear, and socks. I feel kinda bad making her spend money on me, but I really do need them things since my moms ain't let me get my clothes from the room.

"Tyrell," Ms. Jenkins call through the bathroom door when I'm just 'bout to get in the shower. "I found a shirt my husband left here a while back. You have to wear your own jeans though." Ms. Jenkins always call Novisha pops her husband even though they been divorced for almost two years. The man ain't pay no child support or nothing for almost a year 'til Ms. Jenkins finally dragged his ass to court. But she don't hold that against him. It's like she forgot how bad he treated her.

I open the door a crack and she hand me the shirt. "Thanks," I say again. The shirt ain't too bad neither. Just plain blue with white buttons.

"And don't forget to wash that hair. There's some shampoo in the cabinet below the sink."

God, a brotha miss one shower and all of a sudden she actin' like I'm the funkiest nigga alive.

By the time I'm finished taking a shower, Novisha back. She hand me the Rite Aid bag through the door and, 'cause her moms is watching, she cover her eyes so she can't see me naked. Like she ain't seen it all before. And she ain't just get me what her moms sent her for neither. Nah, my girl even got me that $25 card for my cell. I brush my teeth and get dressed feeling good.

Next thing I know, Novisha is sitting on the couch and I'm

sitting on the floor between her legs old-skool style, and she greasing my scalp, combing my hair, and braiding it in neat rows going straight back with the zigzag parts. Shit look real nice.

I ain't gonna lie. I like having my girl take care of me this way. I can't wait 'til she finish high school and we can live together somewhere on our own. I'ma support her while she in college, pay all the bills and shit, and she can take care of me like this everyday. Man, that's the way I wanna be living.

Then Jasmine come into my mind, and I think 'bout what she did to me. I never shoulda let that shit happen. Now here I am and Novisha is treating me so good, and I'm feeling mad guilty. I don't know what I'ma do tonight if my moms don't let me back in the room, but I do know I gotta stay away from Jasmine 'cause I can't let what happened last night happen again.

A couple hours later, I'm sitting in the auditorium of Novisha school, bored out my fuckin' mind. This is s'posed to be a awards ceremony, but the first hour ain't nothing but kids singing church songs. Me and Novisha is sitting together next to her moms, who keep checking the back of the room to see if Novisha pops showed up yet. He said he was gonna meet them here, so he either late or not coming. But it don't matter what time he come 'cause Ms. Jenkins is saving him a seat.

When her moms ain't looking, Novisha whisper in my ear, "I wish she would get over him already. It's embarrassing."

I just shake my head 'cause I know her moms ain't gonna get over him no time soon. No matter what my pops do, my moms still love him. I think females is just like that. When they find they man, that's it. They ain't looking for nobody else no matter what.

The singers finally finish they song, and everybody stand up and clap. I don't feel like getting up, but when Novisha do, I do too, 'cause I wanna make sure all the guys in the auditorium know she with me.

While we standing there, I slip my hand on her waist and kinda rub her hip a little. And I'm real smooth 'bout it, so her moms don't see me. But at the same time, my eyes is going from one guy to the next, trying to catch they reaction. Her school got all kinds of kids, but I'm only checking out the Black dudes 'cause the guy who put them letters in her locker called hisself a brother in one of them.

"I know what you're doing," Novisha say, taking my hand off her hip and looking back to see what I'm looking at.

"I ain't doing nothing."

"He's not here," she say. "So relax."

I don't know if she just saying that or what. She don't be straight-out lying to me, but I know she probably trying to protect herself too. 'Cause she know if I see that dude, I'ma hafta kick some ass up in here. I don't give a fuck 'bout no awards ceremony.

Novisha pops get there 'bout two minutes later. He slide into the seat and give Ms. Jenkins a kiss on the lips. Novisha roll her eyes. Both me and her don't know what her pops is up to and why he be coming 'round again like he ain't never left.

A couple minutes later, they start calling people up to get they award. Most of the kids is getting awards for they grades. Then they say they got four special awards for kids who do stuff for the community. That's my girl. She always doing shit for other people.

Novisha get her award 'cause she volunteer at this nursing home, and she got a lot of other kids to do the same thing. 'Cause of her, something like forty kids from her school is volunteering at six different nursing homes in the Bronx.

When they call her name, I check the room again, trying to see if any of them guys look like they too into her. This one Black guy near the back of the room is standing up, clapping and smiling like a damn fool. I ain't sure if he the kinda guy that be putting shit in people lockers, but I keep my eyes on him anyway.

Novisha don't gotta say nothing when she get her award. She just thank the principal of her school, smile for some pictures, then come back to the seat again. Her moms and pops give her kisses, and she give me the good girl hug again. She show me the little plaque she got. All the money she pay to go to this school, they could give her something a little bigger, you ask me. "Nice," I tell her.

"Yeah," she say. "It's heavy too."

We hold hands again and watch them give out the rest of the special awards. When they call another name, I check back to see if that dude is watching Novisha, but he ain't. He standing up again, clapping and cheesing it up for the guy getting the next award. I guess he do that for everybody. He ain't into Novisha. Nigga just like to clap.

After we leave the school, Novisha pops say he taking us all to Red Lobster. "My little girl don't get an award everyday," he say. He put his arms 'round Novisha shoulders and hug her. "I'm proud of you, baby."

"Thanks, Dad." She smile, but I know she ain't feeling it.

We all walk down the street to where Mr. Jenkins parked his car. On the way to Red Lobster, Novisha moms and pops is just talking to her 'bout the award and how they happy and proud of her and shit. I don't say nothing. Not that I ain't proud 'cause I'm always proud of my girl for all she do, but 'cause I'm thinking 'bout the fight me and my moms had last night. How she gonna tell me to go out there and sell weed just to make money for her? Why she don't care if I get locked up? How she gonna take care of Troy then? Damn.

All through dinner my mind ain't even there. I'm eating 'cause the food is good and I ain't had seafood for a while, but I ain't saying a whole lot. Novisha and her moms and pops is talking 'bout everything, but me, I'm thinking 'bout Bennett and how much I don't feel like going back there. And what I'ma do if my moms don't let me back in the room again? Go back to Jasmine room? Hell no.

When we done eating, Ms. Jenkins order a whole 'nother dinner to go. "It's for your little brother," she tell me.

"You don't need to do that, Ms. Jenkins," I say. 'Cause I know Red Lobster is kinda expensive and her and Mr. Jenkins don't got a lot of money. I mean, it's bad enough they gotta pay for my dinner.

"Yes, I do. That little boy deserves to have some good, hot food on a cold night like tonight."

"Thanks," I say. Then I tell Novisha, "I told you your moms is cool."

"Don't tell her that," Novisha say. "She's getting souped!"

Ms. Jenkins reach 'cross the table like she trying to slap her, but Novisha laugh and move out the way. "Girl, award or no

35

award," she say, "you're not too old for me to put across my knee!"

Everybody is laughing and having fun, and I try to get into it, but it's real hard. The last time my whole family was together having a good time like this was almost four months ago. For my moms thirty-fifth birthday, my pops took us all to this soul food restaurant on 125th Street. Man, we was greasing and joking 'round like Novisha family is doing now, but what we ain't know then was that my pops was gonna get arrested the next day.

That dinner was the last time our family had fun. After that, all we been having is hard times, first trying to hold on to our apartment, and now dealing with the whole shelter bullshit. And it don't look like shit gonna get better neither.

"While we're waiting for the food, let's take a walk," Novisha say to me and grab my hand. "I'm so full. I need to walk some of this off." Then she tell her moms and pops, "We'll be right back."

We go outside and walk 'cross the parking lot real slow. For a few minutes we don't say nothing. Then she ask me if I'm okay.

"Yeah, I'm a'ight."

"You look sad. Is it that place, Bennett?"

"Yeah, kinda," I say. "Hunts Point ain't exactly where I wanted to spend the weekend, know what I mean?"

We still holding hands, so I stop walking and just give her a big bear hug. Her little body feel real good all pressed up against mines. It's like she just fit me perfect. We stand there kissing and hugging 'til a car beep us and tell us to get out the way.

We start walking back to the restaurant. "Are you sure you're okay?" Novisha ask me again.

I kinda wanna tell her 'bout the fight me and my moms had,

but I know if I tell her what my moms want me to do, Novisha gonna get as mad as I was last night. And I don't wanna mess this day up for her. She don't need to get all into my shit on her special day. So I just smile. "Course I'm a'ight," I tell her. "My girl won a big award and made me all proud. How else I'ma be?"

SEVEN

I ain't wanna come back to Bennett, but I know how my moms is, and sometime she don't know how to deal with Troy by herself for too long. My moms get frustrated and she be itching to go out with her friends and shit, 'specially on a Saturday night. A couple times she left Troy alone just 'cause she couldn't take being locked up in the apartment. That's why I made sure Troy know my cell number, so he could call me if our moms ever leave him alone.

I go to our room and knock, but this time my moms don't curse me out and tell me to go away. This time she open the door looking all tired and mad and shit. "Where you been?" she ask with an attitude.

"None of your business." I squeeze past her and go inside. Troy is sitting on the bed watching TV, eating them Cheez Doodles I bought yesterday. Probably ain't eat nothing but junk all day.

My moms close the door. "Your little girlfriend braid your

hair?" I don't say nothing 'cause she know who braided my hair. "What you got in that bag?" she ask.

"None of your business," I say again. "It ain't for you, no way. It's for Troy."

My moms look like she 'bout to argue, but then she change her mind. "I'm going out with Val and Joanne tonight."

"Where y'all going?"

"None of your business."

"A'ight," I say. "Be like that." I open the Red Lobster bag and pull out the plastic container. As soon as I open the bag, the food smell so good it fill up the room. I put the container on the bed.

"Shit," my moms say, sucking her teeth. "How you get this?"

"Novisha moms and pops took us out for dinner."

"I thought they was divorced."

"They are."

My moms shake her head. "Damn shame when two grown-ass people can't stay together for they kid."

I look at her like she out her mind. "Like you and your man, right?" I say. "Y'all doing real good together. You here in a shelter, him locked up at Rikers."

"Shut up, Tyrell." She roll her eyes again and grab a biscuit before I can stop her.

"Here, Troy," I say. "This for you." Then I turn the bag upside down. "Damn, I forgot to get you a fork."

Troy make a face, then he say, "Hey, I got an idea." He run over to his backpack and come back to the bed with two new pencils. "These are chopsticks," he say with a smile on his face. "Watch me, Tyrell."

"You suck on them pencils and you gonna get sick," I say.

"I ain't gonna suck on them. Watch."

I watch him struggle to keep the shrimp and rice on the pencils, then he kinda let the food fall into his mouth. The pencils don't even hardly touch him. He smile. "See?"

"Yeah, that's good," I say. "You smart." I don't say nothing 'bout the mess he making on the bed and floor. A couple more roaches at Bennett ain't gonna change nothing. Least he eating something.

My moms go in the bathroom to take her shower. Me and Troy just talk. I tell him that he can't stay up all night 'cause tomorrow he gonna do all that homework he was s'posed to turn in last week, plus whatever he gotta do for Monday.

"Mommy said I ain't going to school on Monday. We going to see the caseworker."

"You don't gotta go to that meeting. You ain't missing no more school. How you gonna make it outta special ed if you keep being absent?"

"Mommy don't want me to get outta special ed."

"Forget what she say. I'm telling you, if you work hard and stop missing so much school you can be in a regular class next year with regular kids. Ain't nothin' wrong with you."

Troy don't say nothing else, but I can tell he don't believe me. That's 'cause my moms got him thinking he slow when the only reason he even in special ed is 'cause you can get a SSI check every month if you got a retarded kid. My moms probably paid some doctor to evaluate Troy and say he slow, then they put him in special ed, like it ain't matter that there wasn't never nothing wrong with him. Now I don't know if he ever gonna get back to the regular class.

Troy keep eating and eating like someone gonna take the

40

food away if he don't eat everything in, like, five minutes. "Eat them vegetables," I tell him.

He make a face, but he do what I say.

When we had our own apartment and my pops was home, my moms used to cook everyday. That's 'cause my pops wasn't hearing no kinda excuses from her. My moms wasn't working, so what else she had to do but cook? But as soon as my pops got locked up again, it was like she forgot how to cook. All we ate was pizza, McDonald's, and chicken wings and pork fried rice from the Chinese take-out place. The only time Troy ate real food was at school. Me, I only ate good at Novisha house. Being at Bennett is even worse 'cause here we don't got no stove or microwave, so we can't eat no real food even if we wanted.

After my moms leave, I let Troy spend 'bout a half hour playing my Game Boy. Then, when he sleep, I go through his backpack trying to figure out what work he gotta do by Monday. There's a note stapled to the cover of his notebook.

Dear Mrs. Green,

I would like to schedule an appointment to meet with you as soon as possible regarding Troy's schoolwork as well as other important issues. Please indicate when you can meet with me at the bottom of this letter and return it on Monday. I am available after school every day except this Thursday.

Thank you,
Mrs. Kimberly Morton

I know Troy work ain't all that good, but I don't know what Mrs. Morton mean when she say "other important issues." I hope she ain't trying to make a report to ACS for nothing 'cause that's not what I'm trying to hear right now. We ain't had a ACS case in a couple years, ever since my pops got released last time and got us out the system. This time I'ma make sure my moms don't lose custody of us 'cause that foster care shit ain't no joke. Troy don't need to go through that again.

I put all Troy work out on the dresser and take out some of his school clothes so they won't be too wrinkled on Monday. Then I'm just bored as hell, so I call Novisha.

"She's asleep, Tyrell," Ms. Jenkins tell me. "She has to get to church early tomorrow. The Sunday school teacher got the flu, so Novisha's taking her place."

"Man, she really involved in everything."

"That's my girl. I don't know how she manages to do so much for other people, but she does. Tonight's award is proof of that, right?"

"Right," I say. "Oh, yeah, thanks for dinner tonight. Troy loved the food too."

"Good, I'm glad. How's he doing, your brother?"

"He doing a'ight," I say, then I tell her 'bout how much school he been missing and how I'ma try to get him ready for school on Monday.

Ms. Jenkins tell me to work with him but that I gotta have patience and all that. Then she tell me something that really fuck with me. She say, "After we dropped you off at the train, Novisha told me you doing a lot better in school yourself, Tyrell. She said you getting all B's this semester, which is really something, especially with all your family's going through now."

Man, I don't even know what to say to that shit, so I just go, "Can you tell Novisha I called? I just wanted to tell her that I'm, you know, proud of her."

"I will." In my mind I can almost see Ms. Jenkins smiling. I know exactly what to say to keep her liking me. "Good night," she say.

I tell her good night, then flip my cell closed. Damn. Novisha ain't tell her moms I don't be going to school no more. And it ain't like I just stopped going last week or something. I ain't been there in, like, a month now. Novisha been trying to get me to go back, but I ain't hearing none of that. She don't go to the kinda school I used to go to, and she don't know what kinda shit I had to deal with everyday.

And I can see if she just let her moms keep thinking I was in school, but here she is talking 'bout my grades and shit. Straight-out lying. Like she gotta make up shit to make me look good or something. You ask me, it shouldn't matter to Novisha if I'm in school or outta school. School is her thing, not mines.

I lay down on the other bed just feeling myself getting madder and madder. I'm kinda mad at Novisha for lying 'bout me, but most of all I'm just mad at my whole situation.

Why I gotta be here at Bennett with no money and no real apartment? Why I gotta be spending my Saturday night in this nasty room instead of having fun like guys my age is s'posed to? And why my father gotta be locked up instead of here taking care of his family so I don't gotta be worrying 'bout us all the time?

My moms don't get back to Bennett 'til after two and she fucked up. I know she been drinking, and I can tell when she been smoking weed too, 'cause she be talking all loud and shit and making no kinda sense. Damn. She having more fun than me.

"I'm through with your pops," she say way too loud, waking up Troy. "I'm through living like this. You understand me, Ty?" She lean against the door trying to take off her shoes, but she all off balance, so she just slide down to the floor and pull them off. Then she stand up and look at herself in the mirror. "Shit, that club was fulla fine niggas tonight and I coulda had any one of them. Know why?" She smile at herself in the mirror and don't wait for no kinda answer. "'Cause I'm still hot, that's why. 'Cause your moms still got it goin' on. But I don't get to do nothing with none of them, right? No, I gotta be faithful, right? Well, why I gotta be so damn faithful? Shit. I'm tired of wasting my time waiting for your father again and again and again. Let me tell you, Ty. I need me a man now, right here. Right here! Shit, if I had a man, I wouldn't even be here." She sit on the bed Troy trying to sleep on and get all sad and shit. "This ain't right. It ain't fair." Now she get them tears running down her face. "You understand me, Ty? You know where I'm coming from, right?"

I just stare at her 'cause I know better than to answer any of them dumb drunk-ass questions. Not that she gonna stop talking neither. My moms don't get drunk or high all the time, but when she do, ain't nobody getting no sleep. She gonna be talking and crying and laughing and shit all night.

Damn.

EIGHT

Jasmine knock on my door early in the morning, a couple hours after I finally get my moms to shut up and go to bed. "Tyrell," Jasmine say in between knocks. It's like she trying to whisper, but she doing it real loud. "Wake up."

I get outta bed, but I'm not really feeling this. I was trying to get through the weekend without seeing her.

When I open the door, she standing in the hallway wearing her jacket and hat like she 'bout to go somewhere. And she look hot, still in them same tight jeans from the other day.

"Your hair looks nice like that," she tell me. "Your girlfriend braided it?"

"Yeah." I still don't know what she doing here.

"Get dressed," she say. "One of the guards downstairs told me that this church around here gives out free breakfast to homeless people. I don't wanna go alone."

"Church?" I ain't even hardly awake, and the light in the hall is killing my eyes right 'bout now.

"Yeah. The service starts at eight. The only thing is, you have to sit through the whole thing if you wanna eat. So, you coming or what?" She smile, flashing them horrible braces. "Pleeease."

"When you getting them things off your teeth?" I ask, still half 'sleep.

"Why?" she ask, but she know why I'm asking.

"Nah, nothing." I gotta get them thoughts out my head anyway 'cause ain't nothing gonna happen with us no more. I'ma make sure of that.

"C'mon, hurry up," she say again. "Wake up your mother and brother. The guard said the food is good."

I open the door a little wider, and for a second I don't even wanna turn the lights on. Not 'cause my moms is gonna wake up and get mad, but 'cause it's too early to deal with all them roaches.

But I don't got no choice. I flip the light switch and watch the roaches run. I swear, there's more now than before. Probably 'cause of all that rice and shit Troy spilled on the floor last night.

I wake Troy up. "What's the matter?" he ask.

"Nothing," I say. "Get up. We gonna go get a good breakfast."

My moms is 'sleep and I ain't trying to wake her. She real mean and nasty when she hungover. So I grab me and Troy clothes, shake the roaches out our sneakers, and get dressed without even washing up 'cause we don't got no time. I know we funky, but we gotta go.

It's real cold outside and it's dark. Jasmine say she heard it's gonna snow today.

Troy get all happy and shit when he hear that. "I hope we don't have no school tomorrow." He start jumping 'round like it's the best news he ever heard. I remember when I used to be like that, when I was little. Man, snow days used to be real fun.

We walk through the streets real fast, trying to get to this church before eight. We pass burned-out buildings and factories, and empty lots covered with nothin' but garbage. The whole neighborhood is fucked up. A couple blocks later we start seeing some stores and shit. Everything is closed now and the streets is damn-near empty.

"Where were you yesterday?" Jasmine ask me. "I was looking for you. All the other guys were down in the lobby acting like idiots. The guard had to chase them outside because they were making too much noise."

"You hanging with them guys now?"

"No, I was looking for you, but you weren't around. What am I supposed to do? Just sit in my room all day looking at the roaches?"

We walk some more without talking. I don't get this girl. She can't be alone for a second? Now she got me wondering if she did something with them other guys.

Troy is in front of me, and when he get to the curb he just step down into the street without even looking for cars. I run over and grab his arm. "What I say 'bout running in the street?"

He try to get outta my grip. "Stop yelling, Ty."

"You too old for this," I tell him. I'm trying to control my temper, but this shit don't make no kinda sense. "Gimme your hand. You wanna act like a damn two-year-old, then that's how I'ma treat you." I hold his hand tight the whole rest of the way.

The church is called Iglesia de Dios del Bronx. But this ain't no real church like the one Novisha go to. This one is just like a small store on a block with a whole bunch of other stores. I ain't lying when I say this church is mad ghetto. I mean, how you gonna put a church between a barbershop and a 99-cent store?

"Oh, yeah," Jasmine whisper when we just 'bout to go inside. "I forgot to tell you. The whole mass is in Spanish." She smile again like she being funny. "But don't worry about it. Just think about the food."

And that's exactly what I do. I sit there so fucking bored for, like, two hours just waiting to eat. After 'bout five minutes, Troy put his head on my shoulder and he out cold. Jasmine is kinda paying attention. She don't look like the church type, but I can tell she used to go a lot 'cause she still know them Spanish prayers.

The church is real small, but it ain't bad inside. They got red carpet all over and white folding chairs. They don't got no stained glass like at the church where Novisha goes, but they do got posters of stained glass. And they got big statues and a giant cross on the wall. It look kinda like a church. But a real low-budget one.

I ain't really into church myself. Besides when Novisha take me to her church for the Christmas show or some other thing she involved with, I ain't been to church since I was a little kid. Back in the day, my grandmother used to take us to her church every now and then, and that shit used to last all day. All the kids was put in the basement for Sunday school, and we would hafta sing songs and shit. It used to be fun, but no matter what them people said, I never really believed in God 'cause I knew if there was a God he wouldn't never take my pops away from me. And my pops always taught me not to depend on nobody but myself.

This church ain't much different from the church I used to go to with my grandmother, 'cept here I don't understand a word the pastor is saying. When they pass 'round the collection plate, only the people in the front of the church put any money in. The rest of us, in the back, is the homeless people. They don't even bring the plate by us, probably 'cause we more likely to take money than put anything in.

After the service is done, the pastor come down the aisle and say something in Spanish to us in the back. Half the homeless people was 'sleep, so they start stretching and yawning and trying to wake theyself up. I shake Troy a little and he get up. He got lines and shit on his face from pressing into my jacket so long.

"Breakfast is ready downstairs," Jasmine whisper to me. "C'mon."

We all go downstairs and sit down at these round tables with blue plastic tablecloths. There's only 'bout twenty-five people waiting for food, but we the only kids. Everybody else is just old people and a couple crackheads.

The food smell real spicy, and my stomach is talkin'. When they call our table, we line up and the church ladies load our trays up with all kinda Spanish food. I carry our tray back to the table, then we all sit down and tear into our food.

I'm eatin' some kinda eggs with peppers in it, ham, fried plantains, and a lot of other Spanish food I ain't never seen before. I don't really know what the fuck I'm eating, but the shit is good. And I'm eating so fast, I ain't even picking my head up in between bites.

While we eating, the pastor say something else in Spanish and everyone start clapping. "That lady over there," Jasmine tell me and Troy, looking over at a short woman wearing a white apron, "she owns a restaurant around here and she made all this food for us."

I don't say nothing, but I do wanna know what she get outta

49

giving away free food. You ask me, ain't nobody doing something for nothin'.

Then one of the church ladies say something and everyone line up again. "They're gonna pack up the leftovers for us," Jasmine say. "I'm gonna get some for me and Reyna."

"She back?"

"She's coming back today." I'm 'bout to ask her where Reyna went, but she get up from the table too fast. Me and Troy follow her and stand in that long, slow line again. Man, this shit is fucking embarrassing already. How many times they gonna make us line up and beg for food?

Before we leave, the lady from the restaurant come up to Jasmine and they talk for a couple minutes in Spanish. The lady give her a business card. Then Jasmine walk over to the door where me and Troy is standing. "That lady wants me to come to her restaurant and interview for a job." She smiling all big and shiny. "And I need a job too. This is great."

"When you going on the interview?"

"She told me to call her this week to set something up."

When we leave the church, it's already snowing. It's freezing and Troy don't got no hat or gloves, and his coat is ripped up under the arm. But he don't seem to mind. The second we get outside, he start running 'round, making the first footprints in the snow.

Me and Jasmine walk behind him. Jasmine smoking, but I ain't thinking 'bout no cigarette. I don't want nothing to spoil the taste of that food in my mouth.

"You mad at me about the other night?" Jasmine ask after we been walking for a couple minutes without saying nothing.

"Nah," I say. "It's just, you know, I got a girl. So what

happened between me and you wasn't cool. Know what I'm saying?"

She don't say nothing. She just keep on smoking.

We walk a few more minutes. The only thing I hear is the cars and buses driving through the slush in the street. Everything white now when just a couple hours ago there wasn't even no snow yet. The neighborhood actually look halfway decent now.

"How did your family end up at the EAU?" Jasmine ask me. I can tell she trying to change the subject.

To be honest, I was thinking 'bout asking her the same thing on the bus the other day, but I ain't wanna get all up in her business. But now here she is, getting all up in mines.

"My pops is locked up," I tell her. "And my moms can't keep no job. After a couple months of not paying the rent, our landlord took us to court and got us evicted." I say all this like it ain't no big deal, but the truth is, I'm real fuckin' mad 'bout the way my moms handled her shit. She knew what my pops was up to, and she knew he was gonna violate his parole, so why she ain't plan what she was gonna do when he got locked up again? And why my pops ain't plan to take care of his family? What kinda man do that to his wife and kids?

Jasmine shake her head. "Why's your father in jail? Selling?"

"Nah, not this time," I say. I don't really wanna tell her too much, not 'cause I don't trust her, but 'cause I don't really know her. "He violated his parole," I tell her. I know that ain't really saying nothing, but it's the truth.

The whole truth is my pops been in and out of jail three times. He a DJ and he be throwing these wild, off-the-hook parties. The first time he got locked up was for selling drugs at his parties. I was only four or five then so all I knew was one day he was there, and we was living in the projects all happy and shit, and things was good and then the next day my pops was gone and my moms was crying all the time. My grandmother was still alive back then and she came to live with us. She helped my moms out and took care of me, so it wasn't so bad even though I still missed my pops. He got out the day before my eighth birthday, and that night we all went out to dinner and I got to sit next to him. I thought everything was gonna be back to normal.

That feeling ain't lasted long. A couple years later he was locked up again. This time the police was callin' him a pimp, which he ain't and never was. He just threw some real wild parties, and hos would show up just so they could work the men in the crowd. He said they would make more money at one of his parties than they did in two or three days on the streets. And the men ain't had no problem with them being there.

But the police did. They got my pops for selling drugs, selling alcohol without a liquor license, running numbers, and pimping girls. He had to serve three years of a five-year sentence. By the time they let him out, Troy was already five and I was thirteen, and me and him was already in the system.

We get to a corner, and this time Troy wait for me and grab my hand. We cross the street and then he go running off again. He still making footprints in the snow, but now he trying to walk backwards in them same prints. He fall twice, but least he havin' fun. And his coat is already beat down, so it don't really matter none.

And now I'm here thinkin' 'bout my pops and them parties he used to run. He started letting me go to the parties after he got me and Troy outta foster care. I'll never forget seeing my pops up there playing all that old-skool shit like Cameo and Maze. Just jammin'. The place he rented was packed. Niggas was in there getting they party on, like they ain't never been out before. Everybody was drunk and high, and there was the finest females there working them niggas for every cent they had in they pockets.

First time a girl ever blew me was at that first party. Girl was, like, eighteen or nineteen, and she ain't care that I was only thirteen. She pulled me behind one of them big speakers and got down on her knees. She ain't want no money or nothin'. She told me she was doing it just 'cause I was Tyrone kid. I had a smile on my face for two fuckin' weeks after that.

Jasmine is staring at me. "What are you thinking about?"

"Nothin'," I say. "Nothin'." We get to another corner and Troy try to grab my hand again, but this time I don't let him. He too old for that to be a habit. He gotta start taking care of hisself. I watch him look for cars, then run 'cross to the other side.

"I need to stop at that bodega over there," Jasmine say while we crossing the street.

"More cigarettes?"

"That was my last one."

We go in the store and I buy my moms a Pepsi so she won't send me to the store later. I buy a big bag of Cheez Doodles for Troy, but I tell him he can't have none 'til after he finish doing his homework. I leave that store with a little over a dollar. Damn, I need to make some money soon.

NINE

The second we get back to Bennett, the guy at the front desk give us the bad news. "Kids, tell your mothers not to pack nothing. Y'all ain't going nowhere tomorrow. I just got word. The city's expecting the snow to get real heavy tonight, and they gonna be overloaded with homeless people looking for shelter, so y'all gonna have to stay here for a few more days. Spread the word, okay?"

Damn. Why we gotta get stuck at Bennett?

Jasmine get tears in her eyes. "I don't believe this," she say, more to herself than me. "I can't believe Emiliano is doing this to me."

"Emiliano? Who that?"

"My sister's boyfriend. He threw us out. In the middle of winter."

"Man." I think 'bout asking her why, but I can tell by the look on her face, she don't wanna talk no more. She look serious and mad as hell.

"C'mon," Troy say, pulling on the bottom of my jacket. "Stop talking."

"Wait," I tell him. I can't stand when he pull on me like that. He let go but look up at me like I'm being mean or something. "Troy, go sit down and count to a hundred. Then we gonna go upstairs."

He walk away from us real slow and look out the window. A lot of kids from Bennett is out there playing in the snow, and I know he wanna be out there with them. But me and him is both funky, and I told him he can't do nothing 'til we take showers. And 'til he do some of that homework he gotta do. He sit down on the chairs, and a second later start counting real loud and fast. I shoulda made him count to two hundred.

I ask Jasmine, "What you gonna do now?" It's like only a little after 11:00, and I don't wanna just leave her standing in the lobby.

"Nothing. I have to finish reading this stupid play for school, and since there's nothing else to do —"

"You go to school?"

"Yeah. Why you sound so surprised?"

"I just ain't think —"

"Don't you go to school?"

I don't really wanna say nothing 'cause, damn, I don't want her thinking I'm stupid or something, so I just go, "I'm takin' a break from all that right now, with all this shit that's going, know what I mean?"

"Yeah, I missed a few days last week too. Me and Reyna were trying to find a place to stay after Emil changed the locks on us."

Troy up to fifty-seven now. "Why he throw y'all out?" I ask like it don't really matter to me.

"Because he's a control freak, that's why." She got her arms folded in front of her, and she looking really mad now, like she 'bout to explode but don't wanna show it. "I'll see you later," she tell me, and before I can even open my mouth to say something, she down the hall on her way to the stairs.

"One hundred!" Troy scream. The guy at the front desk look over at me like he want me to control Troy. Like Troy my kid or something.

"C'mon," I say, and Troy jump up and run over to me. "Good job."

He run right past me. "Hurry up, Ty. Let's go give Mommy the food."

My moms is still 'sleep when we get to our room. I tell Troy to go wash up and brush his teeth 'cause we gotta spend some time working on all his homework. While he in the bathroom, I try to wake my moms so she can eat some of the food while it's still hot. She ain't happy to get up 'til I tell her I got Spanish food for her.

"You got that food for me?" she ask. She laying there looking tore up from her night partying. I don't know why she think she still young enough to hang.

"Eat it 'fore it get cold," I tell her.

She sit up real slow, and I bring the food to her on the bed. "This shit smell good," she say, opening the foil container. "Now this is what I'm talkin' about!"

I hand her the bag with the Pepsi.

"Damn, you really remembered your mother this time. Can't nobody tell me I ain't raised you right."

I sit on the other bed waiting for Troy to get out the bathroom. "You was fucked up last night," I tell my moms.

"No, I wasn't. I just had a couple drinks." She lying and we both know it. She even got a little smile on her face to prove it.

"Okay, but the next time I get high, you can't say nothin'."

"Bet," she say between bites of some kinda fried codfish thing.

While she eating, I tell her 'bout the snowstorm and that we ain't gonna be going nowhere tomorrow. She don't take it too bad, probably 'cause she eating and happy.

After a while I get up and go through my garbage bag trying to find my black jeans 'cause they still clean. Troy run out the bathroom with no shirt on. "Ty, there's a big giant spider in there. It's black and red."

"So kill it," I tell him. "You a man or a girl?"

I can tell he scared, but he need to get over that. He don't say nothin'. He just grab his sneaker off the floor and go back to the bathroom. A couple seconds later I hear him banging his sneaker 'round like he trying to kill Godzilla or something. Boy can get the job done when he wanna.

By the time I get in the bathroom, Troy got the place all wet with towels all over the floor. And when I get in the shower, the hot water ain't coming out all that hot. Damn. It's too cold outside to be takin' a shower like this. I can't even believe I'm in this place with no money and not even no hot water. There gotta be something else I can do 'cause this shit ain't working.

When I finish getting dressed and come out the bathroom, Troy sitting on my moms bed with her, watching TV and eating them Cheez Doodles I told him he couldn't have yet. I can't stand when my moms do that, let him do whatever he want all the time. Now I'ma hafta be the mean one and make him do work.

I go over and turn the TV off. "What I say 'bout watching TV, Troy? And give me them Cheez Doodles. I said you can't have them 'til you do your homework."

"Oh, man!" He hand over the bag, like it's hurting him or something.

It take me 'bout a half hour to get Troy to sit down and get serious. That boy love to play. When he finally do calm down, it's like torture trying to get through all that work. He crying and whining and complaining. Damn.

I spend a little over an hour with him. We get through all the homework he gotta hand in tomorrow if school gonna be open. He still got a lot of shit to make up, but he can't sit still too long doing work. And here we ain't got no kitchen table to sit at, so we gotta work on the bed, which really don't cut it.

After I tell Troy he free, I get up and tell my moms I'ma be right back. Then I grab my cell and leave the room real fast. I go out into the hall and call Calvin. Me and him been friends since, like, fourth grade. Both our pops was locked up back then, and both is locked up now.

"Yo, Cal."

"Ty?"

"What up?"

"Chillin'. Where you at?"

"Bennett."

"Damn, man."

"Word. Where you at?"

"In fronta my buildin'."

"I'ma be over there."

"A'ight."

"A'ight," I say, and flip my cell closed. My boy Calvin gonna help me out.

I go back in the room for my jacket.

"You going to see Calvin?" my moms ask even though she know where I'm going. Where else I go when I don't got no other choice?

Not that Cal ain't my friend. We been through a lot, me and him, so we can't never be no less than friends, but Cal into some serious shit and I don't wanna go there with him, not if I got any other way to handle my business. To be honest, I don't even like chillin' with him no more 'cause, my luck, I'ma be 'round him when some shit break out and my ass gonna get locked up too. 'Cause Cal the first person to tell you, he gonna end up in jail. Soon. That's just how he livin'.

I don't answer my moms question. I just grab my jacket, shake it out, and leave. I don't want her thinking I'm only going to see Cal 'cause of what she had to say to me the other night.

'Cause the truth is, she was right. I don't wanna be the kinda man my pops turned out to be, the kinda man that don't step up and do what he gotta do. Nah. I'ma hafta do better than him.

On my way out, I see Jasmine in the lobby on the pay phone. I don't want her to see me 'cause I know she gonna wanna talk, so I just walk past her. I try to hear a little of what she sayin', but she speaking that Spanish, all fast and shit, and after that long-ass church service this morning, I had enough Spanish for one day.

TEN

The snow is really coming down hard now. I spend 'bout an hour at the train station swiping people in with my MetroCards, charging them half what the city want. By the time I'm done, I got twelve dollars, which ain't shit, but it beats a blank. I get uptown at just 'bout 3:00 and it's like a fuckin' blizzard out there or something.

Cal live in Bronxwood, but on the other side of the shopping center from where Novisha live at. He standing out in front, probably freezing his ass off. I swear, no matter how cold it is, Cal be standing out there. He all 'bout making cash, and folks want what he selling, winter, spring, summer, and fall. Least he got on a heavy down jacket with a hood and Tims to keep his feet warm. He must be making some good money.

When he see me, he shake his head. "Yo, son, you lookin' busted, man."

"You ain't no Denzel yourself," I tell him. "So stop doggin' a brotha."

"Shut the fuck up," he say, laughing. "Denzel ain't even

Denzel no more." He open the lobby door with his key and we go inside. He know how I feel 'bout standing out there in the cold. Ain't gonna happen. "So, what up with you and Novisha?" He got a smile on his face 'cause he know Novisha, and he know she don't give it up. "You hittin' that yet?"

I don't say nothing 'cause ain't none of it his business. I just laugh a little.

"Damn, man. How you put up with that?"

I decide to change the subject 'cause I don't wanna hear nobody saying shit 'bout my girl, even Cal. "So what up with you and Tina? When she gonna have that baby already? Saw her last week and she look like she 'bout to bust."

Now Cal look mad. "Me and her broke up, a'ight? She —"

"Again?" They be breaking up and getting back together every couple months. They got a real crazy relationship, you ask me. They fight and curse each other out, then they all in love. Next thing, she getting a order of protection against him, then they back together. The only reason she started going out with him in the first place was 'cause he making money. Everybody know she wouldn't look at him before he started selling.

And now that she pregnant by him, he got real problems. Her moms keep calling him and demanding money, talkin' 'bout he need to start taking care of his kid even before it's born. And even if they don't get back together, he gonna hafta put up with her 'til that kid is eighteen. Man, sometimes I'm glad Novisha don't give me no play 'cause I couldn't deal with no baby mama shit right 'bout now.

Cal smile. "Yeah, me and her is through. I got *three* girls now." Then he go on and on with one of his stories 'bout how he gettin' all these fine females now that him and Tina broke up. Cal is my boy, but that nigga can talk some mad shit when he get started.

Finally, when he done, he lean up against the row of metal mailboxes. "So what up? What you need?"

I gotta admit, sometimes I can't stand coming to Cal like this. Me and him is cool and everything, but I wish things was like they used to be, when we was both broke as a joke. Now that he selling weed and making money, things is different. It's like now I gotta come to him for help, like I need him to save me or something.

"Say the word, Ty, and I'll hook you up. You can work for me, make some real money. How long you planning to make that chump change you makin' now?"

"Cal, I ain't working for you."

He shake his head like he don't understand me. "You only fifteen, man," he say, like he ain't fifteen hisself. "You get arrested, you still a juvenile. Ain't nothing gonna happen to you all that bad. What you scared of?"

Me and him had this conversation 'bout twenty times already, and he know how I feel. "I ain't scared of nothin'," I say. I don't want him thinking I'm scared of getting locked up, 'cause that ain't it. "I told you, man, I get locked up, Troy gonna end up back in the system. My moms can't take care of him by herself. You know how she is."

"Yeah, your moms is bugged, man."

"Cal, you ain't never been in the system, but we was, and I ain't going down like that again. I wanna keep things easy. I need to make some money, but I gotta keep myself out of jail, least 'til my pops get out, know what I mean?" For some reason, I'm getting real mad just thinkin' 'bout my pops coming home. "Cal, when he get out, I'm on my own 'cause ain't no way me and him gonna live under the same roof again."

I don't really know why I'm telling all my plans to Cal, but I don't want him thinking I'm turning down his job 'cause I'm scared. When my pops get out, who know? Maybe I will work for Cal for a while, make some quick cash. I wanna make sure I'm ready to move wherever Novisha wanna go to college. It don't matter to me where we go. I just need to be able to take care of her while she studying and shit. And I'ma do whatever it take to make her happy.

After a while me and Cal walk up to the third floor where he live at with his two big brothers. They moms used to live there too, but they got her a apartment in Co-op City. Cal s'posed to be living with her, but he spend most of his time right here. Both his brothers is home when we get there. Greg is sitting on the couch playing some game on the PlayStation. On the screen this man is running down the hall and just killing everybody in sight. Heads is gettin' blown off, and blood is everywhere. The game look so real, and Greg is just smiling and working them controls like this is all he do all day. That and get high.

Andre, the other brother, is in the kitchen on the cell. "What up, Ty?" he ask when he get off the phone. "When you gonna start working with us, man? We expanding our business and we looking for some new guys? You down?"

"Nah, not now," I say.

"You still with that MetroCard bullshit?"

"Yeah, but I wanna talk to y'all 'bout something else."

Andre sit down at the table and light up a blunt. "You want a taste?"

"A'ight."

Next thing I know, me, Calvin, and Andre is sitting at the kitchen table gettin' fucked up. I gotta say, them niggas got the best weed in the Bronx. Greg come into the kitchen after a while, and he look at us and start laughing. I don't know what's so funny, but I start laughing too, and then we start actin' mad stupid, talkin' 'bout how things was back in the day. We talk 'bout how we used to be stealing shit from the candy store 'round the corner, and how Calvin got busted when we was in sixth grade, and they moms had to come down to the store. The Chinese man from the store screamed at they moms for not watching her son and, man, Cal got a beating all the way back to they apartment. And me, Andre, and Greg was out there in front of the building, laughing and eating the candy we just stole our own self. That shit was funny.

After a while, Andre say, "So what you thinking about, Ty?"

"Yeah, what you need?" Cal ask again.

I'm tired of him always asking me that. But I do need something, so I can't front. "I got all my pops equipment and records and CDs and shit," I tell them. "It's in storage."

"You wanna sell?" Greg ask. "'Cause I know a guy that would buy all that shit." Greg always know a guy that wanna buy something.

"Nah, I don't wanna sell his shit. He gettin' out in a couple months. I wanna use it, throw a couple parties like he used to. But for our age. I'ma find a place, and I'ma charge people to come. Y'all can sell your shit outside, and I'ma DJ. What y'all think?"

Greg look at Andre, who the oldest and make the decisions for all of them.

"Sound a'ight to me," Andre say.

"What you need?" Cal ask me for the third fuckin' time.

"I need cash. 'Bout two, three hundred to get the place and set shit up. We pack that place, make this party off-the-hook and we all get paid. But that's only the first one," I say, trying to make them see that this could be big, like my pops parties used to be. "We keep havin' them, folks keep coming, and we start making some real money then."

I don't tell them that all I'm trying to do right now is make enough money to get me, my moms, and Troy our own apartment. 'Cause we been at the EAU over two weeks now, and I'm starting to think they ain't never gonna get us no Tier II.

I mean, most of the time, they only make you stay at the motels a couple nights, then they put you in a Tier II shelter where each family get, like, they own apartment with a kitchen and bedrooms and shit. And yeah, them places ain't all that nice, but they way better than Bennett and least you get to stay there for a while. Least you know where you gonna be sleeping every night.

But they treating my family different now. That's 'cause 'bout three years ago, when my pops was locked up, we was broke and living in a Tier II shelter, and my moms scammed the city. She bought some social security numbers and other shit and was getting welfare money for three different families with all kinds of fake names and shit. She said she only did it 'cause she was desperate.

When the city found out, she was arrested. They ain't put her in jail, but she still on probation for it. She s'posed to be paying the city back, but they givin' her time since they think she got a retarded kid, like that ain't another one of her scams.

The problem is, now that we homeless again, the EAU don't

wanna give us no Tier II again, not when my moms was convicted of welfare fraud. That's why we been at the EAU for two weeks now and they ain't found nothing for us. My moms think they just trying to fuck with us long enough that we give up and find a place to stay on our own. But we don't got nowhere else to go. If we did, why would we be sleeping at Bennett?

Andre reach in his pocket, pull out a big roll of cash, count off three fifty-dollar bills, and just hand it to me like it ain't nothing but a thing. "We in business," he say.

"A'ight," I say. "But for real, y'all gotta keep your shit outside."

They don't say nothing, but I'ma make sure they don't bring no drugs in my party. I do things right, I can make some good money like my pops was makin'. But I ain't trying to go down like the man. Nah. I'ma hafta be smarter than him.

ELEVEN

I only got a hundred fifty in my pocket when I leave the apartment, but least it's something. Now I gotta get my shit together and find a place for the party. And I hafta make sure I make some money outta this. When my pops throw his parties, he be charging people like thirty dollars just to get in, then he make more money selling drugs and drinks. But I can't charge kids that much. And I ain't selling no drugs, that's for damn sure.

The snow is real bad now, and I don't know how I'ma get back to Bennett. The cars on the street is sliding 'round, and I don't see no buses nowhere. I walk down the street trying to keep from busting my ass, which ain't easy with sneakers on. And I'm still fucked up, which really ain't helping none.

When I pass the laundromat where Ms. Jenkins work at, I see her standing inside near the door looking out like she waiting for someone. I wave to her and try to keep on going, but she open the door and lean her head out. "Tyrell, come here a minute."

I stop and go back. "Hi, Ms. Jenkins."

"You coming from seeing Novisha?" she ask. She forever making sure me and Novisha ain't together when she ain't 'round.

"No, I was with Calvin and them 'round the corner."

Ms. Jenkins give me a look like she think I'm up to something. "I hope you're not getting yourself mixed up with them boys, Tyrell. You know what they do, right?"

"Yeah, I know, but you don't gotta worry 'bout me, Ms. Jenkins. I ain't gonna do nothing stupid."

"Good," she say, but I can tell she still not sure she can believe me. "Because you know where those boys are headed, right?"

"I know," I say. "But they don't got a nice girlfriend like I do." I smile 'cause I know she like what I'm saying. "I ain't gonna do nothing to mess things up with my girl."

"Good," she say again. She stare at me for another couple seconds, and I start to get nervous. Damn, I hope she can't tell I'm high. Then she say, "Can you help me with some bags? I'm closing up early here, and I have a lot of groceries to take home. My husband was supposed to pick me up, but I don't know where he is. I guess the snow is holding him up."

I go inside and wait while she turn off all the lights and lock the back door. She got six plastic bags on the floor with all kinds of food inside. She got turkey wings, collard greens, yams, and all kinda stuff. "You making Thanksgiving dinner or something?" I ask.

She laugh. "You know how I do on Sundays, Tyrell. I should invite your mother and brother over sometimes."

"Yeah, my moms would like that. And Troy too. That boy can eat. You should see how big he getting."

68

"Alright. Let me plan something. It would be nice to see your mother again."

I can tell she just saying that to be nice, 'cause the truth is, them two don't really got that much to talk 'bout. When we used to live in the projects, my moms and Ms. Jenkins ain't hardly said more than two words to each other. They was living in like two different worlds. They ain't start conversating 'til me and Novisha started going out, and that was mostly by phone.

I pick up four of them heavy-ass bags, two in each hand, and leave her the two light ones. We go outside, and she lock up the front of the laundromat and pull down the metal gate and padlock it. Then we walk down the street. "I hope Mr. Jenkins don't show up now and find the place closed," she say.

"He got a cell phone?"

"He has one for work, but he's not allowed to give out the phone number. He said they fired a guy for taking personal calls on it."

I wanna tell Ms. Jenkins that her ex-husband is full of shit, but maybe she ain't gonna wanna hear it from me. "You and Mr. Jenkins gonna get back together?" I ask her.

"You sound like Novisha now," she say. "I don't know what we gonna do, but I'm a Catholic, so as far as I'm concerned, he will always be my husband. I don't care what those divorce papers say."

Getting to her building with all them bags take longer than I thought it was gonna take, and I'm getting worried that I ain't gonna be able to get back to Bennett. The snow is deep, and it's hard just walking. And it's so cold I can't even feel my hands or feet no more.

When we get to the apartment, Novisha in the living room on

the computer. She kinda look happy to see me, but at the same time she look like she upset 'bout something. She give me a hug, but she don't seem all that into it. I wanna get a real hug from her, but I don't want her smelling no weed on me, so I just let it go.

"You staying for dinner, right, Ty?" Ms. Jenkins ask.

"You don't mind feeding me three days in a row?"

"Boy, you know I would feed you everyday if I could. Especially with all you and your family going through right now."

"You been doing a lot to help us, Ms. Jenkins, always giving us food and being so nice."

"Does that mean you staying?" She smile and put her hands on her hips like she want a answer already.

I laugh a little bit. "Yeah, I'm staying. Thanks, Ms. Jenkins."

"Now, boy, go relax while I burn up some of these pots and pans!"

Me and Novisha go in the living room and watch TV. We sitting close, but not that close 'cause her moms don't like to see her little girl up under no guy. Before I can even think 'bout it, she whisper to me, "I thought you weren't gonna get high anymore."

"I'm not," I tell her.

She stare at me like she don't believe me or something. She getting that same stare her moms got. "I know what I smell."

"Nah, I was just over at Cal apartment, and you know them niggas is always getting high. I just walked through the door and, next thing I know, my eyes is burning, and I got that weed smell on me."

She look me in the face hard, like she trying to make sure I ain't lying.

"Seriously," I say. "I ain't lying." Her moms ain't looking, so I

70

put my arm 'round her and pull her a little closer to me. But when I try to kiss her real quick, she turn away and tell me to stop.

"I ain't high," I say again.

"It's not that."

"Then what's the matter?"

"Nothing," she say, but she don't look at me when she say it. She look down like she hiding something.

"Novisha, we was just here two days ago, and you told me the same thing, that nothing was wrong. Then you tell me some guy is stalking you, and now —"

"*Shh.*" She get this serious look on her face now. "I don't want my mother to know about that."

"Then just tell me what's wrong."

She look over at her mother again, then she talk real quiet. "That guy, he called here a couple of times today. Like five times."

Damn. I'ma hafta do something 'bout this.

"I don't know how he got my number, but —"

"What he say?"

She take a deep breath. "Well, first he just talked about school stuff, that he wants to help me with the volunteer project I started. I told him I don't need or want his help. Then he said he likes the way I look in my gym shorts, but I don't have gym with boys. It's like he's spying on me or something."

I try to stay calm while she telling me this shit, but it's hard. If I get mad, I know Novisha gonna stop talking, and she gonna stop telling me when this guy do something else. But his shit gotta stop. "Look, Novisha, you tell me who this guy is, and I'ma take care of it. Then you don't gotta worry 'bout him no more."

She whisper, "You don't have to protect me, Ty. I'm in high school now. I can take care of this myself."

"Then what you need me for? What kinda man I'ma be if I can't take care of my girl?"

She just shake her head. "Let me handle this, Ty. I'm a big girl."

Man, that shit just frustrate the hell outta me. What she want from me, to just sit here while she going through all this and not do nothing? 'Cause if that's what she want, I don't know if I can do that. That ain't who I am. Shit, my pops ain't raise me to be no pussy.

I close my eyes for a couple seconds trying not to get mad. I love this girl, but, man, I don't like what she saying to me. She trying to be all grown and shit, but the truth is, she real innocent. How she gonna protect herself from some guy that's so bold he calling her house in the middle of the fuckin' day? To me, that's a nigga that don't care.

When I open my eyes, it take me a while to focus 'cause that weed is still fucking with my head. Damn, man, how I let Ms. Jenkins talk me into coming up here? And how I'ma act like I ain't high through dinner when I can't hardly see straight?

"Are you okay?" Novisha ask me. I know she can tell I'm high.

"Yeah, I'm a'ight."

"So, are we done talking about this?"

I look over at Ms. Jenkins in the kitchen, but she ain't paying us no mind. "We done with this for now," I say, "but I got something I wanna ask you, 'cause I don't understand something. Why you tell your moms I'm getting good grades when we both know

I ain't stepped foot in that school for like a month now? What, you lying now?"

Novisha look like what she is — cold busted. "I'm sorry," she say. "You know my mother. If she finds out you're not going to school, she's not gonna let me go out with you anymore. She's gonna think you're a bad influence on me or something."

"So, you go and lie to her?"

She don't say nothing.

"That ain't cool, Novisha. I'm talking to your moms on the phone, and she telling me all this crap 'bout how proud she is that I'm doing good in school, and I'm like, why Novisha gotta lie like that?" Maybe it's the weed, but all of a sudden I'm just telling her what I really think 'bout what she did. "You ain't had to say nothing to your moms 'bout me, you know. You just making stuff up 'cause you don't think I'm good enough for you the way I am. How you think that make me feel?"

"I'm sorry," she say again. "I just wanted to be able to see you."

"What you two whispering about in there?" Ms. Jenkins ask from the kitchen. She got her hands on her hips and shit, and she got this suspicious look on her face like we planning a bank robbery or something.

"Nothing," Novisha say.

"You do all your homework, girl?"

"Not yet."

"Then let Tyrell watch TV, and get to it. I don't want you up all night."

"They're probably gonna cancel school tomorrow with all that snow out there."

73

"You don't know that yet. So get to work 'til I finish cooking dinner." She start to turn 'round, then change her mind. "You hear from your father?"

"No."

"I just hope he's not stuck out there in that snow."

Novisha roll her eyes. "Don't worry. He'll be fine."

She get up and go back to the computer to finish her homework. I stay on the couch and start watching the news, but the weed is still messing with me. The apartment is warm, and I'm all comfortable and shit. Next thing I know, my eyes is closing.

My stomach wake up before me. The apartment smell real good, and I can tell them turkey wings is gonna be slamming. By the time me and Novisha get married, I hope she know how to cook like her moms, 'cause if she do, I'ma be one happy brotha.

The guy on the news is talking 'bout the snowstorm and how there's gonna be 'bout twelve to eighteen inches before it stop. Shit, ain't no way I'ma get to Bennett now. I'ma hafta go back to Cal apartment 'cause I ain't sure Ms. Jenkins gonna want me to stay here.

My cell ring. I can't tell who it is from the caller ID, but I flip it open anyway. "Hello."

"Where you at?" It's my moms, probably on that pay phone at Bennett. And I can tell she wilding out.

"At Novisha house." Novisha look up from the computer when I say her name. She look like she wanna ask who I'm talking to, so I cover the phone and tell her who it is. I ain't the kinda

74

guy who gonna conversate on my cell when I'm with my girl. That shit just ain't right.

My moms start screaming at me. "Well, you got me and your brother here with no money, waiting for you to bring your ass back with some food and shit."

"How I'ma get there in this snow? You see what's going on out there?"

"Well, what the fuck we s'posed to do? Starve?"

I can't stand when she be making me feel responsible for her and Troy. I ain't her husband, and I ain't Troy father. I wanna curse her out too, but I'm in Ms. Jenkins house and I don't curse in front of her or Novisha. "I can't do nothing," I tell my moms, but the truth is there is something.

So while she cursing and screaming, I'm trying to decide if I should tell her where I keep my emergency money 'cause the second I tell her, I ain't gonna be able to stash nothing there no more. She forever looking though my stuff trying to find money. But, damn, Troy don't got no food, so I don't really got no choice. "A'ight. You know that little black case where I keep the keys for the storage place? I think it's at the bottom of one of the garbage bags. Look in there. I got some dimes and quarters in there, pro'ly a couple dollars' worth. Buy some chips and stuff from the machine on the first floor, and I'll buy some real food on my way back in the morning."

"Ms. Jenkins gonna let you stay there? Do she know you screwing her daughter?"

I just ignore her 'cause she think she know everything when she don't. "I'ma go back to Cal apartment and sleep on his couch."

"You get money from him?"

That's all she care 'bout, but she ain't getting no answer from me. And she ain't getting no money from me neither, not 'til after I make money from the party. "What's Troy doing?"

"Driving me crazy, what you think he doing?"

"You take him out to play in the snow?"

"He went out with them other kids. He don't need me watching him every second of the day."

Damn. She can't do nothing.

"Don't let him out no more," I tell her. "The snow getting too deep, and he don't got no boots. Get him some chips, and tell him I'ma be back in the morning."

"You ain't answer my question," she say. "How much Cal give you?"

"My minutes is running out," I tell her. "I gotta go 'fore the phone cut off. Bye." I flip the cell closed. How I'ma get through this week at Bennett and plan this party with only a hundred fifty? The party gonna hafta be this Saturday, 'cause I need to make some money real fast.

"Come set this table, Tyrell," Ms. Jenkins say from the kitchen.

I get up, kinda glad she making me do something besides just eat. She got four dishes set out like she still waiting for her ex-husband to show up. I start setting the table, but my mind is just thinking and planning.

First thing I'ma hafta do is find a place for the party, and the cheaper the better. Then I'ma hafta find a way to get my pops equipment from the storage place. Maybe Andre or Greg can help me with that 'cause they the only two niggas I know that got a license. Then I'ma hafta promote this party 'cause I need the place to be packed with kids so I can make some real money.

I finish setting the table and ask Ms. Jenkins if I can do something else to help out.

"No," she say. "Just go wash up for dinner. Then come back, sit down, and eat."

I smile.

"And don't think I'm going to let you go back to those boys' apartment, Tyrell. Not with what they're up to. No. You're staying right here. Case closed."

"You sure, Ms. Jenkins? 'Cause I know how you feel 'bout having a boy here with Novisha."

She look me in the eye. "I trust you, Tyrell."

Damn. Now I'm feeling guilty.

She laugh. "And I'm keeping Novisha in my bed with me, so don't get any ideas!"

"Mom!" Novisha say. She still sitting at the computer. "You're embarrassing me."

"Girl, I said I trust Tyrell, right? But I wasn't born yesterday. I was a teenager once myself, you know, and I know what I would've gotten away with if my mother ever turned her back on me and your father. That woman was on me like white on rice, let me tell you. But she knew what she was doing."

Novisha roll her eyes. "I'm not you. And Tyrell's not Daddy. Thank God."

Ms. Jenkins give Novisha one of them stares. "Turn that computer off and come eat dinner. You know they're going to cancel school tomorrow anyway. You don't need to sit there all night."

Me and Novisha look at each other for a couple seconds. She

don't say nothing, but I can tell she thinking what I'm thinking. Her moms is bugging.

A couple hours later, I'm all full and satisfied, and me and Novisha is in her room. We s'posed to be putting clean sheets on her bed, but I'm trying to get some good long kisses from her before she gotta go sleep with her moms. Of course her moms make us keep the door open, so we can't really do much of nothing.

But that don't stop me from trying. I'm grabbing her ass and trying to feel her up whenever she pass by me. And every chance I get, I'm kissing on her like I can't help myself.

"C'mon, Tyrell," she say, checking to make sure her moms ain't watching us. "My mom's gonna wonder what we're doing in here if she doesn't see these sheets changed." She start taking her blankets off the bed, but I stop her and put my arms 'round her waist.

"I wanna sleep on your sheets," I tell her. "So I can smell you all night."

She make a face. "What do I smell like?"

"You know, that peach stuff you use in the shower. I love the way you smell."

"You do?" She smile a little. "But, if you sleep on my sheets, are you gonna —?"

"Pro'ly," I say, and laugh when she get all embarrassed and look away. "But I'ma be thinking 'bout you when I do it. Like when we married, man, me and you gonna be doing all kinda wild things."

Now her smile get real big. "You sure you can wait that long?"

"Yeah," I tell her. "I'm sure." I pull her real close to me and whisper in her ear, "I'ma wait for you 'cause you my girl." I kiss her on her neck a couple times. "Tell me I'm your man."

"You're my man," she say in my ear. Then we kiss on the lips, and this time she don't act like she care if her moms catch us or nothing. She into it. Her lips are so sweet and juicy that, man, it's hard to keep my mind from thinking 'bout what else them lips could do for me.

"You love me?" I ask her.

"I love you," she say. Man, I can't explain, but them words make me feel real good.

After a while, Novisha tell me she better go back out to the kitchen before her moms come looking for her.

"I'ma read your diary," I tell her.

"Which one?"

"Both."

"You better not," she say, but she smiling, so I know she don't mean it. Besides, she let me read her diaries before, so why not now? "Good night," she say, and leave the room. I wish she coulda stayed, but at the same time, I ain't slept in a room by myself since we lost our apartment, so I ain't really complaining 'bout being alone. Sometimes I just need time to chill.

I lay down on the bed, reach under the pillow, and pull out the little purple diary with butterflies on the cover. This is the fake diary, and it's just for her moms to read when she be spying on her daughter. This is the diary I like 'cause this shit is funny.

I open it and turn to the last thing she wrote.

Dear Diary,

I got my award tonight. I still don't understand why they gave it to me. All I did was get other kids to do some volunteer work with me. Isn't that what every Christian should do anyway? Tyrell came to the ceremony, so that made tonight extra special. Then we all went out to dinner. Dad came too. I love him, but I wish Mom would find someone special in her life again. She needs to move forward, not backwards. She deserves to be happy again.

All I gotta say is, my girl is good. It's like she writing this whole diary just so she could tell her moms shit. I flip back a couple pages.

Dear Diary,

Shanice and her boyfriend broke up yesterday. He said he was tired of being in a childish relationship. Those were his exact words. I'm glad Shanice didn't turn her back on her values and give in to that idiot. I don't understand why some boys only think about one thing. Tyrell isn't like that. He respects me and would never pressure me. I'm so lucky to have a boyfriend like him.

No wonder her moms trust me so much. She be reading all this and thinking me and her daughter ain't doing no nasty shit.

I put the diary back under the pillow, then get up to find the real one. That one is just a black and white notebook with GLOBAL HISTORY on the cover, and she keep it on her desk with all her other notebooks. When I find it, I sit in the chair and start reading from the last thing she wrote. It's from yesterday.

I just got back from dinner at Red Lobster with Mom, Dad, and Tyrell. I don't understand Dad at all. He's been hanging around here a lot, giving me money and sleeping with Mom like nothing's changed. If Mom takes him back, I'm going away to boarding school.

I'm so glad Tyrell came to the awards ceremony, but he seemed kind of down. I'm not sure why. I know he loves me and he's happy for me, but maybe it's hard being around me when I'm winning awards and he still doesn't know where he's going yet. Maybe I shouldn't have invited him, but I thought if he came, he would see how great school can be. Sometimes I don't get it when he tells me he's going to support me when I go to college. Tyrell is smart enough to go to college himself. He doesn't have to support me. I don't need him for that.

I wish Tyrell could see how much he's capable of. He's so sweet and sensitive, and he always wants to take care of people. I wish he would love himself and take care of himself first.

I put the notebook back down on the desk. Damn. That shit get to me. What, she just wanna go to college by herself, not with me like we said we was gonna do? I don't know if she mean it, but what she saying is real clear to me. She don't need me.

TWELVE

Novisha wake me up by kissing me all over my face. "They closed all the schools," she say, laughing. "Get up."

Novisha got on this long, thick-ass nightgown. I pull her down on the bed next to me and try to work my hand up that nightgown. "Ty, stop. My mom's sleeping in the next room."

"I just wanna touch you," I say. "I can't even see no skin with that thing you wearing."

She get up off the bed. "That's the idea. My mom made me wear it since there's a *boy* in the house."

"Just pull it up. Let me see your panties. C'mon."

"I'm not wearing any panties," she say.

Now I'm excited. "Come here. Take care of me."

"But my mom —"

"Do it quick," I say.

And she do. She turn 'round the St. Mary statue and get to work. I know she scared 'cause so am I. If her moms catch us, man, we both dead. While Novisha doing her thing, I'm still trying to pull up her nightgown and see her, but she won't let me. She think it's okay if she make me feel good, but I can't do nothing to make her feel good. I don't get it, but I ain't complaining.

When we done, she get up and pick up my jeans from off the floor where I threw them last night. She hand them to me. "Get dressed. Then let's make breakfast together."

She 'bout to leave the room when she bend down to pick something up off the floor. She stand up with my money in her hand, counting it. "A hundred and fifty dollars?" She look at me like she wanna know what's going on. "Where'd you get this?"

I'm laying there trying to hold on to that good feeling in my body, and my mind can't even make up no lie to tell her. "I got it from Cal and them."

"Are you working for them?" She ask it like she don't even wanna hear the answer.

"Nah. You know I ain't gonna do that. I just needed some money 'cause me and my moms is broke. We don't even got money to eat."

"How are you gonna pay them back?"

I don't wanna tell her 'bout the party, so I just say, "I'ma hafta work harder with them MetroCards. Cal said I could pay him back a little at a time."

She hand me the money. "Okay," she say. "I hope you know what you're doing."

"I do," I tell her. "Don't worry. Me and Cal is tight."

After we get dressed, me and Novisha go out to the kitchen and decide to make pancakes. "I wanna make enough for your moms too," I say. "'Cause she been cooking for me, like, everyday."

I ain't never cooked with Novisha before, but we having fun. She mixing the batter and I'm greasing the pan when my cell ring. I don't know the number on the caller ID, so I'm thinking it's probably my moms calling from Bennett again. But it ain't. "Ty, it's me. Jasmine."

Damn, now she tracking me down all over the fucking Bronx. Novisha is like two feet from me, so I don't know what to say. "Yeah, what's up?" I ask Jasmine.

"It's your brother. I went to your room this morning looking for you, and your brother was there all alone."

"What?" I feel the blood pumping through my body real fast now. "Troy okay? Where was my moms?"

"Troy's fine. I don't know where your mother is though. Troy let me in the room because he got scared when he didn't see your mom there. He started crying. I thought your mother must of went out looking for some food or something, so I stood there with Troy waiting for her. But it's been, like, more than two hours, and your mother still isn't back."

"This don't make no sense," I say. "How she gonna do this?" Novisha stop stirring and look at me like she wanna know what's going on. I cover the phone and tell her, "My moms left Troy alone in the motel room."

Jasmine is still talking. "I just wanted to tell you that Troy's with me. He gave me your cell phone number. You wanna talk to him?"

"Yeah," I say. "Put him on."

"Hi, Ty," Troy say in a real low voice. "You mad at me for letting the church girl in our room?"

"No, I ain't mad. You did a good job. But she ain't no church girl. She just took us to church for the food, remember? I'm just glad you remembered my cell phone number. That's good."

"Where Mommy at?"

"I don't know. Was she there when you went to bed last night?"

"Yeah. We went to sleep, but I woke up when the church girl knocked on the door. Mommy wasn't here no more."

"You okay?"

"I like the church girl. She real pretty."

"Yeah, I know. Can you put her back on the phone?"

A second later, Jasmine say, "Ty, your brother is really a great kid."

"Thanks, Jasmine. I'ma try to get back there as soon as I can. You mind watching him?"

"No, we're hanging out together, right, Troy?"

In the background, I hear Troy say, "Yeah."

"A'ight. I'ma leave now," I tell her.

"Where are —?" Jasmine start to ask. "Never mind. That's none of my business."

"I'm with my girl," I say. "All that snow last night, I just got stuck, you know."

"Oh," she say. All of a sudden she quiet now.

"I'ma be back there in a little while, okay?"

"Okay," she say. "Don't worry about Troy. He's gonna be fine with me. It's real bad outside, so take your time, okay."

"A'ight." I flip my cell closed and shove it back in my pocket.

"Who's Jasmine?" Novisha ask, giving me one of them looks.

I don't know what to say, so I just go, "She this girl from Bennett."

"You went to church with her?" Novisha got a little attitude now, which she don't get a lot, so I know she getting jealous.

"Nah, it wasn't like that. She found out 'bout this church that be giving out free food to homeless people, so me and Troy went with her."

"I invite you to church every week, and you hardly ever go with me."

"I ain't wanna go yesterday neither, but Troy was hungry." I pick up the bowl and start stirring the batter, trying to work them lumps out. I can feel Novisha just staring at me, and I know I'm looking mad guilty, but I just can't look at her right now.

"Is she pretty?"

"Novisha, don't start, okay?"

"Is she?"

I put the bowl down on the counter. "Nah, she ain't pretty. That girl is butt ugly. She got braces and acne. You way prettier than her." I look up at her real quick and catch a little bit of a smile. "I ain't looking at no other girl, you know that."

Novisha come over to me and put her arm 'round me. We kiss, but now I'm feeling real guilty even though I ain't even do nothing to Jasmine. She the one that got in bed with me and started touching me and shit. I ain't ask her to do that to me.

"Are you gonna stay and eat?"

"Yeah, but I'ma hafta eat and run. You mind?"

Novisha shake her head. "I understand."

We start making the pancakes. She pour the batter in the pan and I flip them, but the first three pancakes I try to make just fall apart on me.

"You have to wait," Novisha say, laughing. She grab some of the pieces and eat them while I pour more batter on the pan. Then she lean over and kiss me with food still in her mouth. Next thing I know, I got her food in my mouth. The pancakes is cooked on the outside and raw on the inside. Man, them shits is nasty. When I try to spit them out, they just go back in Novisha mouth. And back and forth. Me and her is laughing and kissing for so long, the pancakes on the pan start burning 'cause we ain't paying them no mind. But we having a good time.

Finally, after a while, we make a whole stack of good pancakes and some bacon. Novisha wake her moms up and tell her we made breakfast for her. It take her a while to come out her room, but when she do, she looking real tore up with a scarf on her head, wearing a old beat-up robe. She go on and on 'bout how happy she is that we made breakfast for her. But she don't know how much food we wasted getting this made.

We all sit down to eat. My mind is all over the place. I'm just looking at Novisha and wishing we was grown already and this was our place. She so perfect for me. It's hard to explain, but she got everything I want in a woman. She cute as hell, sexy, sweet, smart, and she love me. What more I'ma ask for?

But to be honest, I'm still thinking 'bout what she wrote in her diary. If she go away to college and don't want me to come with her, I don't know what I'ma do. All I wanna do is take care of her and be her man. I love her. What I don't get is why she keep pushing me away from her.

THIRTEEN

Getting back to Bennett is crazy. Matter of fact, just getting to the train station ain't no joke. The projects is already plowed and the sidewalks is clear, but the second I get near the laundromat and stores, nothing is shoveled 'cause practically everything is closed. Only stores open is the bodega and the Chinese restaurant. Even the liquor store is closed. And in the projects, liquor stores don't be closing for shit. The snow on the sidewalk is too deep to walk through, so I gotta walk in the street and try not to get hit by the cars and buses.

The trains is running, but real slow, and by the time they do come, they just packed. I don't know where all them people is going, but they serious. Nineteen inches of snow on the ground and these assholes can't even stay in they fuckin' house.

When I get back to Hunts Point, it's like the city just forgot 'bout this whole neighborhood 'cause the streets ain't seen a plow yet. I gotta walk four blocks from the train station, which ain't easy, and I'm practically going blind with all the white I'm seeing.

The parked cars is just big white bumps now, and you can't see none of the garbage and shit on the street. Man, I never knew Hunts Point could look this clean and be this quiet.

I don't get back to Bennett 'til 'bout 12:30, and when I do, my feet is all cold and wet, and I'm miserable. I never used to hate snow, but when you ain't got no warm coat or boots, snow ain't cool. Not only that, but I ain't got no other sneakers to put on, so I'ma be stuck in these all fuckin' day.

Jasmine and Troy is in the lobby when I get there. Jasmine is on the pay phone just like she was when I left her yesterday, and just like yesterday, she talking all that Spanish shit. And she look real upset.

Troy is off the hook, running 'round like he lost his mind or something. But least he got other kids to play with now. He chasing two other boys 'round with a long cardboard tube, and they all laughing real loud. The guy at the front desk look like he wanna kill all of them, but I'm like this: If my brother can have some fun while we in this situation, I'ma let him. He don't deserve to be at Bennett. He should be outside with a good coat and boots playing in the snow, so why I'ma stop him from having a good time? So I just sit down on one of the couches and wait for Jasmine to get off the phone so I can thank her for watching him.

But when Jasmine hang up the phone, she look mad as hell. "You okay?" I ask her.

"Not really," she say, sitting next to me, real close. "Reyna — oh, forget it. I don't wanna talk about her."

Man, this girl is so close to me, our legs is all pressed together and shit. "Tell me. What's up with your sister? She still ain't come back yet?"

Jasmine shake her head.

"Where she at?"

"I don't know. She said she wanted to hang out with her friends Friday and Saturday night, but she was supposed to be back yesterday. And now I'm by myself and I only have a dollar left."

"She be leaving you alone like this?"

"No, she never did this. But her boyfriend never let her do nothing. When Emiliano threw us out, Reyna told me she just wanted to have some freedom for a few days, before he lets us move back in with him."

"How you know he gonna let y'all move back in?"

"He will. He's just trying to teach Reyna a lesson, that she needs him."

"You like him?" I ask her.

"Yeah. He's like my father, only better than my real father was. Emiliano is strict, but that's why I like him. He's a real good father, but it's hard for Reyna."

"She love him?"

"No. But he loves her, and he loves me, and he takes care of us. Before I met Emiliano, we didn't have nothing."

"*You* met him?"

Jasmine look like she ain't even know what she said. Then she go, "Yeah. I met him first. We were living with this other guy that Reyna was dating, but I couldn't stand that guy. Then I met Emiliano on my way to school. He got a bread route, and he tried to talk to me while he was unloading his truck. He didn't know I was only fourteen then. So I told him my age and he got all embarrassed, but every time I seen him after that, he would say hi. One morning I was with Reyna, and he started talking to her, and I could tell he thought she was real pretty too. They went out that night, and the next day we moved out of her boyfriend's apartment and in with Emiliano." She stop talking for a while and I don't know if she done or not. Then she say, "He's a great guy. He changed my life."

I can tell she getting sad, so I try to change the subject. "Reyna pro'ly on her way back now," I tell her. "She ain't gonna up and leave you here, right?"

"Right." Jasmine try to smile.

"Who was you on the phone with?" I know it ain't none of my business, but I ask her anyway 'cause she in the mood to talk.

"Emil. I thought she went back there to make up with him, but she's not there. I didn't tell him she's been gone since Friday because he's not gonna like that."

"You still think he gonna take y'all back?"

"Yeah. He told me he wants to work things out with her so we can move back home. He wants her to call him when she gets back. But if she don't come back today, he's gonna know she stood out all night. And he's gonna know she's with other guys." Then she get them tears going again. "I shouldn't of called him."

I put my arm 'round her shoulders. "Relax. She gonna be back. And they gonna get back together, and y'all gonna go back home soon."

She rest her head on my shoulder. "If Reyna doesn't come back, can you stay with me tonight? I can't stand being alone. I'm scared."

Damn. "I don't know," I say. "I don't know if I can trust my moms no more. She gonna mess 'round and get my brother put in foster care again."

"Think about it," Jasmine say. She wipe her face and get

up. "I mean, I know you got Novisha. We don't have to do nothing."

"Thanks for watching Troy and making sure he okay. I owe you."

"Okay, then I'll collect tonight," she say, smiling real sexy. This girl know what she doing, and I gotta tell the truth, saying no to her ain't easy. If Novisha ain't hit me off this morning, I don't know if I woulda been this strong.

"Ty!" Troy finally see me. He leave his two new friends and run over to me, dropping the cardboard tube and jumping on me. Hard.

So I do what a big brother s'posed to do. I stand up and drop him to the floor. Then I get on the floor with him and we play-fight for a while. I be playing real rough with him sometimes 'cause I don't want him growing up all soft and shit. He need to be strong and tough to make it in this world, 'specially here in the Bronx.

Jasmine is still standing there, and she start cheering for Troy. "Get him, Troy. Show me what you can do!"

That get Troy all worked up, and he start fighting back harder. He get on top of me, breathing all heavy and shit.

Jasmine start laughing. "That's it, Troy. Yeah!"

"Don't even try it," I tell him when he throw his arms in the air like he the champ.

I slip out from under him, then we just go at it. Fighting like we on the street. He elbow me in the face, and I punch him in the ribs. I can't believe this little dude is getting my blood pumping this way.

This the way it used to be with me and my pops. Man, when we used to wrestle, we ain't stop 'til both of us was bloody. He

92

used to kick my ass, laughing the whole time. My moms would be yelling at us, that we was gonna get hurt, but that just made us wanna fight harder. She ain't understand that guys gotta act stronger and tougher when females is watching them.

I'm getting tired now, and my wet sneakers is making it hard to move fast, so I just flip Troy over and pin him down on the floor. Then, when Troy can't move no more, I let him get free. I'm thinking we done now, but the next thing I know he on top of me again, trying to pin me this time.

Jasmine is still laughing. "That's it, Troy," she say. "Get him!"

"A'ight. A'ight," I tell Troy, and act like he hurting me. I'm tired as hell, but I like how he don't stop fighting. It's good to know he can take care of hisself if he need to. "You win," I tell him. "You got me, man."

Troy jump up like he fuckin' Muhammad Ali. "I win! I win!" He hug Jasmine. "See, I told you," he say. He got his arms wrapped 'round her waist, and one of his hands is on her ass, I swear. Damn. They got him in special ed, but Troy know what he doing.

"Wow. You're a great fighter!" Jasmine tell him.

I lay there on the floor for a second before getting up. "I'ma get you next time, man," I tell Troy. "Watch your back."

He smile, all proud of hisself.

I kinda wanna smile too, but I don't want him to see that 'cause he gonna know I let him win. Shit, life is so fucked up for Troy right now. Someone need to let him win sometime.

FOURTEEN

By the time my moms get back, me and Troy is upstairs in our room, and he eating the last leftover pancake that I brung back from Novisha house. My moms come through the door carrying three plastic grocery bags like ain't nothing wrong. She even got the nerve to give me a cold look, like she too through with me. "Oh, you couldn't bring your Black ass home last night," she say. "Not even with your little brother starving to death."

I look behind me where Troy is jumping on the bed, trying to touch the ceiling. "He look like he starving to you?"

"You know what I mean," she say, and set the bags down on the dresser.

I can't believe this woman. "Don't try to get outta this," I tell her. "How you gonna leave Troy here by hisself?"

"He was 'sleep."

"You left outta here 'fore nine o'clock," I say. "It's after one now. You think he gonna sleep through the whole day? What you think he was gonna do when he got up and you wasn't here?"

"I thought you was gonna be back by the time he got up."

If Troy wasn't here, I would probably curse her out or something 'cause her attitude is making me so fuckin' mad. She dead wrong and she know it, but she trying to blame me. She do this all the time, and it frustrate the hell outta me. She always acting like she ain't responsible for nothing. Like it's always somebody else fault.

She used to try this shit with my pops too, but he wasn't having it. Matter of fact, even though my pops ain't really no violent guy, I seen him beat the shit outta her twice when she tried to play him like this. Now, I ain't like seeing my moms get a beatdown like that, but at the same time, she the kinda woman that could drive any man to do some fucked-up shit.

The first time my pops beat her was after he got outta prison the first time. He ain't like how much she changed while he was away. The apartment was nasty, and she acted like she forgot how to cook. That's 'cause my grandmother was living with us the whole time he was locked up and my moms ain't had to lift a finger. But my grandmother went back down South a couple weeks before my pops got out, and he kept telling my moms she needed to go back to being the woman he married, but she acted like she ain't know how to do nothing no more.

One night he came home from a party, woke her up, and dragged her ass outta bed. I woke up too, 'cause they was making mad noise and shit. My pops was cursing and screaming, and my moms was crying. He had her in a headlock and he was just dragging her from the kitchen to the living room to the bathroom, showing her everything he thought wasn't clean enough. She tried to talk back to him, but he would just tighten his hold on her and tell her to shut up.

Finally he told her that when he woke up in the morning,

everything had to be clean, but she was still talking back. She said she was tired and couldn't stay up all night cleaning. Man, I thought that man was gonna lose his fuckin' mind. He back-handed her 'cross the face so hard, she fell up against the bathroom door, crying. And I was standing there the whole time with my mouth open, but I couldn't say nothing. What I wanted to tell her was to just shut up and start cleaning before he killed her.

My pops ain't say another word that night. He went in the kitchen, drank a beer at the table, then went to bed. And when he woke up, the apartment was as clean as a apartment in the projects could get. I ain't never gonna forget that. While we was eating breakfast, man, that's when I saw just how jacked-up my moms face was. The whole right side was swole up and her eye was bloodshot red. I couldn't believe my pops actually did something like that to her. Crazy thing is, no one ever said nothing 'bout it. We all just went 'bout our business like nothing ever happened.

The second time was, like, two years ago, right after we moved out the projects. My pops was making some good money, and he was taking care of us. Matter of fact, I was real fuckin' happy 'cause me and him was hanging out all the time. I was at most of his parties, and I would help him DJ sometimes and just chill sometimes. Then me and him used to come back to our new apartment on Pelham Parkway at, like, four or five in the morning, sit on them white plastic chairs on the terrace and just get high and talk 'bout nothing 'til the sun came up.

One morning my moms got up and saw us out there, and she got all mad and shit. She started screaming at him, telling him that he lied to her 'bout the new apartment. She said she thought she was gonna be living in some real nice place, but the new apartment wasn't hardly no better than the projects was. She said he been outta jail for almost a year, and he shoulda been able to set her up in a better place.

Man, she hardly got them last words out her mouth before he stood up and punched her dead in her face like she was a dude. A second later he was back on the terrace like nothing happened. He ain't say nothing to her. He ain't even look back at what he did. That was it. My moms was on the floor looking like she ain't know what happened to her. Her nose and teeth was bleeding, but she couldn't even cry. Me and her was both in shock.

I helped her up and took her into the kitchen, and she ain't cry 'til I started cleaning the blood off her face. Then she cried real hard. I ain't know what to do, so I just kept telling her that he ain't mean to do that to her, and that he was gonna feel sorry for what he did. But we both knew he did exactly what he wanted to do.

My pops don't play. Seeing that shit go down messed with me, but at first I ain't wanna talk to him 'bout it. Then a couple days later, we was on the terrace again, chillin', and I finally asked him why he had to do her like that. He told me that when you a man, you spend all day handling your shit on the streets, and when you get home, you don't need to put up with nothing. And when a man find hisself in a situation that need correcting, he gotta find the easiest way to get the job done.

"Let me school you, Ty," my pops told me that night. "My whole thing is respect. I don't got no respect for a man that be beating his wife all the time for no reason. But I don't got no respect for a man that never beat his wife neither, 'cause every now and then a man gotta show a woman who running things.

He need to get her respect. And if she don't give it to him, he got to demand it."

My pops face was dead serious, and he was talking like what he was saying was real fuckin' important. I ain't say nothing. I just sat and listened. But I gotta be honest. That shit he told me that night was mad deep. And I would be lying if I said it ain't made me think 'bout shit different.

Standing here looking at my moms now, all I can think 'bout is how fast my pops could get control of her. 'Cause no matter what I say to her, she just gonna keep arguing with me and blaming me for whatever she do. And she gonna keep messing up. "Where was you?" I ask her. "Where you get that food from?" But even before she could open her mouth, I know what she gonna say.

"Dante." She put her hands on her hips. "When you ain't wanna come home last night, I called Dante. And you know what? *He* actually helped us. He came by this morning, even with all that snow out there, and he took me shopping 'cause my own son couldn't be bothered."

"Dante don't do nothing 'less he gonna get something outta of it," I tell her.

She don't say nothing. She just take her coat off and throw it over the chair. But I can tell by the look on her face that she not saying something.

Then I get it. I know exactly what she did, and it's my fault for trusting her ass. "I hope you ain't do what I think you did," I say.

My moms sit on the bed and start untying her sneakers. "Yeah, I took the storage room key and lent Dante all your pops equipment."

Damn. Why I had to go and tell her where I hid that key? "You gave him all that for what, three bags of food?"

"I ain't stupid, you know? I'm tired of you actin' like you know more than me."

"Then how much he give you?"

"None of your business."

"I need that equipment back," I tell her. "You ain't had no right to even go in that storage room. I'm the one that's gonna be paying the bill every month, not you."

"Well, Dante paid it for February. So you don't gotta worry about that. And he said he trying to find us a place to live. He know this woman that's moving, and he gonna try to get her place for us." She take off her sneakers and throw them in the corner of the room. "I don't know what you got against that man when he only trying to help us."

"He ain't being nice for nothing. Remember a couple years ago, when he wanted to help us by trying to get with you."

She shake her head like she don't wanna hear what I'm saying. "Why you keep bringing that up? I ain't 'bout to do nothing with no Dante. The only man I want is your father. He the only man I ever had and the only man I ever wanna have."

"Then what was all that crap you was saying the other night when you got home from that club? You was saying you tired of being alone, and there's too many guys out there you could be with."

"I ain't mean it like that."

"That's what you was saying."

"I'm married to your father, Ty. I ain't gonna do nothing with Dante or nobody else, so stay out my business."

"I still need that equipment back," I say again. "And we ain't gonna move nowhere Dante say. You let him find us a place, he gonna want something, and you know it."

She open her mouth like she 'bout to say something, but I don't let her.

"We don't need Dante. I'ma get us outta here."

"I hear you talking, but I don't see you doing nothing. You telling me to feed your brother candy out the machine. That ain't taking care of him. Now, Dante, *he* bought your brother all kind of good food. He got Troy bread, peanut butter and jelly, cookies, soda, and he even got all of us ham and cheese heroes for dinner tonight. *He* looking out for us."

Troy jump off the bed and go right for them bags. He pull out the pack of Oreos and start opening it. "Gimme some," I say, 'cause I can tell he 'bout to go to town on them bad boys.

"Here." By the way he hand me the pack, I can tell he ain't all that into giving up any of them cookies. He acting like I'm asking for one of his kidneys or something. "Don't eat them all," he say.

I grab a couple cookies out the pack. I'm 'bout to sit on the bed, but I gotta knock two roaches off the blanket first. We still got roaches on the bed, walls, and floors, but Troy ain't even crying 'bout them no more. He probably too used to them by now.

"I'ma call Dante to get that equipment back," I say.

"Why you need it all of a sudden? It been sitting there collecting dust for three, four months."

"'Cause I'ma have a party with Cal and them."

"When?"

"Saturday. When Dante gonna have his party?"

"I don't know."

I eat another cookie. Damn. Why I tell her where I hid that fucking storage key? And how she gonna take that equipment and give it to Dante without asking me? What she thinking? Dante probably ain't even give her no real money. And how she know he gonna give it back?

My moms turn the TV on and try to find something to watch, but every channel is just talking 'bout the snowstorm.

I take out my cell and call Dante. The phone ring a couple times then his voicemail come on. "Dante, this is Ty. Call me back." I flip the phone closed. How I'ma put this party together if I don't know when I'ma get the equipment back?

"Can you take me outside?" Troy ask my moms.

"I just came in from out there," she tell him. "Ty, you take him."

"He don't got no boots," I say.

Troy jump off the bed and start taking the food out the plastic bags. "Look, Ty," he say. "I can put my feet in the bags, then put my sneakers on top. Then my feet will be dry."

"You smart," I tell him. "You pro'ly gonna be a inventor when you grow up."

"Yeah!" He sit on the floor and start putting the bags over his socks. "C'mon, Ty. I'm gonna make a million snowballs out there. And me and that church girl gonna be on one team, and you gonna be on the other team by yourself."

"Her name is Jasmine."

"We gonna beat you, watch."

He try to jump up, but I tell him to wait. Then I sit next to him and twist the bags 'til they tight on his calf and put knots on the top so not too much snow could get in. His sneakers is still gonna be wet, but they could dry before school tomorrow. "A'ight, Troy. Let's go, but we only gonna stay out there for a little while 'cause you ain't got no gloves."

I put my wet sneakers back on and grab my jacket.

"C'mon," Troy say, opening the door. "Hurry up."

My moms is still sitting there watching TV, so we just leave. Me and Troy walk down the hall. When we pass Jasmine room, I hear her arguing in Spanish with another female, probably her sister. I'm kinda glad her sister is back, but at the same time, they really going at it in there. For a second, I think 'bout knocking on the door to make sure they alright, but I don't. Besides, Troy is pulling on my jacket, trying to get me to go outside.

Then I hear Jasmine say in English, "I don't care what you say. I'm not going nowhere. You're not gonna put me through that again!" She crying. I can hear it in her voice.

"That the church girl?" Troy ask me.

"Yeah."

"Let's get her."

"Nah," I say. "She busy. C'mon." We walk past the door, but I can still hear them screaming in there. I don't know what's going on with them two, but I do know Jasmine is mad as hell. And I don't know where Reyna wanna take her, but if Jasmine don't wanna go, I hope she don't gotta.

A few minutes later, me and Troy is in the middle of a all-out snowball fight — some of them Hunts Point kids against us, the Bennett kids. I don't know how this shit got started 'cause it was going on when we got out here. But we in it now, and it's war.

All the cars is covered with snow, so we end up using them like they our forts, ducking behind them to build up our ammunition, then jumping out and bombing kids with the fat-ass snowballs we got piled up. A couple of the other guys is out with they little brothers and sisters, so least I ain't the only dude my age throwing snowballs 'cross Hunts Point Avenue. And them guys is mad funny too, so, I gotta be honest, we all having a good time actin' like we still ten years old and shit. Before I know it, it's getting dark outside.

It take me 'bout half hour to get Troy inside. He arguing with me and begging me for more time, but our sneakers and jeans is soaking wet, and I know his hands is cold 'cause mines is froze. And Troy need to dry off and get warm so he don't get sick and miss no more school.

My moms is laying down when we get back to the room. Me and Troy change into dry clothes and put our sneakers in front of the one heat vent that actually work. Then I get on my bed and listen to my cheap, no-name CD player while Troy watch cartoons.

The hip-hop music is so loud in my headphones that I can feel the bass through my whole body. I always listen to music when I got things on my mind. I don't know, but music just get my mind going 'specially when it's the right kinda music. The kind with a strong beat that block out everything else and get your blood pumping real hard.

Rap music used to be my whole life back when me and Troy was in foster care starting from when I was, like, eleven. But back then I only listened to that loud, angry gangsta shit like Mobb Deep and DMX—dudes that was just pissed off and wanted everybody to know it. And even though them niggas was rappin' 'bout being in gangs and jail and all that shit, I could relate to them. 'Cause I was in the system and that shit was fucked up.

Only good thing was that me and Troy was together in the same foster home. I used to go in our room and blast my music, and just lay on the bed and feel all the shit boiling up inside me. My foster mother, Miss Niles, was always screaming at me, telling me to turn my music down or she was gonna call my caseworker and get me put in a group home, but I used to just ignore that woman. Man, she threatened me with that everyday. Meanwhile, I knew she ain't want me there from jump. She liked Troy and them other little kids she had, but she ain't want no older kids like me living there. But, being that the city ain't wanna split me and Troy up, she got stuck with me too. And she let me know I wasn't wanted there every chance she got.

But I ain't care how much she hated me or how much she yelled at me 'cause nothing mattered to me back then. Nothing. My pops was locked up, my moms couldn't take care of us by herself, and my grandmother, who used to be there to help us out, was already dead. So we was all stuck where we was at.

Shit, my music was mad and so was I. Them rappers was saying shit I couldn't say to no one 'cause no one was listening to me. But Miss Niles complained so much 'bout the noise, my caseworker gave me this cheap-ass CD player at the agency Christmas party just so I could listen to my music and not bother no one. And that was fine with me.

Only thing, I don't listen to that gangsta shit too much no more. Yeah, I'm up on all the new music, but the CDs I play the most is the rap from back in the day, brothas like Rakim, Big Daddy Kane, KRS-1, and Tupac, 'cause them niggas had some real deep shit to say. My pops got me into them 'cause that's the only kinda rap he play at his parties, and when I took the time to listen to the words, man, I started to respect them dudes. They was the real deal. Not like now when most of the rappers is just frontin' like they from the streets or starting beef with other rappers over nothing just so they could be in some fake war and sell more CDs. The new rap is alright, but there ain't never gonna be another Public Enemy. Never.

But the truth is, I'ma need to get some new music soon 'cause the old stuff ain't gonna work for this party. Patrick, this guy I know from Bronxwood, always got all the new stuff. He be making bootleg CDs and DVDs and selling them 'round the projects. Me and him ain't really friends or nothing, but he cool, and we could probably work something out.

But there's someone I need to get ahold of first. I take my headphones off and try calling Dante again, but he don't answer. And I know he ain't gonna call me back neither. Nigga know what I want, and he ain't gonna wanna give up that equipment for shit. 'Specially after he gave my moms money for it.

I get off the bed and put my room key in my pocket. "I'ma be back," I tell my moms. "Don't leave Troy alone no more."

She don't say nothing, but she look mad that I even said that. I walk down the hall to Jasmine room feeling kinda stupid with no shoes on. I knock on the door, but nobody there. Damn. I hope Jasmine ain't had to go with her sister 'cause she sounded real upset 'bout that.

Then Wayne, one of the guys I was out there in the snow with, come down the hall. "Lost your girl?" he ask me.

"Nah," I say. "She went out with her sister and ain't got back yet."

"Yo, man," he say, then he just stop hisself. "Forget it."

"What?" I'm here in the hall with no shoes on my feet, and I ain't got time for no bullshit.

"Nothin', man."

"You got something to say 'bout Jasmine?"

Wayne shake his head. "It's just, how good you know that girl, man?"

"I know her."

"'Cause last night she was hanging with, you know that tall light-skin dude with the Sean John jacket? Him. She was downstairs with him for a while talking and crying and shit. Then she took him to her room." Wayne raise his hands like he ain't in it. "Now, I don't know what happened, but I do know that guy is going 'round saying he hit that all night."

"She ain't do nothin' with him," I say, but both of us know I'm talking mad shit 'cause Jasmine coulda did anything she wanted with him.

I tell Wayne I'ma check him later and walk back to my room. I'm mad, but I ain't even sure why. Ain't like Jasmine my girl or nothing.

FIFTEEN

Later that night, when my moms and Troy is both 'sleep, I'm in the room still working on the party. I already called Patrick, and me and him worked out a deal. I'ma get all the new CDs and he gonna get to sell all his bootleg shit at my party. Not only that, but I told him he could DJ for me when I wanna take a break. So the music ain't cost me nothing.

But I still don't got a place. I'm sitting on the bed thinking, but I gotta be honest, I'm stuck. All the places my pops use for his parties cost more money than I got, and they probably ain't gonna let a bunch of teenagers use they place no way. And the snow ain't helping none 'cause it's gonna be hard to get 'round and find something on my own.

When I can't think of nothing else to do, I don't got no choice 'cept to call my pops friend Regg on his cell. When my pops throw his parties, he hire Regg to handle the money 'cause he the kinda guy you could trust no matter what. He also the size of a Hummer, so ain't nobody gonna mess with him.

I ain't looking to call all my pops friends 'cause most of them is into the same kinda illegal shit he into, and I don't wanna end up where he at, but Regg ain't like the rest of them. I been knowing him since I was real young, and outta all my pops friends, he the only one that keep it real no matter what. He ain't slick like Dante, and he ain't only out for hisself. Not to say he don't wanna get paid, 'cause he do, but he the kinda guy that got your back even if there ain't nothing in it for him.

And Regg is a scary dude when he hafta be. One time, a couple years ago, my pops was throwing this after-hours party in the basement of this take-out restaurant. As usual, the place was packed. My pops was DJing and Regg was at the door collecting the money and giving out the drink tickets. I was helping my pops pull the records he needed, and putting them away when he was done. Then I would just sit next to him, watching him mix the records, smooth, like the music for the whole night was just one long song.

When my pops needed a break, I would take over, trying to copy what he was doing. Most of the people at his parties was, like, in they thirties and forties, but for some reason at this party there was a lot of people there in they twenties too, so I was mixing the music up, going from old to new. Females was yelling out shit like, "Ooh, that's my song!" and "That used to be the jam!" Most important, everybody was dancing. And since folks was liking what I was doing, my pops left me up there for a while and he was dancing with a group of girls, pointing to me, and probably telling them that I was his kid. I was feeling all good and shit.

That's when everything broke out. Three niggas rolled up and tried to get by Regg without paying nothing. They was actin' like they wasn't coming to party, like they was just looking for somebody. Regg was blocking the door and not moving 'til he saw some cash. They was arguing, but I couldn't hear what no one was saying 'cause of the music.

Then all I seen was Regg grab one of the guys by the neck, whip out his nine, and beat the dude face with it. The guy was bleeding and screaming, and none of his friends did jack to help him. I thought bullets was gonna be flying next 'cause them niggas looked like they was packing, but after what Regg did to that first guy, all three of them just cut out like a bunch of pussies. Regg ain't even break a sweat.

After a couple rings, Regg answer the phone and we talk for a couple minutes. He tell me he in Atlanta taking care of some business, but he don't give no more details than that. Fact is, nobody know exactly what Regg do to make money, and nobody ever ask. "When your pops getting out?" he ask me.

"S'posed to be in August, if he got good behavior."

"That shit is fucked up."

"True that," I say. Then I tell him 'bout how we in a shelter and how I'm trying to make some money by throwing a party on Saturday.

"Yeah, you can make some good money, Ty. I seen you DJ for your pops, and you got his skills. You good. You got a place yet?"

"Nah."

"How much cash you got?"

"A hundred fifty."

"You ain't gonna get no place with that." Then he start with the math. He tell me if I wanna get a decent place that can fit two or three hundred kids, I'ma have to spend 'bout $500, and I'ma need that money up front. "You got any friends with a house you can use?"

"Nah. Not really." Only kids I know that don't got they moms 'round is Cal and them, but they apartment is way too small for what I'm planning.

"Then you gonna need to see this guy, Leon. He can find you a place, but it ain't gonna be on the up-and-up. Your pops know him. Remember that party he threw at that factory in Harlem? Leon set that shit up."

I remember that party 'cause we had to do the whole thing, even the setup and break down, between the time the night shift left at 9:00 and the day shift got there at 6:00. It was wild. At 'bout 5:30 in the morning, we was throwing niggas out and breaking down the equipment like we was crazy. The whole factory was tore up. Machines was broke, garbage was all over the place, the bathroom was flooded, but we ain't care 'bout that. We just ain't wanna get caught.

I start laughing. "Why my pops go to a guy like Leon?"

"He ain't had no money, why you think?"

"Like me."

"Yeah. But you gonna make money if you get the word out and promote it."

I ask him how much I could make.

"If you charge everybody ten, you make anywhere from two to three thousand, minus expenses. You gonna need some guys you trust working for you, and you pay them each two hundred for the night."

$200. Each. That's gonna be a big chunk out my money. But I can't complain. I ain't got nothing right now. "Ten is a lot," I tell Regg. "Kids ain't gonna have that kinda money." Not only that, but I know if I charge everybody $10, girls ain't gonna wanna pay that. And the party ain't gonna be no good 'less it's packed with females.

My pops be charging like $30 for his parties, but he give a couple free drinks with that. And with him, his parties is so big, he don't leave outta there with less than $6,000 after he pay for the place and give everyone that work for him they cut. But some of his money come from selling drugs and shit, and I ain't gonna do that.

Me and Regg start going over the math again. He so quick with the numbers, now I know why my pops put him in charge of the money. No matter what numbers I throw at him, in a couple seconds he come up with what I'ma take home. After a while, I figure it out, and I know it's gonna work. "A'ight. A'ight. Fifteen for guys, free for females. How much I'ma make then?"

In a second, Regg say, "You come home with about two thousand two hundred and fifty minus expenses, if you can get half the place filled with guys. But that ain't gonna be a problem, not with girls coming free."

$2250 sound good, but it ain't really shit if I'ma have to pay everybody $200 and pay for the place. I'ma be lucky to leave outta there with $1500.

When I tell Regg my plan to get a apartment, he tell me it ain't that easy. "You gotta have two, three months' rent up front. They don't just let you move in like that. You gonna need more money, Ty, so why don't you do like your pops do?"

"Nah, Regg. I ain't going down like that."

"It's your call, man. I just don't know if you gonna get enough for an apartment. What about beer? You could sell beers for double the price you get them for at the wholesale place. You get someone to handle the beer and the money, you cut him in for twenty-five percent and that would still get you another two, three hundred."

A extra three hundred would be sweet, but no, I ain't gonna let no $300 get me locked up. "Nah, Regg. I ain't looking to go to jail for selling no beer."

"You only, what, fifteen?" he ask me. "They arrest you, you not gonna do no real time."

"You sure 'bout that?"

"You been knowing me since you was a kid," he say. "And you ain't never know me to say shit I ain't sure of. Cops come in, they gonna lock my Black ass up before you 'cause I'm the adult. Look, Ty, you want money, you take chances. That's how it go."

Maybe he right, but I don't know. Shit getting too complicated. I just wanna throw a party, have some fun, make some money, and get us outta Bennett. Why I gotta be worried 'bout getting locked up all the time?

"You gonna be back by Saturday?" I ask him. "'Cause I'ma need someone I could trust to work the door and collect the money and shit."

"I'm there," he say. "And I ain't gonna take twenty-five percent of the door money like I do with your pops. Whatever you make, you keep. I want your family out that shelter."

"You sure?"

"Now your *next* party, I'm in it for my cut, understand?" He laugh a little. Then he give me Leon cell number. "And tell him you with me, okay?"

"A'ight," I tell him. I wanna tell Regg 'bout Dante and the equipment, but what Regg gonna do 'bout that when he in Atlanta? Nah, I'ma hafta handle Dante on my own.

"And when you see your pops, tell him I got his back, okay?"

"A'ight," I say again even though I ain't seen my pops since he was arrested and don't plan on seeing him no time soon. I don't say nothing to Regg, but the truth is, I don't do the whole prison bus-ride thing. I can't even stand seeing them women lined up on Grand Concourse and 149th Street every morning waiting for them buses. That whole scene don't make no sense to me.

Saturdays and Sundays is even worse 'cause them women drag they kids with them. Dress them up like they going to a birthday party or something. Like there ain't nothing else them kids wanna do but go through metal detectors and get searched by guards just so they could spend a couple hours in the prison visiting area with they pops. With more guards watching they every move.

I know how them kids feel 'cause I used to be one of them. My moms used to make me wear my best clothes and take me on them buses with her. The whole way there, all us kids used to play 'round in the back of the bus like we was friends or something. Nobody talked 'bout they pops. We just acted like we wasn't even going to prison.

But I ain't never going through that shit again. I'm too old for that now. If my pops wanna see me, he need to keep his ass home.

SIXTEEN

It's practically midnight and I'm hungry. I still got that ham and cheese hero my moms brung home, but I wasn't even gonna eat it 'cause I ain't want shit from Dante. But then I remember all them cookies I already ate and say fuck it.

The bags Troy used in his sneakers got ripped up, so my moms put all the food and shit in the other bag. I open it and, damn, there ain't nothing but roaches in there. Like fifty roaches all on the cookies and crackers. My sandwich is in some kinda plastic wrap, and I don't know if the roaches got in there, but I ain't reaching my hand in the bag to find out. That shit is nasty.

I take the whole bag and tie it up with the roaches inside. If I leave this bag in the room, every roach in Bennett gonna be up in here. I put my key in my back pocket and go out in the hall to find a garbage can, but there ain't none on my floor.

On my way downstairs to the lobby I knock on Jasmine door again. This time I can hear the TV on in her room, but nobody still don't answer the door. She must be back 'cause I don't remember hearing no TV when I knocked on the door before. But if she is back, then where she at?

I go down the stairs, but I still don't got no sneakers on, so I'm trying not to walk in no wet spots. And this ain't easy 'cause there's a lot of wet boot prints and dirty, melting snow all over the lobby floor. But least there's a garbage can by the candy machine.

"Your girl still missing?"

Wayne.

I throw the bag away and try to act like I don't care what he say. "I ain't looking for her," I tell him. "I'm throwing away a bag of roaches."

Wayne start laughing. "Them niggas wasn't lying about Bennett the other night, was they?"

"Nah," I say. "This place is bugged." We both start laughing then. Next thing I know, we sitting on them busted chairs in the lobby just talking 'bout nothing. He all into the Knicks, like my pops is, so we talk 'bout the team for a while. I used to be into them too, but now I ain't got time to be no Knick fan. And even when I do catch a game on TV, it ain't the same no more.

"What you doing on Saturday night?" I ask him.

"I don't know. I hope I ain't still here though."

I tell him 'bout the party I'ma have and that I need some people to work.

"How much?" he ask.

"Two hundred for the night. But you gotta help set up and shit."

He don't even think 'bout it. "I'm in. You need some other guys?"

"A couple, but not that guy you seen Jasmine with. I don't trust him."

"He probably just talking shit, man."

"I know."

We stay down there in the lobby for 'bout fifteen minutes just chillin'. And since there ain't nobody at the front desk, Wayne give me a cigarette and we both light up and smoke. I don't hardly know Wayne, but he alright, least from what I seen of him so far.

Me and him is just getting ready to go back upstairs to our rooms when the door behind the front desk open and Jasmine come out. She got her head down so I can't hardly see her face.

A second later the night manager come out behind her. He fixing his hair with his hands and looking at Jasmine body with a real nasty smile on his face. And I can tell that something went on in there. Ain't no doubt in my mind. And I don't gotta think 'bout what I'ma do. I'ma kick his Puerto Rican ass.

It don't take me more than a second before I'm jumping over the front desk and rushing the night manager. I grab him by the neck hard, and when I slam his head back into the wall, he look at me like he don't even know what the fuck is going on. I can hear Jasmine screaming, but I'm so mad there ain't no way to stop myself.

I punch the night manager in the stomach and he go down and, man, I wish I had my sneakers on so I could stomp him on the face. But before I could fuck him up anymore, Wayne grab me and pull me away from him. "C'mon, man," he say. "C'mon, man."

Next thing I know, two security guards is there, too. One is grabbing my arm, pulling me away from Wayne, and the other is helping the night manager get up off the floor.

"You okay, Mr. Mendoza?" the guard with the dreadlocks ask the night manager.

"I . . . I think so. Yeah." He standing up on his own, but his nose is bleeding and his face and neck is all red and shit.

"Get off me," I say to the other guard, and try to pull away from him, but he got me in a hold and I ain't going nowhere. "Get the fuck off me. I ain't done with him yet." I look the night manager in the face. "You like little girls? What, you a fuckin' child molester?"

The guard tighten his hold. "Shut up."

"Fuck you," I tell him, still fighting to get loose.

Jasmine is just standing there crying. "Ty, stop!" she keep saying. "What are you doing? Stop!"

Finally I break away from the guard, and in a second, I'm on Mr. Mendoza again. And when my fist connect with his jaw, I can hear the cracking sound, and I know he gonna be feeling that for a while.

Then the guard I just got away from come after me again. He look me in the face with some jacked-up teeth and say, "Get away from him."

The guard with the dreadlocks pick up the phone. "I'm gonna call the police, Mr. Mendoza."

Teeth grab me up in a headlock and, I gotta be honest, that shit hurt. I'm trying everything I can to get free again, but he too strong.

"Let him go," Jasmine say. "Let him go!"

"What you trying to do?" Wayne ask. "Break his neck?"

"Put the phone down," Mr. Mendoza tell Dreadlocks. "We don't need to get the police involved in this. Everything's fine now."

Dreadlocks drop the phone. "You sure, boss?" he ask.

When Mr. Mendoza nod, Teeth release his hold on me. Now I'm the one that's in pain, but I still wanna fight. I still gotta teach that nasty asshole a lesson. But just like that, Dreadlocks stand in front of him like he his personal bodyguard or something.

Wayne put his hand on my back and start pushing me away from the whole scene. "C'mon, man. Let's go."

I let Wayne push me away and try to calm myself down, but it ain't easy. Just seeing the look that man gave Jasmine when he came out that room make me wanna hurt him. Damn. What he do to her in there?

Me and Wayne get to the stairs, and Jasmine is behind us crying. I swear I don't get this female. Why she gonna let that man do whatever the fuck he did to her? I just wanna grab her and ask her what she doing, but if I put my hands on her, I ain't gonna be able to control myself. Not now. Not when I'm so fuckin' mad.

We get upstairs and Wayne leave us in front of Jasmine door. She crying real hard, and her hands is covering her face. "Open the door," I tell her. "Where your key at?"

When she don't move, I just reach my hand in the front pockets of her tight jeans and pull out all kinda shit: a Chap Stick, a twenty-dollar bill, the business card she got from the lady at the church, a dollar bill, and then the room key. "Here." I give her back her money and the other stuff and open the door. We go inside, but I don't even know what to say to her. The TV is on so loud and my blood is pumping so hard and fast, it feel like my head gonna bust open or something. It's gonna take a while to get myself calmed down.

"I'm gonna take a shower," Jasmine say. She don't wait for me to say nothing. She just grab her towel and some clothes and go into the bathroom, slamming the door behind her.

First I sit on the bed, then I lay back and look up at the ceiling. There's a couple roaches up there and I hope they don't fall on me, but at the same time, I don't move out from under them. This girl got me going through mad changes. I know she like me and wanna get with me, but the second I ain't with her, she off screwing the guy in the Sean John jacket or that asshole downstairs. What she doing?

But that don't mean I ain't still pissed off at that night manager 'cause he the one that shoulda knew better. No matter how Jasmine look and what she do, he a grown-ass man and don't got no right doing nothing with her. That shit is just wrong.

Jasmine come out the bathroom only wearing this big pink T-shirt with BORICUA 'cross the front and no bra on. She still not saying nothing to me. She just stand in front of the mirror and start brushing her hair. Only thing is, every time she raise her arms up, her T-shirt lift up in the back and I get a look at the little red panties she got on. And with half her ass hanging out, she definitely got my attention. Damn. Her body is off the chart. She got a big ass, a small waist, and big titties. I ain't so mad at her that I don't like what I see.

When she finish putting her hair up, she turn 'round and ask me if I'm staying. I wish I could say no, but something is keeping me there. "Yeah, I'ma stay," I say.

"You gonna sleep in your clothes again?"

"Yeah."

She turn off the light and we both get under the covers in the dark. At first she on one side of the bed and I'm on the other, and we ain't touching. Then she move closer to me and whisper, "Thanks for staying with me. I really hate being alone, especially at night."

"Why?"

"I just don't feel safe when I'm alone."

Next thing I know, our feet is touching. I got my socks on, but still, it feel nice. Jasmine give me a little kiss on the cheek. "That's for beating that guy up," she say. "I didn't know you could fight like that."

"I can take care of myself," I say, and I gotta admit, it kinda feel good hearing her say that. Like she respect me for doing what I had to do.

Novisha wouldn't be like that. She woulda got mad at me for fighting and almost getting in trouble. Then she woulda got all worried that I'ma end up like my pops. Least Jasmine understand that sometime a man gotta step up.

Me and Jasmine start talking in the dark. She tell me all 'bout her life and how much fun she used to have when she was little, living in the South Bronx, not all that far from Hunts Point. Her family used to go to Puerto Rico for Christmas and Disney World every summer. They was a real tight family.

But when Jasmine was five, her moms and little brother died in a car accident. "It was just me, Reyna, and my dad left," she say. "We were so sad all the time. It was terrible. Terrible."

She stop talking and I don't know if she want me to say something or not, so I don't.

120

"My dad, he had a lot of problems." Jasmine is whispering now. "He was on methadone. Do you know what that is?"

"Yeah," I say, but all I know is that they got a methadone clinic a couple blocks from Bronxwood and every morning there ain't nothing but skinny-ass drug addicts lined up in front of it waiting for the place to open, no matter how cold it is outside. Whatever that methadone is, folks be wanting it, that's for damn sure.

"Well, he was on methadone for a long time and it was helping him stay away from heroin, and he could still work and take care of us. But sometimes he would start using again and lose his job, and he wouldn't come home and we couldn't find him. Me and Reyna would be all alone and scared and worried."

"Was y'all ever put in foster care?"

"No. Nobody ever knew we were alone. Reyna always used to feed me and take care of me. We would go to school and act like nothing was wrong. Everything was a secret. Then my dad would come home after a few days or a week. Just like that."

"And he would be okay?"

"No. When he came back he would look terrible and dirty, like he was sleeping on the streets or something. Reyna used to take care of him, put him in the bathtub, give him food, make him sleep. Then he would promise us he would stop using. And he would. Just for us. He was a strong man, Ty, but the drugs, they made his heart weak. When I was eleven, I came home from school one day and found him on the floor in the hallway. He was dead. They told me he had a heart attack. A forty-one-year-old man."

"Damn," I say. "That's messed up."

"And he wasn't even using nothing then. He was clean. I'll never forget that day, coming home all alone and seeing him like that. I'll never forget it."

I put my arm 'round her and we move even closer together. Her legs is pressed up against mines and the only thing between us is my jeans and them red panties. I gotta be honest. It ain't easy holding myself back.

But I do. She here talkin' 'bout her family, and I ain't the kinda guy that would try to get with a girl when she all sad and shit. That ain't right, and that ain't me. Plus, I don't wanna do nothing with her if she just been with that nasty night manager. And I ain't looking to mess up what I got with Novisha.

"What your mother say when she got back?" Jasmine ask, and I know she trying to change the subject. "Did she say why she left your brother all alone?"

"Nah. She just blamed me for everything."

"Is she always like that?"

"Only when my pops is locked up. When he 'round, she a'ight. She like a regular mother. But when he gone, she don't know how to act. She just lose it."

"Well, you still lucky you got a mother," Jasmine say. "Even if she's not perfect." Then she tell me 'bout how Reyna been trying to be her mother for the last four years, but that things ain't working out. "She was only eighteen when our father died, so she didn't know what she was doing, and I went wild. Ay! She couldn't control me for nothing. Then when I met Emiliano and we moved in with him, everything changed. He calmed me down and tried to teach me how to respect myself and only date boys who respected me. He was so strict with me. He used to take me to school and pick me up everyday. In the bread truck. It was

122

so embarrassing! I had to prove to him that I wasn't gonna do nothing wrong before he stopped doing that." She stop talking for a while, then she say, "You know something, Ty? I really, really need him. I don't know what I'm doing without him."

"That why you was with Mr. Mendoza? I mean, I know it ain't none of my business, but, c'mon. Ain't he kinda old?"

I hear her start crying, and it's a real long time before she talk again. "Reyna came back here this afternoon and she took me to some guy's apartment. And guess what? She's moving in with him, just another guy she met in some club. Well, I'm not doing that no more. He was looking at me . . . funny. He gave me the creeps. Reyna said if I don't move with her she's not coming back here, and she doesn't care if ACS finds out I'm all alone and puts me in a group home. But I left anyway and took the bus back here." She stop talking again, but she still crying. "Then I got hungry, but I only had a dollar left. So I went downstairs to the machine for some chips or something, but the machine wouldn't take my dollar bill. I went up to Mr. Mendoza and I asked him if he could change my dollar, and he said if I'm hungry he would split his sandwich with me. So I said okay."

"You know a guy like that ain't gonna give you something for nothing," I tell her. "You ever look at yourself?"

"I know what I look like, Ty. Guys been trying to get with me since I was twelve. I know how to handle men."

She try to sound like she all confident and shit, but I ain't buying it. Just 'cause she hooked up with a lot of guys don't mean she wasn't being used by them. "And you was gonna handle Mr. Mendoza?"

"I was gonna eat for free!" she say. Then she tell me that he took her in his office and they ate his sandwich together. That's when he started in on her, asking her if she needed money. And when she told him yeah, he told her he would pay her for sex. "I told him hell no, but that didn't stop him. He was, like, trying to see what I would do for how much, treating me like I'm one of those Hunts Point hookers out there."

My body tense up and my breathing get heavy. I don't like what the fuck I'm hearing.

"I told him that I'm only fifteen and I wasn't gonna let him touch me," Jasmine say. "But I really needed some money, Ty. My sister abandoned me with nothing."

"He gave you the twenty, right?"

"Yeah."

"What he do to you?"

"He didn't do nothing to me." But then them tears start again, and we so close now, the side of my face is getting wet from them. "I, um, I just stripped for him and . . . and I gave him, like, a lap dance, and . . . he touched himself."

"A'ight, that's it." I move away from her and get out the bed. "I'ma go back down there and finish kicking his ass." I turn the light on and look for my sneakers. Then I remember I ain't had them.

"Ty, no. It was me. I wanted the money." Jasmine get off the bed and pull on my arm to try and stop me. "I don't want you to go down there. All you gonna do is get arrested. Come. Come back to bed. Stay with me."

But I can't hardly hear what she saying. I'm heated. How I'ma let that dude get away with what he did? Any man that's gonna see a girl like Jasmine and take advantage of her just 'cause she homeless and hot need to get his face broke, you ask me.

Jasmine stand in front of the door, blocking it. "Stay with

me," she say again. "I don't wanna be here alone." She scared. I can tell by the look on her face. Only thing is, she ain't scared of being alone. She probably scared of what she gonna end up doing just to get somebody to be with her.

Damn. How I'ma leave when she looking at me like she need me or something? I try to cool myself down and breathe regular again. "A'ight. A'ight," I say. "I ain't going nowhere. I'ma stay."

She sigh. "Thanks, Ty." Next thing I know, her arms is wrapped 'round me, and we standing at the door hugging for a long time. Her body feel real good next to mines and I start relaxing. After a while I ain't even thinking 'bout Mr. Mendoza no more.

Then, when I'm all calm and shit, she whisper something in my ear in Spanish. I don't know what she saying, but it get me excited.

"What that mean?"

"It means, 'Too bad you have a girlfriend!'" She laugh a little and let go of me. "Come back to bed. You keeping me nice and warm." Then she climb back on the bed, and I see them red panties again.

I shake my head and turn the light off, but ain't no way I'ma get to sleep tonight, not next to her I'm not. I know I'ma be thinking 'bout them panties and that ass all night, and my head is gonna be spinning. I don't know why I'ma torture myself like this all night when I'm just trying to look out for this girl. But this situation ain't natural, and I'ma hafta be real strong to get through it.

SEVENTEEN

When I wake up, Jasmine is already up and dressed. And finally, she ain't wearing them same jeans no more. Now she wearing nice black jeans with a red sweater. She got her hair out, and she standing in front of the mirror putting on eye makeup.

"Where you going?" I ask her.

"To school," she say. "Remember, *I* go to school."

"What time is it?"

"Six forty." She lean closer to the mirror. "I hate my skin so much."

"You ain't gonna have acne forever," I tell her, but I'm half 'sleep and don't really know what the fuck I'm saying.

"I have a dermatologist appointment on Monday, but Emiliano's probably not gonna keep paying for me now. Oh, yeah, I almost forgot, I have an orthodontist appointment in two weeks. Man, I'm too expensive."

I make a sound so she think I'm paying attention, but it's hard to follow what she saying. I ain't hardly get no sleep laying in bed with that girl. It took a couple hours just to get my mind off her body and what I could be doing to it. Females don't know how hard it is sleeping with them when you ain't doing nothing. Shit ain't right. My whole body was hurting to get with her. "What time you gotta be at school?"

"Eight, but I wanna go early and talk to my teachers and explain why I missed so much school last week. I know they were wondering where I was."

"My teachers ain't even know my name," I say.

"I go to an alternative school. It's real small."

"Damn. Alternative schools is for bad kids. How bad was you?"

She turn 'round to face me. "I wasn't *bad*," she say. "I was *at risk*!"

We both gotta laugh at that shit. Starting in first grade, them teachers took one look at me and started putting me in programs for at-risk kids, then at-risk boys, then at-risk teenagers. Personally, I ain't never knew what the fuck I was s'posed to be at risk of, except growing up Black, but ain't no program I know of gonna change that.

Jasmine come over and pull the blanket off me. "Get up!"

"A'ight. I'm up. I'm up. I gotta go wake Troy up anyway. If he get to school by seven forty-five, he could get free breakfast."

I stand up and look at myself in the mirror. My face is jacked up. My braids is still alright, but living at Bennett got me looking all tired and shit. In the mirror, I check out Jasmine as she stick her books in her backpack then sit on the bed to put on her boots and, I gotta admit, she look real nice.

"Why are you staring at me?"

"I ain't staring," I say.

"I know what you're thinking!" She start laughing.

"What I'm thinking? Tell me."

She don't say nothing. She just keep smiling all sexy and shit.

"What?" I ask again.

She put her jacket on and throw her backpack over her shoulder. "I gotta go now." She open the door. "C'mon."

"A'ight," I say. "Be like that." I go out into the hall and she lock the door behind us. "You the one pro'ly thinking nasty stuff 'bout me," I tell her. "You pro'ly can't keep your hands off a fine brotha like me. Tell the truth."

She lean over and give me a kiss on my cheek. Then she whisper some Spanish shit in my ear again.

"What that mean?"

"It means, 'If I wanted you, I would of had you by now!'" She laugh again, and I'm like, damn. Even with all that metal in her mouth, she look so good today, man, it's hard to let her go. But I gotta. I tell Jasmine I'ma see her later, and she walk to the stairs and I go to my room.

Getting Troy up ain't hard, but I can't say the same thing 'bout my moms. Still, I ain't 'bout to let her sleep all day, not when I'ma be out there working to make money for her.

I finally remember to show her the letter from Troy teacher. She read it and get all nervous and shit. "I hope she ain't trying to get ACS on us, 'cause I'm a good mother."

"She just wanna see you," I say, 'cause it's too early to hear

128

her talk 'bout what a good mother she is. She staring at the note and I can tell she don't know what to do. "Write on the bottom of the letter that you can see her today after school," I tell her.

She nod and start writing. Troy sitting on the other bed, getting dressed in his uniform. "I'm hungry," he say.

My moms point to the dresser. "Eat some of them crackers Dante got for you."

"It ain't there," I say before Troy even move. "I had to throw it out 'cause of the roaches."

"All that food?" my moms ask.

"You wanna eat roaches?"

That just get Troy started then. "Ty, Mommy wants to eat a roach sandwich!" He start laughing, cracking hisself up. "With roach ham and roach cheese and roach bread . . ." He don't stop neither, but 'long as he getting dressed I don't say nothing. I just find some clean clothes in my garbage bag and get myself in that shower.

When we both dressed and ready to go, I tell my moms to get to the school early so the teacher don't gotta wait for her. "And act nice and don't argue with her no matter what she say. If she talk 'bout ACS, tell her that things is hard now 'cause we homeless, but when we get a apartment, Troy gonna do all his homework and he ain't gonna miss no more school. And tell her you trying to get him a new coat and some boots."

She nod. "Okay."

It look like she don't mind me giving her orders, so I keep going. "And you need to call the caseworker from the EAU. We was s'posed to have a meeting with her yesterday, remember? Tell her you need a new appointment."

"Yeah, okay."

I think 'bout telling her to wash all the dirty clothes too, but if I give her too much to do, she ain't gonna do nothing. She just gonna get on one of them prison buses like she do every time I tell her to go look for a job.

Me and Troy leave the room and he take off down the hallway like he got nothing but energy. "Hurry up!" he yell.

I'm too tired to go running after him today, so I just take my time.

"C'mon, Ty," he say again, turning the corner.

"Just wait for me downstairs," I tell him.

I got a lot I need to do and I gotta save the little bit of energy I got. First thing I gotta do is find a place for this party so I can get out there and start promoting. I'ma hafta call this guy Leon, 'cause I ain't got time to waste looking for someplace on my own. I don't know shit 'bout him, but if my pops and Regg trust him, he probably alright.

And it ain't like I got no other choice.

EIGHTEEN

After I take Troy to school, I spend a hour swiping MetroCards at the 149th Street, Third Avenue station. It's rush hour, and them working people be looking for kids like me so they could get to work cheap. In a little over a hour, I make $21, which I need 'cause I don't wanna dip into none of the money Cal and them gave me. Plus, I don't know how much Leon gonna charge to find me a place for the party.

I call him and when I tell him I'm Tyrone son, he tell me to meet him at the McDonald's on Fordham and Soundview at 10:30. When I get there, this skinny dude with a doo-rag on his head call me over to the booth he sitting at. He look like he damn near forty, but he wearing baggy jeans, Tims, and all the name-brand clothes kids my age be wearing. I go over to him, but I don't know how he know me. I ain't never seen him before in my life.

I sit down 'cross from him and for a while he don't say nothing to me. He just sit there scarfing down his pancakes and

131

sausage like I ain't even there. Finally he look up at me and say, "You look just like your old man." Then he reach in his pocket and pull out a roll of bills. He flip through all the hundreds, fifties, and twenties, and hand me a ten. "Order breakfast 'fore they switch to the lunch menu."

I still don't say nothing. I just get up and get in line. I don't know this guy, but I ain't too proud to take his money. 'Specially when I ain't eat nothing yet.

When I get my food, I sit down again and for the next half hour, me and him eat breakfast, just conversating 'bout all kinds of shit like the snowstorm, crime in the city, the new video games. Meanwhile I wolf down two Egg McMuffins in like five minutes, then start in on the hash browns.

After a while we start talking 'bout my pops. He say, "I got much respect for your old man, Tyrell. He a good man, and everything he did, right or wrong, was for y'all."

"I know," I say, but, truth is, I do got my doubts 'bout that. I know my pops worked mad hard to make us happy, 'specially my moms, but I still don't get how he could keep doing shit that he knew was gonna take him away from his family. He just kept taking chances and not thinking 'bout what was gonna happen to us.

And now, 'cause of him, I gotta be the one thinking 'bout how to take care of my moms and Troy. My pops is sitting on his ass in jail and I'm meeting with this shady dude, trying to make some money and not end up in jail my damn self. I mean, I ain't even sixteen yet. Why I gotta be dealing with all of this?

When we done eating, Leon lean back and ask me, "How many kids you expectin' at this party?"

"I'ma try to get like two fifty, three hundred if I can."

"How important is heat to you?"

"Heat?"

"Yeah, you need a place with heat?"

It feel like two degrees outside today, and I don't think it's gonna get no hotter by Saturday. "Yeah. I need heat," I tell him. "And electricity."

He nod. "I got a couple places. You wanna stay in Hunts Point or go uptown?"

"I don't care. Long as people can find the place."

"C'mon."

We get up and go outside. My jacket ain't no kinda match for this cold air. We cross the parking lot and I'm thinking we going to the corner to take the bus or something, but he go straight to this brand-new silver Escalade and unlock the doors with the remote key chain. The truck is the shit. I climb in and I'm like, damn. That's how he rolling?

It take us a while to get out the parking lot 'cause they bulldozed all the snow into big piles that be taking up most of the spaces. The parking lot look more like a maze or something. When we finally on the street, Leon crank the radio and we drive off in style.

After a couple hours with Leon, I gotta say one thing 'bout the brotha: He mad creative. The first place he show me is a elementary school a couple blocks from Bennett. We get out the car and stand in front just looking up at the three-story building. "This is a good spot," he say. "The train is right here, and there ain't nothing else on this block. No neighbors to call the police and complain about the noise or nothing."

"It's a school," I say. The windows got paper snowflakes taped on the inside, and I can even see the little kids sitting at they desks inside.

"You need to open your mind, Tyrell. Schools ain't open on Saturday nights, right?"

"No."

"Then what's your problem?"

Damn.

We get back in the car and get on the Bruckner Expressway heading north. After 'bout a half hour, Leon pull up in front of a school bus depot not too far from Bronxwood. We don't get out the car this time. He just circle 'round the place one time, then park in front. 'Bout a hundred yellow buses is parked in front, and while we sitting there, buses come and go. "They got some buses inside, too," Leon say. "But there's gonna be enough floor space in there for your party."

The depot is a huge, flat building that take up most of the block. The parking lot take up the rest. And there ain't nothing else 'round here neither. No buildings or stores or nothing. "How you get in a place like this?" I finally ask him.

"You don't gotta worry about that. I'm gonna have all that took care of."

I wanna ask him how. Like, do he just break in, or do he pay someone off that work there? But something tell me I don't wanna know the answer. All I know is, if he pulled off that factory party with my pops, he can probably do anything he want.

"Another good thing about this place," he say with a smile on his face, "is the buses. Kids can use them to, ya know, get some privacy. Know what I'm sayin'?"

I smile. Now Leon making sense.

Leon drive me 'round to a couple more places, some factories and warehouses, but I ain't feeling none of them. Matter of fact, I ain't really feeling this whole breaking-in thing, but I don't got no choice really. My pops probably felt he ain't had no choice neither when he did business with Leon, but he did and shit worked out alright. That time.

Leon stop the car in the parking lot of the McDonald's, the same one from before. "Let's talk business while we eat," he say.

Now he gonna make me hand over the little bit of money I got from Cal and them. And since that ain't shit, he probably gonna want some of what I make on Saturday, too. I ain't even made a dime yet, and his hand gonna be in my pocket already.

"You don't eat nowhere else?" I ask him.

"Yeah, but this is my office."

"What kinda business you in, other than parties?"

"I do a little of this, a little of that," he say, and open his door to get out.

What kinda answer is that? Why he ain't just tell me to mind my fuckin' business?

Leon ain't lying when he say that McDonald's is his office. He go straight to the same booth, and he give me another ten-dollar bill to get lunch. "You want something?" I ask him.

"I'm good," he say. Then he take out his cell.

While I'm on line, every time I look over at him he either talking on the phone or dialing someone else. He even got a pad out to write shit down. When I come back to the table with my tray, I hear him tell someone, "You know what I need, and

135

if you ain't gonna set that shit up, I'm gonna find someone who will."

I sit down, but I ain't sure if he want me to hear what he saying. So I just unwrap my Quarter Pounder and act like I ain't listening. I do get a quick look at the pad and all I see is numbers and little symbols and shit, like he writing in code or something.

"Alright, good. I'm gonna expect that by tomorrow." He flip his cell closed.

"You had enough money?" he ask me.

"Yeah, thanks," I say. "You ain't had to pay for me."

"I know."

I'm 'bout to ask him if he sure he don't want no food when one of the cashiers come over to the table with a tray full of food for him. She a cute Black girl that look like she 'round nineteen or twenty.

"Thanks, Sherry." Leon slip her a fifty. "How that little boy of yours doing?"

"He's fine," she say, smiling. "He's trying to walk already."

"I told you he gonna be an athlete, you watch."

Sherry leave the table and come back with his change. But Leon don't take it. "Buy that little boy some sneakers," he tell her.

Sherry look over like she making sure none of the other workers is watching and slip the money in her pocket. "Thanks, Leon," she say.

Leon check her out as she walk away. "She look good," he say. "She don't need to be working here."

I wanna ask him where she should be working, but I don't. I just wanna get this whole thing over with. My cell ring, and I reach in my pocket for it. It's Cal. I flip it open. "What up?"

136

"Chillin'. You got a spot yet? I'm trying to talk this shit up 'round here, but niggas need to know where it's gonna be at."

"I'm doing that now. Let me holla at you later."

"A'ight."

I close the cell. "That's my boy," I tell Leon. "He helping me with the party."

Leon lean forward in his seat and look me straight in the eyes. "Let's talk business then."

NINETEEN

A couple hours later, I'm standing in front of Novisha school freezing my ass off waiting for her to get out. Her school get out at 2:30, fifteen minutes before the public school 'cross the street, the high school I woulda ended up at if we ain't move from the projects. I think Novisha school let them out early so all the kids could get out the area before the thugs is released. And most of the time, the Catholic school kids be walking to the bus and train real fast like they know time is running out.

But them public school kids ain't what I'm thinking 'bout today. I'm just looking to make sure Novisha is safe from that nigga that think he can just write her and call her when he wanna. My opinion, he getting too bold. Next thing, he gonna try to follow her home or something. And, man, if something happen to my girl, I'ma hafta kill somebody.

Then I see her. She come out the building looking so cute in her short red jacket and red hat, all warm and shit. But she ain't alone. She with a whole group of kids. I know her best friends

Shanice and Ana, but they got three guys with them too, and it kinda look like they three couples or something. 'Specially 'cause two of the guys is Black and the other one is Dominican like Ana.

I'm just standing there watching them come down the walk, just talking and laughing and shit. I know Novisha ain't ask me to come pick her up today, but she looking too happy with them other guys and, straight up, I don't like what I'm seeing.

Course I look them brothas over real fast, not like they competition or nothing, but 'cause I wanna make sure none of them is the guy writing her them letters and calling her at home. But can't none of them be him. Not only 'cause they look like three punks, but 'cause Novisha look too comfortable with them. I just hope none of them is trying to step to my girl 'cause I'm not having that.

When Novisha see me she smile real big, but I can tell she surprised I'm there. But, still, she do run over and give me a big hug, even though it's only the good girl hug. "Ty, what are you doing here? What's going on?" I know she ain't mean it like this, but it kinda sound like she ain't all that happy to see me.

I slip one hand 'round her tiny little waist and cop a feel of her ass with the other. Not only 'cause I like feeling her up, but 'cause I want them chumps she with to see that she mines. "I wanna walk you home," I say in her ear.

She let go of me. "I can't. I'm not going home now. I'm going to the nursing home."

"It's Tuesday," I say. She only do her volunteer work on Mondays now that she got a lot of other kids to help out on the other days.

"I know, but yesterday, you know, there wasn't any school,

and I don't want a whole week to go by without seeing the residents. They'll miss me."

I take her arm and kinda move her away from the other kids so we can talk. "Who them boys?"

She look at me like I'm acting crazy or something. "Them? They volunteer at the home on Tuesdays, so we decided to all go together today. We're gonna have fun."

"That dude write you today?"

"No." She sound like she tired of me asking her that. "Why are you bringing that up? C'mon. They're all waiting for me."

"Let them go without you. I wanna talk to you." I put my arm 'round her again and lean over to kiss her on her neck, which ain't easy with that thick jacket she got on. Her skin smell clean and peachy, and all of a sudden there ain't nothing I wanna do more than just be alone with her.

She kiss me back, but she pulling away at the same time. "This is embarrassing, Ty. My friends are watching us."

But I can't even see straight no more. "I love you," I tell her. "You look so beautiful today." And she do. I'm looking at the short uniform skirt and her legs in them thick black tights and I just wanna touch her and feel her touch me. Her lips taste so sweet and my mind is spinning with nasty thoughts.

She grab hold of both my hands. "I love you too," she say with a little smile. "But I have to go. Don't be mad."

I wanna keep her there and convince her to stay with me, but I don't. I want her to wanna be with me. I don't wanna beg. So I take a deep breath and tell her I ain't mad. "I'm a'ight," I say. "Go on. Go with your friends."

She look at me for a few seconds like she still ain't sure if I'm mad or not. Then she turn and go back over to where her friends is standing. She look back one time, smile, and wave at me. But I don't wave back. And I don't go nowhere for a while. I just watch them walk down the street, talking and having a good time. I know she doing something good, spending her time with them old folks that don't got no family visiting them or nothing, but at the same time I'm, like, damn, who more important to her, them or me?

I gotta say, since she started high school, things ain't the same no more. When we first started going out, we was tight. We was always together or on the phone with each other. And if I showed up at her middle school, she always used to spend time with me.

Now she into so much, she don't be making time for me no more. The only day she save for me is Wednesdays 'cause her moms work a double shift and we can be alone. But on the other days, it's like everybody and everything come first. Instead of me.

I ain't sure why, but shit between us don't feel right no more.

From Novisha school, I go straight over to see Cal. He out in front of his building where he usually at. Myself, I don't get how he can just stand there everyday 'specially in this kinda weather.

"Yo, son," he say. "That jacket keeping you warm?"

"Oh, you got jokes?" I kinda ain't in the mood for Cal shit today, not after what just happened with Novisha. Not only that, but he know the only reason I'm wearing this old jacket is 'cause my pops got locked up before he could get me a new one. And 'cause the little money we did have, we wasted trying to keep him outta jail and hold on to our apartment. I give Cal a look that say don't mess with me today.

"Damn, man. What's your problem?"

"You my problem, asshole," I tell him.

"Well, fuck you too," Cal say, and start laughing 'cause he don't really mean what he saying. And 'cause he know that even when I'm mad at him, he still my boy. We been through too much together for that to change now.

We go inside and stand in the lobby. The whole floor is wet and nasty with black puddles of water from the front door all the way to the elevator. Someone put big pieces of cardboard down so folks won't slip, but even the cardboard is soaking wet now.

Man, when I used to live here in the projects, I thought buildings with wet lobby floors and pee in the elevators was normal. It wasn't 'til we moved to Pelham Parkway that I found out landlords is s'posed to hire people to clean they buildings and keep things safe. Over there, if our lobby ever looked like this, folks woulda lost they minds, 'specially with all the rent money we was paying to live there.

Me and Cal stand there talking for a while, and when buyers pull up in front of the building, I just wait in the lobby while he go outside and do his business. When Cal selling, he a different guy. Nigga be macking like he be running things at Bronxwood. Like he ain't the asshole doing all the work out there in the cold while his brothers ain't hardly doing shit.

After 'bout a hour, we go upstairs. His brothers ain't home, so we just chill in the living room watching videos on BET, getting high and drinking forties. To be honest, I don't think even Cal and them got weed strong enough to make me forget 'bout Novisha and how she just walked away with her friends and left me standing there like a chump. Man, I'ma hafta be real fucked up for that not to mess with my head.

I fill Cal in 'bout Leon and all them places he showed me. "The bus depot is the best spot," I say. "So Leon gonna set it up."

"How much he charge?"

"I had to give him the whole hundred fifty y'all gave me, and he said he want another two at the party. I'ma hafta tell Regg to give him the money when he show up to collect."

"Damn."

"Nigga kept telling me he was giving me a break 'cause of my pops, but three fifty ain't cheap."

Cal shake his head and keep drinking. "So he gonna make sure we don't get caught or what?"

"I don't know, but when my pops went to him, we ain't had no kinda trouble." I'm on my second forty now, and I'm really feeling buzzed. "We was shitting our pants the whole time, but we ain't got caught."

We don't say nothing for a while. I don't know why, but between the weed and the beer, I'm getting mad depressed. Like, I'm starting to think this party ain't gonna make me no money, and we ain't never gonna get outta Bennett, and me and Novisha ain't gonna end up together.

Finally Cal say, "I got this letter from my pops last week, talking about they transferring him upstate somewhere and he wanna see me before he get sent up."

Cal don't never talk 'bout his pops so I'm kinda surprised he telling me this. His moms and pops wasn't never married so even the one time his pops got out, back when we was in sixth grade, Cal hardly ever seen him. I swear, that man was out for like five, six months tops before he was right back in. And this time he got

143

like twenty years for killing a guy over a bad drug deal or something. Before that, he did eight years for attempted murder. Man, Cal has a pops so bad, he make my pops look like one of them TV fathers.

"What you gonna do? Go see him?"

"And waste my time? For what? Ain't like he getting out no time soon." Cal reach down for his forty on the floor. "And even if he did get out, you know he going right back in. My pops don't even know how to act when he ain't locked up. Last time they let him out, you shoulda seen him, walking around in clothes from, like, fifteen years ago, trying to pick up young girls with his old-ass self." Cal drink the rest of the bottle, then his face get kinda serious. "And he never did nothing to help my moms out with us, even after he was making money on the streets again. Remember how broke we was back then?"

"We was all broke back then," I say. "I'm still broke."

"Yeah, but when your pops get out, he coming back home to y'all. I ain't never had a pops like that. My moms *was* my pops. But your pops, he real."

"Word." I must be drunk 'cause Cal almost sound like he making sense. Okay, yeah, my pops keep getting hisself locked up, but I know he really wanna be home with us. He a good father that way.

"You believe in a couple weeks I'm gonna be some kid pops?" Cal shake his head. "Man, that shit is wild. I don't even know what a father s'posed to do."

"You scared?"

"Nah, I ain't scared of nothing. But, damn, them babies is mad small when they come out. I ain't even gonna touch that kid 'til he old enough to shoot hoops." He start laughing. "I just hope it ain't no girl 'cause when you got girls you always gotta be worrying about them and chasing dudes away from them. Man, I'm gonna be one of them fathers boys is scared of. Nobody never gonna ask my daughter out 'cause they gonna hafta get past me first."

He laugh again, but I can only work up a smile 'cause I ain't feeling all that happy right 'bout now. Cal a happy drunk, but I'm like one of them sorry-ass drunks you see crying on theyself on the train.

"What your problem, man?" Cal ask me.

"Nothing."

"How long I know you? Man, you ain't look this bad since you and Lynette broke up."

"I wasn't like this when me and her broke up," I tell him. "I'm the one that dropped her for Novisha."

"Yeah, right," he say.

"Fuck you, bitch. What you know?" I look at Cal and just wanna hurt him all of a sudden. "I'm tired of you trying to tell me shit you don't know."

"Man, you bugging." Cal shake his head and get up to go to the bathroom, and I just rest my head back on the couch.

Lynette. Damn. I ain't thought 'bout that girl for a long time but, the truth is, me and her had a nice time together back in eighth grade. Lynette wasn't only real pretty, but she was real smart too.

My pops liked Lynette, but he ain't think she was the right kinda girl for me. I was forever trying to defend our relationship to him, telling him she a nice girl that do good in school and all that, but he wasn't hearing none of it. He would just shake his head and be like, "The girl too smart."

145

One time I got mad and asked him, "What, you saying she too smart for me?"

"I didn't say that," my pops said. "You need to listen to your father. Listen. What I'm saying is, I know the kinda man you gonna grow up to be 'cause you gonna be like me, and me and you is strong men. We need women we can take care of. Now Lynette, she a nice girl, but smart girls like that ain't gonna let a man take care of them. They independent. They wanna take care of theyself."

Of course I ain't listen to him, and me and Lynette kept going out. She was the girl I was with before I flipped the script with Novisha and started being her man instead of just one of the guys she grew up with.

When my pops found out I was with Novisha, all he said was, "Another smart girl." I knew what he was thinking. Novisha another girl that ain't gonna let me take care of her, but I still ain't listened to the man. Course now I know how right he was.

Cal come back in the living room. "You wanna talk about what the fuck bothering you? Novisha and you still kicking it?"

"Yeah. Pro'ly."

"What that mean?"

I can't stand talking to Cal 'bout Novisha 'cause they live in the same projects and I don't really want him knowing nothing personal 'bout her. But for some reason I start telling him what's going on. "Novisha got some dude at her school writing her letters and calling her at home, like stalking her and shit."

"Let's go kick the nigga ass then," Cal say right away, like he ain't even have to think 'bout it.

"She don't want me knowing who the guy is. She trying to protect me. Or him."

I tell Cal how I'm trying to keep her safe, but she making it real hard. "She don't want me pickin' her up from school no more. Matter of fact, she actin' like she don't even want me 'round her when she with her friends. And she be writing in her diary that she don't want me there with her when she go to college, like she wanna go somewhere for four years without me."

Cal lean forward on the couch. "The problem is, you still ain't hitting that, you know what I mean? She don't need you 'cause you ain't doing the right thing where it count. Now the first time she give it up to you, she ain't gonna wanna go nowhere without you. That's how you gonna get to be her man for real."

"I am her man."

"You keep telling yourself that, but females need you to show them that. Show her, man, then she gonna be hooked on you and things is gonna change, watch."

I rub my eyes. Damn. Cal is making mad sense today. But the problem is, Novisha ain't gonna give me none. She told me that from jump. I knew that shit even before I broke up with Lynette, who was giving it up on the regular. But I had to have Novisha.

I mean, me and Novisha was always friends, but we ain't get real close 'til the summer before she started eighth grade. Her pops stepped out on them in, like, May, and her moms was a mess. The man left them with nothing. And I ain't never seen Novisha madder at nobody than she was at him.

Then when her school gave her a scholarship to some Bible camp, her moms just sent her away. For six weeks. Ms. Jenkins said she needed to get herself together and all that, but Novisha was just madder then.

Me and her got real close when she got back. We would

have some deep conversations 'bout everything, and I stopped looking at her like the little girl from Building G. Yeah, I'm older than her, but it ain't matter no more. I mean, she was always pretty and all that, but we connected that summer, and there wasn't no way I could be with Lynette no more.

My cell ring and I reach in my pocket for it. It's Novisha. Like, she musta knew I was thinking 'bout her or something. But, to be honest, I ain't in the mood to deal with her now. And the second she hear me, she gonna know I'm high and drunk, and I don't feel like hearing shit from her. The cell keep ringing.

"Who that?" Cal ask.

"Novisha."

"You ain't gonna talk to her?"

"Nah."

"Take my advice, man. You start giving it to her, all your problems is over. Trust me. I know what I'm talking about."

"How you know?" The cell stop ringing and I put it back in my pocket. "You and Tina back together?"

"Yeah, man." He put on one of them Kool-Aid smiles. "She gonna be the mother of my kid. How I'm gonna stay mad at her?"

"When she gonna drop that kid?"

"Two weeks, man. Two weeks."

He look kinda happy, too, but that couldn't be me. I ain't trying to be no fifteen-year-old father. Shit, I got enough to worry 'bout taking care of Troy everyday.

"Check that out," Cal say, pointing to the TV. Two girls with the biggest asses I ever seen is dancing in some video, and they look real good. "Where they find girls like that?"

"I know a female at Bennett with a body like that. You should see this girl." I shake my head, thinking of Jasmine in them red panties.

"And you ain't doing nothing with her?" Cal look at me like I'm stupid.

"Nah. We just hanging out. She real nice."

"Something wrong with you, man," Cal say, smiling. "I don't even know you no more."

Then, all of a sudden, the door fly open and Andre and Greg come busting in like they the police or something. I know I'm high, but I can tell by the wild look in Andre eyes that something 'bout to go down. "Cal," he say, "you got a minute to get up outta here. Starting now."

Cal sit up straight on the couch. "Where I'm s'posed to go?"

"Go to Ma's."

Cal start smiling, actin' all cool and shit, probably 'cause I'm there. "Nah, man, I ain't going nowhere."

"Look, I ain't playing with you. You don't need to be here."

Cal face get a little more serious now. "Why? What up?"

"Shit 'bout to happen. Get out 'fore you get caught up it in."

Cal get up off the couch. "A'ight, give me a second." He don't ask no more questions. He just leave the room, and before I know what to think, he back in the living room with a backpack. "C'mon, Ty."

And we out. Just like that.

It's dark when we get out in front of the building, and I'm like, "What's going on?"

He shrug. "Andre trying to keep me outta his shit 'cause he think I'm too young and can't handle nothing."

I can't tell if he upset or glad he don't gotta be in it.

We start walking down the path to the street and he pull out his cell and call for a cab. "This shit making me mad," he say when he flip his cell closed. "Andre trying to be my pops and keep me outta shit, but he ain't my pops. He don't get that."

"Why you don't just live with your moms? Fuck Andre."

"Yeah, I should do that. But I work here and my moms don't wanna be part of what we do. She try to act like she don't know what we gotta do to pay her rent and buy her stuff. But that's cool. She a good mother and she deserve what we doing for her."

We stand on the corner 'cross from the laundromat and wait for the cab. My cell ring again, but I know it's Novisha, so I don't even take it out my pocket. I keep looking down the street to Cal building, but I don't see nothing happening. There ain't hardly no people out. "What you think gonna happen tonight?" I ask.

"I hope nothing, so I can come back tomorrow. When I'm at my moms apartment, she try to treat me like a kid. She cook for me and make my bed. I can only take one or two days of that shit."

When the cab come I'm 'bout to tell Cal bye and walk to the train. But he get in the cab and leave the door open for me, and I hear him tell the driver that there gonna be two stops. So I get in and tell Cal that it's probably gonna cost 'bout $20 to go all the way to Hunts Point.

"Twenty ain't shit," he say. "I make that in, like, three minutes."

TWENTY

When I get back to Bennett I'm real tired and miserable, and I just wanna get in bed and sleep the weed and beer off. But Troy is 'sleep on one bed, all spread out and shit, and my moms is sitting on the other with her arms folded like she mad at me or something. "Where was you all this time?" she ask me. "You don't think your brother wanna see you when he get home from school?"

Damn. I gotta come back to this kinda attitude? "I was with Cal. We working on the party."

"Well, you got responsibilities here too."

"I know." She using Troy to make me feel guilty, but I'm used to it by now, so I don't let it get to me most of the time. I sit on the end of the bed where Troy sleeping. "Look," I tell her. "Straight up, I'ma be mad busy this week. You know how it is a couple days 'fore a party. So you gonna hafta spend more time with Troy by yourself while I'm out making money." I try to keep my voice calm 'cause I don't wanna get in no argument tonight.

"You sound like your father," she say, but I don't know if she mean it as a good thing or not. Most of the time when she tell me I'm like my pops, it ain't no compliment. It's like she looking at me, thinking I'ma end up just like him.

"A'ight then," I say. I'm real fucked up and there ain't nothing more I wanna do but lay down and let all that shit work they way out my system. My eyes is closing and I can't hardly stop them.

"You been drinking?"

I nod.

"Thought you was planning the party."

"I was." I open my eyes to see if she buying any of what I'm saying, but she looking at me like she know I'm full of shit. "I was," I say again.

She still looking at me, but I'm too tired to keep talking. I just want everything to be quiet and dark for like ten hours, but she don't stop. "I went to school and spoke to that teacher, Mrs. Morton."

I can't hardly talk no more. "What she say?" Three words is all I can get out.

"She told me she don't think Troy need to be in special ed, that she wanna put him in one of them regular classes and see how he do."

"That's good."

"No, it ain't. What that bitch know 'bout my kid? What if they put him in that regular class and he don't learn nothing or them other kids treat him bad? What then?"

I don't say nothing 'cause I can't stand when she act so negative, putting Troy down before he even get a chance to try.

"And she told me 'bout some kinda after-school program they

152

got with tutoring and art classes and karate. And she want Troy to stay for that and get help with his homework and make friends and shit."

"How much money?"

"It cost fifty dollars a week, but she think we ain't gonna have to pay nothing 'cause we homeless, so she gave me a application to fill out and our caseworker from the EAU gotta sign it."

Okay, she ain't gonna stop talking so I try to focus on what she saying, so I could get this whole thing over with. "The caseworker?"

"Yeah, I called her and I got another appointment for Friday. I just hope she don't sign that application."

I stare at her for a couple seconds. "Why not?"

"'Cause I want Troy to stay where he at. There ain't no reason to change nothing. He doing fine."

My mind is working kinda slow, but the bullshit she saying wake it up. And now I get it. The only reason she saying all this is 'cause if Troy ain't in special ed no more, we probably ain't gonna get them SSI checks every month.

I stand up. "I'ma be back." Maybe if I go check up on Jasmine for a while, I won't hafta think 'bout any of this, 'cause it's just making me mad.

I ain't even at the door yet when my cell ring. It's Novisha again. But this time I flip it open. "Hi."

Novisha sigh. "Ty! I've been trying to call you all night."

"Yeah, I know. I had the cell in my backpack and I ain't hear it ring."

"I just wanted to apologize for this afternoon. I felt so bad leaving you there like that."

"A'ight." I walk out to the hallway and close the door behind me so my moms can't hear my conversation. "That all you wanna say?"

"Wow, I didn't know you were that mad," Novisha say.

"Who said I was mad? I ain't mad."

"I'm sorry, Ty, but I didn't know you were coming today. Do you really think I would've left you if I knew you were gonna be there?" It sound like she 'bout to cry or something.

"Look, Novisha. You don't gotta do nothing for me, okay? You keep doing what you doing, and I'ma keep doing what I'm doing. And what I'ma do is make sure you okay. And if something ever happen to you, I'ma hafta go to jail 'cause somebody gonna die."

"Nothing's gonna happen to me. I'm fine." I hear her take a deep breath. "Now, am I gonna see you tomorrow?" She changing the subject, but that's alright with me 'cause I'm too depressed to keep talking 'bout the same shit over and over.

"Yeah. I'ma be there."

"Good. Oh, yeah, my mother wants to talk to your mom."

"What's up?"

"She wants to invite your family to dinner. Are you guys free on Friday night?"

"Yeah, pro'ly."

"Okay, can you put your mom on the phone so my mother can talk to her? I'll see you tomorrow. I love you."

"Yeah, I love you too." All of a sudden I get this sick feeling in my stomach, like I'ma throw up or something. "Hold on."

I go back inside. "Here," I tell my moms. "Ms. Jenkins wanna talk to you. Novisha bringing her to the phone." I don't wait for my moms to say nothing. I just give her the cell and go to the bathroom. I really wanna throw up all the shit I put in my body 'cause I'm feeling mad sick, but when I lean over the toilet, I'm gagging but nothing come up. Man, my stomach is tore up. Why I do this to myself?

When I come out the bathroom, my moms say, "We all going over to Ms. Jenkins apartment on Friday night. She talkin' 'bout how me and her need to be friends since you and Novisha is get- tin' serious. Do Ms. Jenkins know you screwing her daughter?"

I take my cell back from her and head for the door. "I'ma be back in the morning. Don't leave Troy alone."

Just as I'm 'bout to slam the door behind me, she yell, "Do Novisha know you screwing that Puerto Rican girl?"

TWENTY-ONE

"I was waiting for you," Jasmine tell me when I get to her room. She walking 'round in that same BORICUA T-shirt, but tonight she wearing panties with zebra stripes on them.

"How you know I was coming?"

"You love sleeping with me. I'm real soft and I smell nice." She stand in front of the mirror and start brushing her hair.

"You right, but it's killing me." I ain't take my eyes off her ass yet.

She start laughing. "Oh. Guess what I did today?"

"Do I wanna hear this?"

"Yeah. I called that lady from the church, the one with the restaurant. She asked me if I need a job and I said yes and she said I can come in tomorrow for an interview to be a waitress."

"You know how to be a waitress?"

"No, but it can't be that hard. And I can make a lot of money from tips."

"True that." I sit down on her bed and start to feel a little dizzy. Not only that, but my stomach still hurt.

After a couple minutes, Jasmine turn 'round and look me in the eye. "Are you high? I didn't know you got high."

"It's nothing," I say. "I ain't that high." I get that taste in the back of my throat that I always get right before I throw up, and I just wanna do it and get it over with already 'cause I feel like shit.

"Liar." She put her hair in a ponytail. "You wanna watch TV or just go to sleep?"

My stomach twist hard and I know it's finally gonna happen. I run to the bathroom and make it just in time. Then I'm throwing up, not only in the toilet, but all over the toilet seat and the floor. And it's real nasty. Then I just stand there hunched over gagging and gagging 'til there ain't nothing left inside me.

Jasmine stand in the doorway, freaking out in Spanish like she ain't never seen nobody throw up before. I don't know what she saying, but it ain't making me feel no better. "What's the matter?" she finally ask me in English. "You drunk or something?"

I nod my head and go over to the sink to wash my face. The water is coming out cold no matter how much hot water I try to put on to warm it up, but it still feel good on my skin. Then I rinse out my mouth a few times.

"Why were you drinking?"

I don't say nothing 'cause I don't even know why I drank so much. My opinion, weed ain't nothing compared to alcohol. They made the wrong thing legal.

I grab some toilet paper and try to clean up the mess I made on the floor. And Jasmine start helping me, which, I gotta say, is mad nice of her 'cause I don't know if I would do that for somebody else.

When we done, I take off my sweatshirt, wash the stains out in the sink, then hang it up on the shower rod.

157

"I'm gonna get you some soda from the machine," Jasmine say.

"No, don't go down there. Mr. Mendoza shift pro'ly started and I ain't in no condition to kick ass tonight." I walk real slow over to the bed and lay down.

But Jasmine don't listen. She out the room in a second, but she do come right back with a can of ginger ale. "Here, drink this." She hand me the can.

"You seen him?"

"Yeah, but he didn't say nothing to me. He looked at me, then put his head down. I think he's afraid of you."

I sit up on the bed and drink the ginger ale. Jasmine sit next to me and rub my head and my back, and with no shirt on, her hands feel real nice on my back. "You feeling better, Papi?" she whisper in my ear.

Damn. I ain't never had a girl call me Papi before and it's so fucking sexy. And she sitting so close to me that I don't wanna do nothing 'cept kiss her. So I do. I turn my head and, next thing I know, my lips is on hers, and my tongue is in her mouth and her arms is 'round my back. I don't want the kiss to end 'cause I need this after the way Novisha treated me today. I need a female like this that know how to treat me right.

After a long time, the kiss end and Jasmine smile at me. "You a good kisser," she say. Then she bust out laughing. "But your tongue tastes like vomit."

"A'ight," I say. "Just for that, I'ma brush my teeth with your toothbrush." I run back to the bathroom and lock the door before she can get in.

She bang on the door. "Ty, no. That's *my* toothbrush!"

I rub some of her toothpaste on my finger and brush my teeth and tongue that way, but she don't know what I'm doing. "Ty, that's disgusting!" she screaming.

Before I leave the bathroom, I wet her toothbrush. Then I walk out and watch her go in and check her toothbrush. "*Ay, dios mio!*" she say. "I can't believe you did that!"

"Sharing a toothbrush ain't no different from kissing." I sit back on the bed.

"That's not true. Kissing is nothing."

"Well, then come back over here and kiss me some more," I say. "And call me Papi again."

Kissing Jasmine is real nice, but I don't take things to the next level which I could do real easy. Jasmine ain't the kinda girl I wanna just use like that. It ain't right. And, truth is, she ain't the one I really wanna be with right 'bout now.

After a while, I get up and turn off the light. Then me and her lay in bed with our legs wrapped 'round each other. She stroking my head and I'm kinda getting into it when she say, "Why you so sad, Papi?"

"Sad? I ain't sad." I'm mad, I wanna tell her.

"Girlfriend problems?"

"Something like that," I say. Then I tell her everything I told Cal, 'bout the stalker and how Novisha ain't letting me protect her. And I tell Jasmine how Novisha just walked away from me at her school like she wanted to be anywhere else 'cept for with me.

"She still love you?"

"She say she do. But I don't know. Things is just different, you know what I mean?"

"Yeah. Things always change, but they can change back again, so don't worry so much."

Me and her talk for a while and, I gotta say, it's real easy talking to her. And I'm real comfortable being with her like this. I don't know, but when I'm with Jasmine I don't gotta act like everything is okay when it ain't. I can just relax and let my guard down.

Novisha don't got a clue how I'm living. She don't know that all my clothes and shit is in garbage bags and my little brother is 'sleep in a room full of roaches. And she don't know how bad I feel that I can't get my family outta this situation faster.

But Jasmine do know what I'm going through 'cause she in it with me. Me and her is the same. And that's something me and Novisha ain't never gonna be.

TWENTY-TWO

I wake up 'cause there's someone knocking on Jasmine door. I don't know what time it is, and I don't got no clue who it could be. Jasmine is 'sleep with her arms 'round my waist, but she wake up fast and grab ahold of me a little tighter.

"You think it's Mr. Mendoza?" she ask.

"It better not be," I say. My stomach is feeling a little better now and I could probably kick ass if I hafta. "What time is it?"

She let go of me and check the little alarm clock she got on the floor by the bed. "Five twenty-two."

Whoever it is knock a couple more times. Then I hear, "Ty, it's me." Troy sound real little this time in the morning. "Ty, you gotta open this door and wake up. But, I mean, the other way around."

I jump outta bed and open the door real fast 'cause I don't want my brother in the hall by hisself, 'specially here at Bennett where I don't know who the fuck could be out there. Troy standing in the hall wearing just his sweatpants and T-shirt, and he ain't got no sneakers or socks on. "What you doin' here?"

"I woke up and you still wasn't there," he say. "Mommy told me you was in room two-oh-seven and I found it by myself."

"She let you out alone?"

"She said you was here." He point to the number on the door. "See."

What my moms thinking? "Get in here." I turn the light on so he can see where he going and, man, I swear them roaches musta been having they own party 'cause they all up in here. Troy hop up on the bed with Jasmine while them roaches book 'cross the floor like they on the highway or something. There's even some centipede-looking things running by. Troy stare at everything like he at the zoo.

I just stand there for a second thinking how crazy this shit is. I mean, something ain't right when Troy don't even get scared no more. Matter of fact, when most of the roaches is gone, he just shrug his shoulders and start jumping up and down on the bed like ain't nothing wrong with this place. I'ma hafta get us outta here. Fast.

"Troy, no!" Jasmine scream and try to move out his way. She laying in bed barely awake and now she got this kid jumping, like, two inches from her head.

"Watch me," Troy say loud, like it's three o'clock in the afternoon. "I can do a flip. Watch."

I go over and grab him off the bed before he stomp on Jasmine face. "No flips today, man. I ain't got no money to take you to the emergency room."

"I ain't gonna get hurt, Ty. I promise."

"No." I set him down on the floor. He try to get back up on the bed a couple times, but I don't let him, and finally he give up and just sit on the bed.

"I didn't see you last night," he say, sticking out his bottom lip like he a three-year-old. "You wasn't even there when I went to bed."

Now I got a seven-year-old making me feel guilty. "I'm working this week," I tell him, and sit down next to him. "I'm trying to get us outta here, so I need to make a lot of money."

"Like a thousand million dollars?"

"Nah, not that much. But a lot." It's hard talking to Troy sometimes 'cause I don't want him growing up to be like me. I want him to stay in school and do everything right and not think a man always gotta do shit to make fast money. I mean, there's some men out there that work hard and don't take no chances with they freedom. Problem is, my pops ain't one of them.

And me, I ain't trying to be one of them men that always gotta be looking over they shoulder for the police neither. I know if I'm with Novisha, she ain't gonna let me end up like that. But if me and her ain't together, I don't know what kinda man I'ma be. I could go any ol' way.

I sit there and answer a couple more questions from Troy, then tell him to lay down with us for a few minutes 'cause it's too early to get up for school. I start to slide over next to Jasmine, but Troy don't let me. Nah, my man just climb right in the middle of us. He get under the blanket and rest his head against her arm. And he got a big-ass smile on his face like he right where he wanna be.

I don't blame him neither. Jasmine is a nice female to sleep with. Yeah, it's hard keeping things PG-13 with a girl as fine as her, but if you could get past that, she got the right kinda body to make you comfortable.

The three of us sleep for 'bout another half hour, then Jasmine wake up to get ready for school, so I take Troy back to our room. My moms is 'sleep, so while Troy is in the bathroom, I wake her up to yell at her.

"He left by hisself," she tell me when I'm done breaking on her. She don't even sit up in bed to talk to me. She just lay there like this ain't no big deal. "He woke me up and asked me where you was, and I told him. He musta left when I went back to sleep."

Something 'bout the way she say it, I know she telling the truth for a change. Leaving the room by hisself do sound like something Troy would do. The only thing I wish is that she was as upset 'bout this as me.

While I'm waiting for Troy, I put all the dirty clothes in one garbage bag and tell my moms that she gotta do the laundry today. Shit, just 'cause we in a shelter don't mean we gotta look broke down. That's one thing I ain't having. Brotha like me gotta keep my shit together at all times. You never know.

"I need money," she tell me.

"What you do with the money Dante gave you?"

"I only got ten dollars left." Now she sit up in bed and look at me like I did something wrong. "You wasn't around yesterday. I had to feed myself and your brother. Don't you think we need to eat?"

"Use the ten dollars for the laundry," I tell her. "If you want more money, you need to get ahold of Dante and get that equipment back."

"What I'm s'posed to tell him?"

"Tell him I need the equipment by Saturday. And if I don't

164

hear from him today, me and my friends is gonna roll up to his place and kick his ass."

Troy come out the bathroom and I go in. I don't say nothing to him 'bout what he did yet. Me and him is gonna hafta have a man-to-man on the way to his school.

When me and Troy get downstairs to the lobby, they got signs taped up on the walls and doors. Folks couldn't miss them if they wanted.

TO ALL GUESTS
DUE TO INCLEMENT WEATHER AND THE SUBSEQUENT LACK OF SHELTER BEDS, ALL UNDOMICILED FAMILIES CURRENTLY STAYING AT THE BENNETT FAMILY CENTER WILL REMAIN AT THAT LOCATION UNTIL MONDAY MORNING AT 7:00.

THE NYC EMERGENCY ASSISTANCE UNIT APPRECIATES EVERYONE'S ONGOING PATIENCE.
—THE MANAGEMENT

"What them signs say?" Troy ask.

"They say we ain't leaving here no time soon," I tell him. "We stuck."

More reason I gotta make us some real money this weekend, I'm thinking as we go outside and get slapped in the face with the freezing cold air. This party gonna hafta work. This is serious now.

And I can't believe them assholes actually called us guests. That shit gonna have me bugging all day.

On the way to the train station, I let Troy know how mad I am that he left the room by hisself. I tell him 'bout all them people that wanna steal kids and that he gotta be careful, 'specially at Bennett. Then, when I see he ain't paying me no mind, I break it down for him and tell him if he leave the room alone again, I'ma hit him.

"You can't hit me 'cause you ain't my father."

"Yeah, I am," I tell him. "'Til August, I'm your pops, got that?" I keep my voice strong like my pops do when he mad at us and want us to stop doing something. "You got that?"

"Yeah," he say. "I said I wasn't gonna do that no more, right?"

I can't stand when he get fresh like that. Actin' all grown and shit. I gotta work on that 'cause he wasn't never that way when my pops was home. He gotta know that he s'posed to act right no matter if our pops is home or not.

TWENTY-THREE

At 2:20, I'm in front of Novisha school waiting for her the way I do every Wednesday. Wednesday is our day, so least I know she ain't gonna dog me like she did yesterday.

It take a while, but finally some kids start coming out the front doors. Funny thing 'bout this school is when the kids leave outta here, they look like they had a good time all day. They be laughing with they friends and waving bye to they teachers and shit. You wouldn't even know they been in school all day by the way they actin'.

My school wasn't nothing like this. It was more like a prison, you ask me. We had to go through metal detectors just to get in, and if them alarms went off, we had to go to another room to get searched again with one of them hand wands like they use at the airport. And no matter what you had on you, they would say it was a weapon and take it away from you, even when you was bringing it for school. Shit like compasses for geometry and them little staplers wasn't allowed in my school. Even rulers. Like we was gonna file them down and make knives outta them or something. The whole thing never made no sense to me. They was s'posed to be getting us ready for college, not a life behind bars.

Man, I couldn't stand that place. When last period was over I would just book outta there, trying to get to the train fast before it got too crowded. I just ain't wanna deal with nothing. And when I would get home, my moms wouldn't never be there 'cause she had to pick up Troy from school, so most of the time it was just me and my pops. He would always ask me 'bout school, but not like a lot of parents do. He would be like, "How much you fail that quiz by?" or "How many classes you cut today?" Crazy thing is, I wasn't even failing or cutting when he was 'round and he knew that. He was just trying to let me know he was up on my grades and shit.

After he got arrested, everything changed. Yeah, I was still going to school and all that, but things at home was so jacked up I couldn't even think straight. And at school, I just wasn't having it. If a nigga looked at me wrong, there was gonna be a fight. Anything used to just set me off. The vice principal was always threatening me, saying if I kept fighting he was gonna throw me outta school. Like I woulda cared.

I mean, I was getting in trouble just 'bout every day and I got suspended twice, so I just ain't go back after Christmas vacation. The whole first half of the year was wasted anyway. I only passed math and music, and I was gonna end up in night school or summer school no matter what. What difference did it make if I stopped going?

I look up and finally see Novisha. She coming out the school talking to Shanice and Ana like she always is. I don't know what she tell her friends she do with me on Wednesdays, but I know for a fact them girls don't know what she really up to. When it come to us, she got a lot of folks fooled.

Today when she see me, she actually look like she happy I'm there. She smile real big and bright, and just seeing that smile make me wanna forget the way she dissed me yesterday. Man, that smile could make me forget anything. And I'm like, that's how my girl s'posed to act when she see me.

After she say bye to her friends, she run over to me like she ain't seen me in weeks and throw her arms 'round me. And she kiss me. It ain't one of the real long, real juicy kisses we famous for, but it's good. It work. And this time she don't act all embarrassed kissing me in front of her friends. She into it.

"Your lips are frozen," she say.

"I know. I been waiting a while."

"I'm sorry. I forgot my bio book in my locker and I had to go all the way up to the third floor for it."

"You don't need no biology book," I tell her. "I'ma teach you all you need to know 'bout the body. Watch."

"Well, unless you're gonna teach me everything I need to know about a cow's body, I'm gonna need my book!" She start laughing.

"A cow?"

"Yeah. Cows have four compartments in their stomachs and we're supposed to know what each one does."

"Man, next time I eat a burger I'ma be thinking 'bout that."

"And they're gonna make us dissect a cow's eye next month." She make her nasty face, but at the same time, she do look like she kinda into all this biology stuff. She probably gonna end up some big-time doctor or something.

We start walking down the street holding hands. "You wanna

169

go to the diner?" she ask me. "They have the best hot chocolate there. With whipped cream."

I ain't really in the mood for nothing 'cept getting her back to her apartment and being alone with her. That's 'cause today is the day I'ma make my move and take Cal advice for the first time since I knew him. I'ma show Novisha what I can do and give her a preview of how good things is gonna be when we finally hook up.

The last two nights was real tough, sleeping with Jasmine and not doing nothing with her. That girl is like a test, to see how much I love Novisha, and so far, I been passing. Now I know I ain't getting no A or B on the test, but I'm least getting a C+ 'cause I been just 'bout as good as a normal guy could be. 'Specially a guy that ain't getting none from his girl. If she only knew what I was turning down for her.

We get close to the diner and I tell her I ain't feeling no hot chocolate today. "The only kinda hot chocolate I want is you," I say with my smooth self, and she giggle. "But we could still get that whipped cream if you wanna."

She laugh and punch me on the shoulder. "You're nasty."

"No doubt."

She punch me again, harder, but she still got that smile on her face. I don't know if it's just me, but I think when Novisha finally do give it up, she gonna be real into sex. Course I'm hoping she don't actually make me wait 'til we married. I'm hoping she get so worked up, she just tell me to go for it one day. One day like today.

Me and Novisha got our Wednesdays worked out. I pick her up from school and walk her to 'bout a block from Bronxwood. Then she stop by her moms job while I kill thirty to forty-five minutes. Most of the time, I go see Cal 'cause, fact is, he the only guy I know who always 'round. Novisha talk to her moms for a while, then act like she gotta go home to do her homework or something. Then when she get home, she call my cell and I go over there and we get to be alone together 'til 7:30 or 8:00.

Most of the time, we don't get to do nothing no other day 'cause her moms is always home by 4:00 at the latest. And her moms don't want me in the apartment when she ain't there. Yeah, she trust me, but not that much. It's like she alright with Novisha having a boyfriend long as she can watch us all the time.

So today I kiss Novisha when we get to the corner by the check-cashing place and she walk to her moms job. I decide to go see Patrick and make sure the music at the party gonna be jammin'. He live in the same building with Cal but on the twelfth floor. When I get near the building, I'm kinda surprised to see Cal out there working 'cause I thought he wasn't gonna be 'round Bronxwood for a couple days after the way Andre threw him out last night and made him go to his moms place. Like a war was 'bout to break out or something. But Cal out there doing business so I just give him a little nod and walk by him. He don't say nothing to me neither 'cause he too cool to talk when he working. I'm used to it, but I still don't get him sometimes. Shit, when I start making money DJing, I ain't gonna be like that with no one.

I can hear Patrick music blasting as soon as I get off the elevator. His moms let me in the apartment and tell me he in his room, which she don't even gotta say 'cause that's where all the music coming from. Patrick got the whole apartment pumping. Shit sound nice too.

Patrick room is all 'bout music and movies. The first thing

you see when you go in there is all the computers. He got three regular computers and two laptops and all they do is copy DVDs and CDs 24/7. Blank CDs and DVDs and plastic cases is stacked on one side of the room and all the finished ones is on the other, just waiting to be sold. He got all the new movies and CDs and his products look good, too, almost like the real deal. Really don't make no sense buying them nowhere else.

And he got DJ equipment too — turntables, a CD deck, mixers, and speakers, but not like what my pops got. He do got enough for a real nice house party though. If Dante keep actin' a fool, I could use some of Patrick equipment, but his speakers ain't gonna work in a room the size of the bus depot. I'm still gonna need speakers like my pops got or the music gonna sound like shit.

Me and Patrick spend 'bout a half hour going over all the new music he got. He got some good stuff, like he got instrumental versions of some of the rap songs, which, I gotta say, sound a whole lot better without the rapper. The music and the beat sound real nice, and my mind is flying thinking of how I can use them in remixes and shit. Another song he got, the rapper keep saying, "I like it when the honeys shake it, shake it." The rest of the song is garbage, but I could definitely mix that line with something else.

The good thing 'bout going over to Patrick apartment is that I get to use his equipment and do some mixing on the CD deck, which I ain't never did. My pops don't be playing no CDs at his parties, so I need this kinda practice. And Patrick use the Denon deck, which got all kinda features and shit. And 'cause I'm just learning, I wanna try them all out. After a while, I'm jammin' so loud in his room that his moms come in and tell us to turn the

172

noise down. The woman look like she just 'bout had it with Patrick and his music.

When Novisha call and tell me she home, that's all I gotta hear for me to fly outta Patrick apartment. I mean, why I'ma sit up there with this guy when I could be with my girl, right? I see Cal again downstairs, but I still don't talk to him 'cause this time he in the lobby by the mailboxes, and Andre is standing real close to him, whispering. It ain't no friendly conversation neither. Andre got his finger pointing in Cal face and it's real obvious he pissed off 'bout something. Course I'm trying to find out what's going on, and if it got anything to do with whatever the fuck happened last night after me and Cal left. Just the fact that Andre alive and don't got no broken bones or open wounds probably mean it wasn't all that serious, but still, I wanna know what's up.

I walk real slow through the lobby and when I get near them, I hear Andre say, "This is a business, man. You either working or you ain't working." He still pointing and actin' like the boss man, and Cal just standing there staring out the window like he trying not to hear what his brother saying. Cal look mad too, but he don't never talk back to Andre 'cause, fact is, he a little scared of him.

Cal don't see me 'til I get to the lobby door and when he do, he just look at me for a second then down at the floor like he embarrassed or something. I don't know why he like that. He always too busy actin' like he running things that he can't even keep it real with me, his friend. Don't make no sense.

But I ain't really got time to think 'bout him right now. He be alright. I'ma go see my baby. And I got plans.

TWENTY-FOUR

I'm like a spy or something trying to sneak into Novisha apartment without none of her nosy neighbors seeing me and telling her moms that I was there. But the second I'm in there, I don't waste no time waiting to kiss her. We kiss from the living room to the kitchen, then, finally I back her up into her bedroom. I got my hands on her waist and I'm pulling her real close to me and I know she can tell how excited I am.

Finally Novisha come up for air. "Wow. You're on fire. I need to catch my breath."

"I'ma give you two minutes, tops." I sit on her bed and try to cool myself down so I can take my time with her. It's Wednesday. We don't gotta rush today.

While she take off her uniform blazer and shoes, I grab the fake diary from under her pillow and start reading.

Dear Diary,
    I don't understand how my mother could forgive my father so easily. It hasn't even been two years since he left us.

Why doesn't she remember crying all night and having to beg him for money to pay my tuition and the other bills? I definitely remember how he didn't even show up to my graduation last year.

My mother has me thinking too. She tells me she's a good Catholic, but she's having sex without being married. Does that make it right? I'm confused.

I put the diary back under the pillow. "Just 'cause your moms read that, don't mean she gonna stop letting your pops come 'round. He pro'ly doing the right thing in bed."

Novisha make that face again, like she just ate something nasty. "I don't wanna hear about my mom's sex life, Ty. It's disgusting."

"Yeah, but it's true. My pops beat my moms down, twice, and she still with him."

"That's because she's dependent on him for money. My mother was like that too, when they were married. He cheated all the time and she pretended it wasn't going on because she needed him, but now that she's working full-time there's no reason to get back with him. He's only going to walk out on us again." Novisha get all sad and her eyes get all watery, but she don't really cry.

"Next time he walk out, y'all gonna be prepared," I tell her. "It ain't gonna be no surprise, so y'all gonna be okay." What I'm saying is bullshit and I know it. Like, we all knew my pops was gonna get locked up again and we wasn't prepared for shit. The first couple weeks after he was locked up, all three of us was walking 'round in shock like we couldn't believe what the fuck happened to our family.

"You're right," Novisha say, and wipe her eyes. "But I just

hope my mother will read that and do what I'm telling her to do and dump him. I know what's best for her."

"Look at you, thinking you can get people to do what you want them to."

She put her hands on her hips. "It's not like that!"

"Forget all that and come over here, girl." This conversation is getting too sad, and I ain't looking to ruin the mood.

She walk over to the bed and turn St. Mary 'round.

"Now that's what I'm talkin' 'bout!" I say, getting all excited again.

She unbutton her uniform blouse and I'm liking the cute little black bra she got on. Then she take off her skirt and she wearing matching black panties, and I know she wearing her sexiest underwear just for me. And her body is so tight, damn, I don't know how long I'ma be able to wait to get me some of that.

So before she can even start to do her thing on me, I tell her, "Females first."

"What does that mean?" She look a little scared and I don't know why.

"I wanna do you," I say.

She start to move away from me, but I just grab her waist and, 'cause she so light, I just flip her on the bed next to me. She start laughing but try to get away at the same time. "Relax," I tell her, tickling her stomach. "You gonna like it."

She scream 'cause she hate getting tickled. Man, watching her laugh and wiggle 'round on the bed get me even more excited. 'Specially the way she arching her back all sexy. Damn.

"Ty, stop. Stop!"

I stop, but then I go for that bra, trying to reach 'round and

176

unhook it. Then I see it's one of them bras that hook in the front, the ones they make just to confuse dudes.

"Ty, c'mon. You know how I feel about this." Then she go into all that shit she always say 'bout how she Catholic and she wanna wait and all that, but this time I ain't paying her no mind.

"I respect you," I tell her. "But I wanna get closer to you."

"But —"

"I love you. I wanna make love to you, but I'm cool with waiting, you know that. But we been together, like, a year and a half, and I wanna show you how much I love you. And I want you to trust me, a'ight?" I look her in the eyes with my real serious face.

She just stare at me and I see how scared she is. "Ty, I don't want one thing to lead to another. I know how boys are."

"Not all boys is the same," I say. "And I ain't no boy. I'm a man. Your man. And I ain't gonna take it too far. You gonna hafta marry me 'fore I give you any."

She laugh a little and I take that as a green light. And I go. I take that bra off and I kiss her all over. And when I start slipping them black panties off, for the first time she let me, and I'm like, man, this is easier than I thought it was gonna be. I keep kissing her everywhere. Matter of fact, there ain't a spot I don't miss. And when she all relaxed and smiling, I go down on her and finish her off real slow. When I'm through, she breathing all heavy and shit, and I'm feeling, like, finally I'm the man.

Then we just lay there kissing. "You a'ight with that?" I ask her.

"Yeah," she say. "I'm happy."

177

I put my arm 'round her waist. "Tell me I'm your man."

"You're my man."

We kiss some more. Then after a while she try to take the sheet and cover herself up, but I ain't having none of that. Not after all this time it took me to see her naked. I take the sheets and blankets and kick them off the bed. "Nah," I tell her. "You too beautiful to cover up."

She smile and we lay next to each other kissing and talking. Personally, I'm feeling real good 'bout this, like we now tighter than we ever was. A couple more Wednesdays like this and she ain't gonna be thinking 'bout going away to no college without me. She gonna know she need me.

Later, after we both satisfied, I get dressed and Novisha fix me a plate and let me eat in her room while she go call her moms to make sure she ain't gonna close the laundromat early and bust us.

I sit at her desk and scarf back them leftover turkey wings, white rice, and spinach. From the kitchen phone, I hear Novisha lying to her moms on the phone, talking 'bout how she was doing her homework, but got real hungry and practically ate all them leftover turkey wings herself. The girl is a good liar, I gotta say that. There's a whole 'notha side to her that her moms don't know nothing 'bout.

While I'm sitting there, I find her real diary and do what I always do, read the last thing she wrote.

Yesterday, Shanice asked me what school Ty goes to and I finally admitted to her that he hasn't gone back to school since Christmas break. She told me she would never go out with a boy who dropped out of school, and while she was talking I felt really embarrassed. I'm not proud of myself for feeling that way, but I did. Am I going to have to live my whole life feeling embarrassed because my man doesn't even have a high school diploma? I hope not.

Man, every time I read this diary, she got something in it that make me feel like crap. And after the fun we just had together, I ain't really in the mood for this. To be honest, I'm kinda tired of reading how she too good for me.

"Okay, she's closing the laundromat in forty-five minutes," Novisha say, coming back in her room.

"I'm out," I say, kinda glad I got a excuse to leave. All of a sudden I just wanna be by myself.

Novisha walk me to the door and she kiss me, but I don't drag it out. I just kiss her and grab the doorknob to get outta there. "You don't have to pick me up tomorrow," she say. "I'll call you the second I get home, so you won't worry about me."

I nod. "A'ight. That's a'ight."

"Are you okay?" She try to take my hand, but I don't let her. I just open the door. "Did I do something?"

"Nah, we good," I tell her. "Don't forget to call me tomorrow."

"I won't." She smile, but I can tell she still trying to figure out what's wrong with me. "I had a nice time today."

"Me too." And I leave, go out in the hall and press the DOWN button for the elevator. I know I shoulda said something 'bout what I read, but I ain't looking to get into no argument with Novisha 'bout the shit she be writing in her diary. I'm trying to hold on to her, not push her away. She all I got.

TWENTY-FIVE

My moms is in a real good mood when I get back to our room. And for the first time since my pops got locked up, she actually look kinda nice too. She went and got her hair braided with long extensions, and she smiling. That's probably why she look different.

Troy is sitting on the bed playing something on the Game Boy and my moms is sitting next to him watching. And she into it too. She telling him shit like, "Watch out for them aliens," and "Jump over that black hole."

For a second I think he using my Game Boy 'cause he always playing with my stuff when I ain't 'round, but then I look closer and see he got the new Game Boy that just came out, the one I wanted to get. "Where he get that from?"

My moms look up at me, and all she gotta say is one word: "Dante."

Damn. I shoulda knew it was him. Who else gonna go outta his way to get on my moms good side? And Troy is sitting there playing his game, not caring what kinda asshole got it for him. He just happy. "Troy, you know how to talk?"

Troy put the game on pause and finally look at me. "Hi, Ty. Look what Dante got for me." He hold up the Game Boy like I ain't seen it already. "I'm on level two."

"That's good." I try to sound happy but, truth is, I'm way past pissed. I unzip my jacket, but before I can even take it off, I look 'round the room and see that not only did Dante buy Troy a Game Boy and pay to get my moms hair did, but he been food shopping for us again. We got more crackers and cookies and shit on the dresser, and this time all of it is in plastic containers with lids to keep the roaches out. Dante thinking of everything. "When I'ma get the equipment back?" I ask my moms.

"He need it for Friday, so you can get it back Saturday."

"How I'ma get it from him?" My pops got a lot of equipment and huge speakers. Ain't like I could just roll up there and carry the shit out by myself. I'ma need a couple guys and a van or truck to do that.

"He said he could bring it where you want on Saturday, but you gotta find a way to get it back to the storage place on your own."

"A'ight." I know what Dante after, trying to be nice to me, and if he keep on doing what he doing, he gonna get my moms and my pops equipment for hisself. Just like that.

Troy start laughing 'cause he winning the game and my moms is clapping for him. "See, I said you could get past them aliens." She got way too much energy all of a sudden.

"You do laundry?" I ask her.

"Yeah, it's all folded in the bag over by the door."

"Y'all eat?"

"Dante took us out for pizza, after we finished shopping. You seen all the food he got us?"

"Yeah."

"If you hungry, there's some peanut butter crackers in one of them plastic containers, but save some for your brother."

"Watch me, Mommy," Troy say. "Look."

"Troy, you gonna hafta start gettin' ready for bed," I tell him. And I don't even know why I gotta be the one to tell him that. I can't stand when my moms do that, make me the one that gotta stop all his fun. She used to do that with my pops too. Make him the bad guy.

"I need more time, Ty," he say, like he doing some real important work. "I'm almost finished this level."

"Well, you better finish that level in five minutes. What 'bout your homework? You did it?"

"Yeah."

"Let me check it."

"The church girl checked it already."

"Jasmine?"

"Yeah, her."

I look to my moms for some kinda explanation.

"That Puerto Rican girl came by looking for you," she say. "Me and Troy was doing his homework. She said she could help him if I wanted, so I let her. She a nice girl. We talked for a long time."

"'Bout what?

Troy stomp his foot on the floor. "Mommy, keep watching me."

"Everything," she say. "We talked 'bout you. I think she like you."

"Nah. We just friends."

"I can't believe you standing up there lying to your mother like I don't know no better."

"It's true."

"I like her," Troy say. "She the prettiest, most beautifulest girl I ever saw."

I'm just 'bout to ask my moms what she told Jasmine 'bout me, when she get up off the bed and say, "Let me show you what else Dante got for your brother."

She walk 'round to the side of the bed and pick up two big shopping bags. From one of them she pull out a thick black North Face jacket, the kind that got a hood with fake fur inside. "See, this the kinda jacket he need 'cause the one he got is all ripped up," she say. Then she pull a big Timberland box out the other bag. She open it up and show me new boots. "And you know he really need boots with all that snow out there." She close the box and start putting everything away. "I don't know why you don't like Dante. Look at everything he doing to help us. And he went to the management office of his building 'cause that apartment gonna be empty soon. They told him we could have the place as long as we have the two months' rent and one month security deposit up front."

"Why don't Dante give you that too?"

"He would if he could, but he don't got that kind of money. If you bring home enough from the party, we could get that apartment."

Yeah, that's what I want. A apartment in Dante building.

Close enough so that asshole could come by whenever he want.

My moms is staring at me. "What's your problem?"

"Nothing. You know what you doing with Dante, right?"

"I told you, I ain't doing nothing with Dante." She fold her arms in front of her like she a little kid.

"A'ight. You ain't gotta convince me of nothing. I ain't your man." All I know is I really hafta get outta this room. The longer I stay here, the madder I'ma get. "Make sure Troy go to bed when he finish that level. I'ma see y'all in the morning."

I say bye to Troy, but he don't hardly hear me 'cause he too into the game. I can't believe my moms don't see what Dante is doing. He think he could just step in and take my pops place. Now that might be okay with my moms and Troy, but it ain't never gonna be okay with me.

"Did you used to walk 'round like this in fronta Emiliano?" I ask Jasmine when I get to her room 'cause as usual she half naked.

"All the time," she say.

"And he never tried nothing with you?"

"Never."

I sit on her bed. "Then either he blind or gay 'cause no other guy could take it."

"Well, you been sleeping with me, how many days now? And you never tried nothing. So what does that say about you?"

"That I'm stupid. Or crazy."

She laugh. "Or faithful to your girlfriend. I think it's cute."

"Great. I'm cute, but what's that doing for me? Being cute

ain't gettin' me outta Bennett. It damn sure ain't gettin' me no money. It ain't even working with Novisha no more." I'm in a real fucked-up mood, but, still, I wasn't looking to say all this to Jasmine. She ain't ask for none of this shit.

Jasmine come over and sit next to me on the bed. She grab ahold of one of my hands. "What's the matter with you? You drunk again?"

"Nah."

"Then why you so sad? You getting depressed being here?"

I shake my head. "I don't know. Pro'ly."

"You having more problems with your mom?"

"Yeah," I say. "But that ain't it." Then, next thing I know, I just tell her what I'm going through, 'bout how I thought I was gonna be in a good mood tonight 'cause I was spending the day with my girl and we was gonna get closer than we ever was, and how things ain't go the way I wanted. "She wrote in her diary that she embarrassed 'cause I ain't in school, and she ain't gonna wanna end up with nobody that don't got a high school diploma. Like that's the only thing that matter to her."

"She lets you read her diary?" Jasmine ask, like that's the only thing she heard.

"Yeah."

She shake her head. "I bet she's not writing what she really thinks. Not if someone else is reading it."

"Nah. That's the thing with us. We tell each other everything."

Jasmine get this half smile on her face. "You tell her you been sleeping with me every night?"

Damn. Why she had to go there?

"I didn't think so." She start laughing. "I'm just saying, you keeping stuff from her and she's keeping stuff from you. All girls keep secrets."

"Not her. You don't know her."

"Okay, you right, but, c'mon, if she knows you reading her diary, she's not gonna write everything. She's gonna leave some things out. It just makes sense."

I ain't in the mood for this tonight. "Look, let's go to bed. I'm tired."

She stand up and go to the mirror and start putting her hair in a ponytail like she always do. "I came by looking for you today," she tell me like I ain't already know that. "I wanted to tell you about my interview at the restaurant. The lady, she was so nice to me and it was so easy talking to her. And you know what? I think I'm gonna get the job."

"Nice," I say.

"But I have to call her back Friday to find out. I could tell she liked me though. She let me stay and eat for free. And you know how good her food is, right?"

"Yeah."

"Your mother was nice to me too," Jasmine say, still looking at herself in the mirror. Man, I ain't never seen nobody stare at theyself more than her. "She told me all about you, when you were little, how you knew all the words to the rap songs your father used to play." She giggle. "And I helped your brother with his homework. He's really a cute little boy."

"First you tell me I'm cute, now you say he cute."

"Both of you are cute."

"Yeah, right." I gotta get outta here too. I need to get away from her bullshit for a couple minutes. "Look, Jasmine, I'ma be back, a'ight?" I get up and walk out the door real fast, before she can try to stop me.

In the hall, it hit me. I really don't got nowhere to go. For real. I mean, I don't feel like staying with Jasmine tonight, but I damn sure ain't going back to my room and hafta stare at the jacket and boots Dante got Troy.

So I go downstairs to the lobby and, man, every time I go through there, the place look more and more tore up. It's downright nasty now with all kinds of garbage, soda cans, and cigarette butts and shit on the floor and tables. There's some kinda red juice or something spilled on one of the couches, and course nobody did nothing to clean it up.

I swear, this place probably ain't been cleaned for months. And the smell is a whole 'nother story. Bennett stink like the inside of a garbage truck. I mean, the rotting fast food, stale cigarettes, and funky people is definitely giving the room a kick. Man.

Two women is sitting on them nasty chairs drinking beer outta brown paper bags while they kids is going buckwild, running 'round and making all kinds of noise. Mr. Mendoza is at the front desk on the phone and he look like he too through with them kids. A couple guys my age is standing 'round too. They by the candy machine talking and eating Doritos. I give them a nod and a what up, then I see Wayne outside in front of the building smoking, so I go out there to let him know the party is on for Saturday and tell him what time I'ma need him there.

I zip up my jacket and step out in the cold. Wayne is leaning up against a car talkin' to some other guy. I think his name is Rafael or some shit. I give them a what up too, and bum a

187

cigarette from Wayne. Then I just lean against the car and chill. Try to relax.

Wayne and Rafael is talking 'bout the subway fare hike that's gonna start next month. "That shit's crazy," Rafael say. "How they gonna charge that much to ride them dirty-ass trains?"

"Word," Wayne say. "And all them homeless people they got on them trains. Shit, man. They charging us more money and they ain't doing nothing to get rid of them bums."

I just smoke and listen to them talk, but, in a way, it don't feel like none of this is really happening. I mean, I can't believe I really been stuck here at Bennett for so long. Or that I'm really homeless. Me. Two weeks ago, I had a address. When I was hungry, I went in the kitchen and got something to eat, and when I ain't wanna deal with my moms, I went in my room and closed the fucking door and ain't had to put up with nothing for a while.

Now what I got? Some clothes in a garbage bag, a cell phone with, like, ten minutes left on my prepaid, a jacked-up CD player, and a couple MetroCards. Oh, yeah, I got a room in a disgusting roach-filled motel. I don't even got my own bed.

When they stop talking, I tell Wayne 'bout the party, and I ask Rafael what he doing that night. "Nothing," he say. "You need help?"

"Yeah, setting up and keeping shit running."

"It's two hundred for the night," Wayne tell him, and I wanna punch him 'cause I was 'bout to tell Rafael I would give him $150.

"Yeah, I'll be there," Rafael say.

I give him all the info. "But you gotta help break down the equipment and load up the van." Course I don't actually got no van right now. That's another thing I gotta set up.

"Two hundred." Rafael look real happy, like he already got the money in his pocket. "Cool, man."

"There you are!" I hear, and when I look up I see Jasmine standing in the doorway. She got her clothes back on, but she ain't wearing no jacket. She come outside anyway. "I didn't know where you went."

She stand next to me, close, so I put my arm 'round her shoulder. She take the cigarette out my hand and start smoking it. "That ain't right," I tell her, trying to get it back. "And you smoke too much anyway."

She start laughing and fight me off. "I'm not the one out here smoking in the cold."

I get the cigarette back. "Yeah, but I don't gotta smoke, like you."

"At least I got an excuse for doing something this stupid," she say. "I'm addicted." She put her arm 'round my waist and whisper, "When are you gonna come back to bed?"

"Gimme a minute."

We share the cigarette, passing it back and forth, and out the corner of my eye, I see Wayne and Rafael looking at each other. I know they heard what she said and they trying to figure out what's up with us. They probably jealous too. Yeah, I know me and Jasmine ain't doing nothing, but they don't know that. All they know is what they see, a hot girl like her begging a brotha like me to come back to bed. And that's all good.

"I'm cold," Jasmine say.

"Okay, I'ma be back up there in a while." I don't got nothing more to do out here with them dudes, but, truth is, I wanna hear what they gonna say when Jasmine leave.

"Hurry up," she say. Then she run back inside. I keep a eye

on Mr. Mendoza through the window, but he don't move when she walk past the desk. He barely look at her. The man got one beat-down, and now he scared. Pussy.

"Man, I can't believe you hittin' that," Wayne say. "She wild or what?"

I smile like I'm thinking 'bout all the good times me and Jasmine had. "She a nice girl," I tell him. "But I ain't the kinda guy that talk 'bout what a girl do or don't do, know what I mean? All I'm saying is she nice." I take a deep breath and watch them waiting for me to give them more details. Then I just go, "I'll check y'all tomorrow," and that's it.

As I walk away, I can hear Wayne and Rafael saying shit like, "That ain't right," and "That shorty need to be with me, not him."

I got my back to them, which is good 'cause I'm cheesing it up real big. Yeah, I gotta admit, messing with them dudes heads was definitely worth staying outside for. And I'm feeling a lot better now.

TWENTY-SIX

Jasmine is sitting up in bed reading some schoolbook when I get back to the room. "You gotta keep your door locked," I tell her.

"You said you were coming right back."

"Yeah, but you seen the kinda folks they let up in here. Lock your door."

"Yes, Daddy." She look cute sitting on the bed with her legs crossed. The jeans is off again and she showing off them sexy panties she like to wear.

Pain shoot through my whole body. "I don't know why I'm putting myself through this," I say under my breath, but loud enough for her to hear. "Girl like to kill me, teasing me like this every night."

Jasmine start laughing. "Stop talking to yourself."

I take off my sneakers and put them by the vent so they could dry.

"Take off your pants," Jasmine tell me. But she don't look up from her book, so I don't know what she mean by it. Is she gonna do something to me again? And if she try, am I gonna let her?

Being that I ain't one to argue, I sit on the bed and take off my pants. Then I just wait, but she don't do nothing. She just keep on reading.

Then, after a while, she say, "Can you sleep with the light on? I need to finish this chapter."

"A'ight," I say, confused.

"It's only, like, three more pages."

"A'ight."

I get under the covers, but I ain't really all that sleepy, and I'm still waiting to see if Jasmine gonna do something to me. So after 'bout ten minutes, I turn over and watch her. She highlighting something in the book and she kinda look like she really thinking hard 'bout whatever she reading. "What you studying?" I ask.

"Latin American history. The Mexican Revolution."

"Sound mad boring to me."

"You don't like nothing about school?"

"Nah. I used to just go 'cause I had to. 'Cause if I cut, my pops woulda kicked my ass."

"You gotta do things for yourself, not just your father."

"I know that."

"You going to college?"

"Nah."

"Well, you should at least finish high school. You gotta think about your future. And Novisha's. If you love her, then you gonna have to get a good job and pay half the bills."

I sit up in the bed. "I'ma pay all the bills. See, I'ma be a DJ, so I ain't gonna need no high school diploma."

"You definitely not gonna go back to school?"

"I don't know." For some reason, I ain't all that sure I'm never going back. For now, I ain't, but I know when my pops get out, he ain't gonna let me stay outta school. And he gonna be pissed that I messed this year up and I'ma hafta do the tenth grade over.

Jasmine go back to her book and I just lay there watching her. I don't get why everybody care if I go to school or not. It's my fuckin' life. I ain't bothering no one.

When Jasmine finish studying, she get up to turn the light off and I lose my head for a while staring at her body. And I make a decision right there. I'ma get me some of that tonight. Shit, I'm tired of trying to do the right thing. Why I gotta be faithful to my girl when all she do is constantly put me down?

So when Jasmine climb back on the bed, I put my arms 'round her waist and pull her on top of me, and we start kissing in the dark. The thing I like 'bout kissing Jasmine is her kisses ain't like the ones Novisha give me, them sweet, love kisses. Jasmine kisses is hot and sexy and exciting.

And wrong. But I don't care 'bout that right now. I'm ready to close this deal. Shit, I can always feel guilty later. Only thing, after a couple minutes, Jasmine pull her mouth away from mines, so I'm like, "If you worried, I got a condom."

"Good," she tell me. "Keep it for your girlfriend."

Damn. That hurt. I kiss her again. "C'mon. Help a brotha out." No, I ain't too proud to beg.

She push herself off me. "Ty, you know I like you. But I'm not gonna let you use me." She get under the covers and start getting all comfortable.

"But I ain't using you."

"Well, you the one who told me you have a girlfriend and you just wanna be friends with me, right? Remember that?"

"Yeah, but —" I can't stand when females use your own words against you. It ain't right. "Why you tell me to take my jeans off, then?"

"I wanted you to relax," Jasmine say, like that's the only reason why a girl would tell a guy to take his clothes off. "You know, Ty, before I met Emiliano, I might of done it with you. But now I respect myself and I even respect your girlfriend too much for that."

Emiliano. I'm tired of hearing 'bout that guy. And how come Jasmine ain't had no respect for herself the first night we was together or when she was stripping for Mr. Mendoza? Why she only got respect now?

"Let's cuddle." Jasmine slide her body next to mines, but all that do is put me in more pain.

I turn my body away from hers. I ain't looking to cuddle. I'm tired of all that. How many days I'm s'posed to put up with that shit?

But she don't leave me alone. She start rubbing my back, first in big circles, then in little ones. "Don't be mad," she say.

"I ain't mad."

"Then talk to me."

I don't move and she keep rubbing my back and shoulders.

"Talk to me," she say again, but this time it sound like she mean it. "You don't have to keep everything inside, you know."

Jasmine hands feel real nice and warm on my back. I kinda don't want her to stop, but after a while, I turn back 'round to face her. It's hard to really see her good in the dark and maybe that help 'cause I start talking and it's like I'm talking to myself. Yeah, Jasmine say things to let me know she listening, and she hold my hand the whole time, but she don't cut me off or nothin'. She just let me keep talking.

So I tell her everything. 'Bout why my pops is locked up and what my moms want me to do to make money. And 'bout Dante and how he trying to move in on my family. "And it ain't that I don't want Troy to have that jacket or them boots 'cause he need them to stay warm," I tell her. "But that ain't the point."

"What is the point then?"

"The point is, I was gonna be the one that got them things for him. Me. We don't need Dante. And my pops is sitting there in prison thinking things is gonna be the same when he get out, but my moms can't even wait for the man. You know what I mean?"

"Uh-huh."

"I mean, I don't get women sometimes. They say they want a man that's gonna love them, but when they got a good man, they disrespect him or lie to him or cheat on him. Make a man wanna give up on them."

"You talking about your father or you?"

"Both. Novisha don't be lying to me or cheating or nothing like that, but she do be disrespecting me. But she don't get that. I mean, why I gotta read her diary to know what she really thinking 'bout me? She s'posed to talk to me. We ain't s'posed to be keeping nothing from each other."

Talking 'bout this make me even more mad. I shoulda said something to Novisha before I left outta there. I shoulda told her that when her friends say some shit that put her man down, she s'posed to have my back. Not be embarrassed by me.

Before I know it, Jasmine actually get me to cuddle with her, and I gotta admit, it's all good. She wrap her arms 'round my waist real tight and we kiss a couple more times. Course I got both my hands on her ass. I ain't the kinda guy to give up that easy.

"You a good DJ?" she ask me after a while.

"I'm a'ight," I say, but truth is, I don't really know how good I am. Yeah, I could fill in for my pops when he on a break, but I ain't never had my own party. I ain't never had to think 'bout how to keep the music pumping and how to get people dancing and shit. And I ain't never said more than a couple words at a time on the mic. Plus I damn sure ain't never had to promote no party and try to get people to pay they hard-earned money to hear me play.

I tell all that to Jasmine.

"I know you nervous, but I can help you promote if you want." She sound kinda excited now. "I know everybody. Not just at my school but at the two other schools I used to go to before, um, before they asked me to leave." She start laughing.

"You got kicked outta two schools?"

"Yeah."

"Man, you wasn't no joke."

"I told you I used to be wild, right? But the good thing is that now I got friends all over. I could tell the right people about the party, and you gonna have that place packed."

"And I could go back to my old school and do the same thing," I say. "I mean, yeah, I had to kick some ass at that school, but some of them kids was a'ight. And there's this school 'cross the street from Novisha school that I could promote at too."

"Ooh. In December, me and my friends danced at the talent show at my school. We could dance at your party if you want."

"What kinda dance?"

196

"We do all kinds of dances, mostly salsa. And all five of us are pretty girls, and we know how to get the crowd going."

"I ain't gonna pimp you, Jasmine."

"Stop being stupid! We don't strip or nothing. It's just fun. And if the party starts getting boring and we come out there, all the kids will start clapping and cheering and having fun."

"A'ight. That could be good." I hope Patrick got some Spanish music in all them CDs he got.

"I'm gonna talk to the girls tomorrow and see if they could come to the party. And I need to get my outfit from Emiliano's apartment."

That name again.

"Can you meet me at my school tomorrow?" she ask me. "I get out early, at one fifty. Then we could start going around to the schools."

I ain't doing nothin' tomorrow so I tell her yeah. I'm kinda glad she gonna help me out. Truth is, walking 'round with a girl that look like her could only help bring the guys in. And that's a good thing, 'cause the guys is the only ones that's paying.

Jasmine fall asleep before me, and I just lay there for a while awake. Thinking. Not 'bout Novisha 'cause I'm way too tired to think 'bout her tonight. No, I'm thinking 'bout my moms. I gotta say, she don't make no sense to me no more. First she tell me to step up and provide for my family, but then she don't even give me a chance to do nothing. She been married to my pops more than seventeen years, so she know how much time it take to put a party together. But, still, as soon as she get desperate, she turn to someone else.

The way I see it, the only way to keep shit together 'til my pops get out is for this party to be bangin'. I need to walk away from there with some real decent money, then start working on the next party right away. That way, my moms won't hafta look to Dante for help all the time, and Troy won't hafta take handouts from a guy that say he my pops friend, a guy that be stabbing my pops in the back every chance he get.

I mean, I know my pops been gone a long time, but my moms gotta know that Dante ain't gonna make nothing better. He just gonna make new problems for us. Like we don't got enough problems now.

TWENTY-SEVEN

Troy walking mad stupid the next morning on our way to the train. He picking his feet up real high like a horse or something, trying to get used to them heavy-ass boots. He got me cracking up, shit's so funny. "Stop walking like that," I tell him. "Just walk normal."

"I can't," he say, but I know them boots ain't all that heavy. He just bugging.

Even though I don't wanna admit it, he do look good in his new jacket and boots. And I know he warm. "Don't let no one take your jacket," I warn him. "'Cause all them other kids is gonna be jealous. If you gotta fight for your stuff, you fight."

"I ain't gonna let nobody take nothing from me." He actin' all tough and shit. "Someone try to take my jacket, I'm gonna do karate on them." He try to lift his foot to do a karate kick, but he forget how heavy them boots is, and he practically fall back and bust his ass. I catch him in time then scream on him. He go, "That ain't funny, Ty. Stop laughing at me."

"C'mon, karate-man, we gonna miss the train."

We pick up the pace and cross Whitlock Avenue, then walk up the steps to the 6. I can hear a train coming, but I don't know if it's going uptown or down. Troy school is way uptown near where we used to live. Most of the motels we was sent to the past couple weeks wasn't as far away from his school as Bennett is. We out in the boondocks now.

When we get to the school, Troy teacher is in the cafeteria, keeping an eye on all the special-ed kids. They keep them on they own side of the room, like they can't mix with them other kids or something. "Wow, Troy," she say, smiling at him the way teachers do. "I love your new jacket."

Troy hold out his foot so she can get a look at his Tims.

"And new boots too!" She look over at me. "I'm so glad your mother was able to get those things for him. She told me what a difficult time your family is going through."

"Yeah," I say, nodding. "But we gonna be a'ight real soon."

"That would be wonderful."

"Um, Ms. Morton, can I ask you a question?"

"Of course."

"You really think Troy don't need to be in special ed no more? I mean, I know he smart, but sometimes he don't think 'fore he do things, he just do it."

"He is smart," she tell me. "But sometimes children adapt to their surroundings."

Man, was she saying something bad 'bout my family? That he only actin' that way 'cause his family so messed up?

But before I can ask her what she mean, she say, "He's been in special education for almost five months, and some of the

200

children in the class have behavioral and emotional problems. I think if Troy is placed back in regular education, some of those behaviors he's picked up may disappear."

I nod. "That sound good. When you gonna move him?"

"Monday. We're going to slowly transition him out of special education. And since he's so strong in math and science, we'll put him in the mainstream classes for those subjects first and see how he does. If all goes well, he'll be completely mainstreamed in two or three months."

I look over at Troy, who's at one of the tables eating a English muffin next to his best friend, Malcolm. He eating and talking, and I'm just hoping he ain't got so comfortable with them special-ed kids that he not gonna know how to act when he back in the regular class.

"Thanks, Ms. Morton," I say. "I better get outta here."

"Tyrell," she say. "I don't want to hold you up from getting to school on time, but could you wait for me at the front door for a minute?"

"A'ight," I say. I walk out the cafeteria and down the hall, but I don't know what's going on. What she want me to wait for? I hope she ain't gonna ask me no questions 'bout my moms and try to say Troy getting neglected or nothing 'cause that ain't true. Long as I'm 'round, my moms can handle Troy.

I stand by the front door, freezing as kids come running in from the streets, the door opening every five seconds letting in all that cold air. Finally after two or three minutes, Ms. Morton come over and hand me something wrapped in foil. "Here. Something for you to eat before school." She smile again.

Damn. She giving me handouts. I mean, I know she being nice and everything, but all I feel is embarrassed.

And what's messed up is that I'm really hungry too. Starving. I need this food.

I thank Ms. Morton, but she tell me don't worry 'bout it, that they always got extra food and it's better to let someone eat it or it's gonna go to waste. Man, I can't even hardly look her in the eye though. I leave outta there and walk down the street real fast.

On the train heading back downtown, I unwrap the foil and bite into the English muffin that got eggs and something that kinda look like sausage in it. People is giving me dirty looks 'cause the eggs is stinking up the train, but I don't care. I'm hungry. And the shit taste alright for school food.

I get off the train at 149th Street and Third Avenue 'cause it's still rush hour and I can make some decent money at a busy station like this. I take up position by the turnstile and flash my MetroCards so folks can see them, but, at the same time, I try to keep things on the down low so the cops don't catch me.

The thing 'bout the city is that they try to be slick. They don't want nobody buying a 30-day unlimited card and swiping in all they friends and shit, so once you swipe your card, you can't use that same card again for like fifteen minutes, which ain't right. So I got me five cards. And I don't pay what the city charge for them neither. Cal brother, Greg, told me 'bout this guy he know that be selling 30-day cards for $25. First I thought the cards he was selling wasn't gonna work, but they do, so a couple weeks ago, after we got evicted, I went back to him and got five so I wouldn't hafta waste no time standing 'round in between swipes. Spent my last dollar on them cards and made a profit two days later.

I ain't there a minute before some guy come up beside me

and slip me a dollar. I use one of my cards to get him through. Then for the next hour and a half, I'm mad busy. The only time I stop is when cops go by. I know the guy selling MetroCards in the booth see what I'm up to, but he don't pay me no mind. He probably glad I'm there 'cause now he got less work to do hisself. I'm doing half his work. But I don't care though. All I know is I'm getting paid up in here.

TWENTY-EIGHT

Jasmine set me up. And I'm so damn stupid, I walked right in her trap. Course I don't even see the trap at first. I'm just chillin', standing outside her school at 1:50 eating a buttered roll from the truck in front of the building. All I got on my mind is business and how I'ma hype the party so kids is gonna wanna come. I'm all 'bout numbers, gettin' as many kids up in there as possible.

The thing is, I know when me and Jasmine go 'round to the schools, them kids is gonna be sizing me up, trying to see if I'm the kinda brotha that could throw a good party. Now I know I'm looking good, 'cause I always do, but my jacket look like shit. I mean, it ain't tore up or nothing, but it ain't new like what Troy got.

Standing out here waiting for Jasmine, I'm kinda tired, 'specially 'cause I been working on my feet all day. The good thing is I'm up $66, which I need 'cause I been walking 'round broke after Leon took all the money Cal and them gave me. But I still could use even more money before the party. In case some last-minute shit come up.

I called Leon a couple hours ago to let him know I'ma have the equipment back, so the party is definitely on. He told me he gonna be at the depot to let us in at 5:30 when it's dark enough out that we could get all the equipment in without nobody seeing us. Before I hung up from him, he reminded me that I still gotta give him the extra $200, like I forgot 'bout that or something. Asshole. I just hope he do a good job setting the party up and keeping us from getting locked up. 'Cause that's what I'm paying his ass for.

Jasmine go to a school called The Bronx High School for Cultural Expression. I don't know what the fuck that mean, but the school is mad small, so probably a lot of kids don't want they culture expressed. The school is in the basement of a office building just a couple blocks from Yankee Stadium, and while I'm standing there, all kinds of people with briefcases and shit come in and out the building.

Me, I know I could never work in no office all day. I would probably lose my mind locked up in a building from nine to five. That just ain't me. I'm the kinda guy that need to be his own boss. Like my pops always say, people spend they day working for somebody else only to get nothing but chump change. But when you work for yourself, everything you make is yours.

After 'bout fifteen minutes, I go inside to warm up. This female guard is standing by the door. "You making a delivery?" she ask me, and I'm thinking, do she see me carrying a package or something?

But I just go, "No, I'm waiting for my friend."

"What's your name?"

"Tyrell Green, why?"

She flip though some sheets of paper on a clipboard. "Oh, go on downstairs. They're waiting for you in the guidance counsel-or's office." She write my name on one of them visitor stickers and tell me to put it on. I'm confused as hell, but I put it on and take the stairs down to the basement where they got a big banner with the school name on it. What the fuck is Jasmine up to? She ain't say nothing 'bout me coming inside her school. I thought she was gonna meet me outside. And why she waiting for me with the guidance counselor?

Course this is before it hit me that I been set up.

When I get to the office, Jasmine tell me some bullshit 'bout how she sorry she kept me waiting, but her and the guidance counselor, who she be calling by her first name, had to talk 'bout something. So for a while I'm just sitting there listening to them talk 'bout some teacher that Jasmine having trouble with 'cause all he do is give tests and shit.

"I'm not kidding, Yolanda," Jasmine say. "He doesn't under-stand that this is an alternative school. This is the kinda school that's supposed to help kids that had trouble at other schools."

I lean my head back and close my eyes for a second. Damn. Why is Jasmine doing this to me? She so fuckin' obvious it ain't even funny.

Them two go on and on trying to show me what a good school this is, and the only thing that keep my attention even a little is that Yolanda is hot. For real. She can't be no more than twenty-five, she Dominican-looking, and her body is tight. Shit, man, the guidance counselor at my school look like Cedric the Entertainer in a wig. I ain't lying neither.

Finally Yolanda turn to me and say, "What school do you go to, Tyrell?"

"I don't go to school no more," I tell her, like she don't already know. "I'm taking a break." I look over to Jasmine who's doing everything she can not to make eye contact with me. She looking at her nails, then at her watch, then at the floor, actin' as guilty as she gonna get.

Yolanda ask me how long I ain't been to school and I tell her I only missed 'bout a month, and how I'm trying to work and make money so we could get out the shelter system. All that. She look at me while I'm talking and it's kinda like she actually listening to what I gotta say.

"How old are you?"

"Fifteen, but I'ma be sixteen in March, so I could drop out then, right?"

"Is that what you want?"

"Nah. I mean, maybe. I don't know."

Jasmine elbow me in the side. "C'mon, Ty. You could come to this school. Tell him, Yolanda."

Yolanda laugh a little. "You just did." She stand up and come from behind the desk. She sit in the chair on the other side of me. "You've only missed a month. That's not too bad right now. As Jasmine said, we're an alternative school, so we have various schedules and programs here. Some kids are on the traditional four-year track. Some would rather take five or six years to graduate, so they can work more hours at their jobs. If you transfer here, you can choose your own plan, and we'll do everything we can to help you achieve your goals." She stand up again. "Okay. That's my sales pitch. Tell me what you're thinking."

"I'm thinking I got played by a fine girl."

Jasmine start giggling next to me.

"Well," Yolanda say, "boys have done crazier things than go back to high school for a girl they like. Jasmine is a very sweet girl who cares about you. And you can never have too many people who care about you."

"True that," I say. But still, I don't like being set up.

Before we leave, Yolanda make me give her my information so she can contact my school and get my records faxed to her. "And why don't we meet Monday at ten to discuss your options? No pressure." She smile. "Seriously. We'll just talk." When I don't say nothing right away, she say, "Okay, okay. I'll even steal some donuts from the teachers' lounge and we'll have a late breakfast together for fifteen minutes, which is about all the time I'll have before students like your friend here come knocking on the door."

"I don't know."

"The donuts are fresh on Mondays," she say. "By Wednesday, they're like ashtrays with holes in the middle."

I laugh. "A'ight. We can talk, but I ain't saying I'ma come back to school or nothing."

"I'll see you Monday." She reach her hand out.

We shake. "Monday," I say.

When we get outside, Jasmine rip the visitor sticker off my jacket, and I'm, like, "Why you do that for?"

"Because you look like a *pendejo*, that's why."

"I ain't talking 'bout the sticker, I'm talking 'bout that whole thing with Yolanda just now. Why you set me up like that?"

Jasmine put her hands on her hips. "Set you up?"

"Don't start."

She laugh like this is a joke or something. "You can't get mad at me for trying to help you. And if you come here to my school, me and you are gonna have so much fun everyday."

I just shake my head 'cause I can tell she got the whole thing worked out in her mind already. It don't matter what I say. I don't know why, but females always think they know what guys need. Like we too dumb to run our own life or something.

TWENTY-NINE

We don't talk no more 'bout Yolanda or school for the rest of the day. We just get to work. Jasmine tell me she already got the word out at her school, so we go straight to one of her old schools 'cause they get out at 2:35. We gonna promote there for 'bout fifteen or twenty minutes, then go a couple blocks to the other school that kicked her out. They don't get out 'til 3:00.

The first school ain't too far from the criminal court where me and my moms spent way too much time in September going to hearings and meeting with my pops lawyer who ain't know shit 'bout how to keep a man outta jail. The lawyer had, like, fifty thousand cases, and no matter how many times he seen us, he still ain't know who we was. That's 'cause he was one of them free lawyers you get when you can't afford no better. And the truth is, when you pay nothin', you get nothin'.

When we get to the school, it look like half the kids is in front of the building like it's summer or something. They talking and smoking, and taking they time walking down the block. Man, I woulda been long gone by now if this was my school.

Jasmine go right to work like she gettin' paid to promote my party. And she wasn't lying when she said she know everyone. And it don't matter the race neither. When she went to this school, she musta been down with the Blacks, Puerto Ricans, Dominicans, Koreans, Cambodians, and even the couple White kids 'cause everybody know her and come up to her to say they miss her and shit like that. Everyone kiss her too.

She a new person when she with all them other kids. She all friendly and happy, and that smile don't never leave her face. Jasmine introduce me to some of her friends. "He's the best DJ. You gotta come hear him," she tell a group of girls. She give them the time and place. "And I'm gonna be there, and I'm inviting a lot of cute guys, so you gotta come." One girl write the info on the back of her notebook. "And, Marisol, you gotta bring your brother. And all his cute friends."

"Okay," Marisol say. She look like she would do anything Jasmine tell her to.

Jasmine hug her. "Tell everyone you know, okay? Spread the word."

Then, later, when she talk to two guys, she tell them, "Girls are getting in for free, so you know there's gonna be a lot of them there. I invited all my friends. And I'm gonna be there, and I wanna dance with both of you."

She say the same thing to every guy. The way I figure it, by the time we through with both schools, she done promised to dance with, like, forty-something guys. And the way them dudes was looking at her, and putting they arms 'round her waist and kissing her on the cheek and shit, I ain't really like it. How they know me and her wasn't together? Why they think they could get with her when I'm standing right there?

Matter of fact, most of the time that's just what I was doing — standing 'round, not doing much of nothin'. Yeah, Jasmine introduced me to just 'bout everyone she know, but I ain't had to say nothing. She did all the talking, and she was doing just fine selling my party all by herself.

And now I know there's a whole 'nother side to Jasmine I ain't seen before. The whole time we was promoting, she looked like she was in heaven, just eating up all the attention them kids was giving her. Looking at her like that, she ain't even seem like the same girl that's scared to be alone, that be sad and crying all the time.

When we done, Jasmine grab my hand and start pulling me up the street. "Come with me to Emiliano's. I need to get my dance outfit."

We walk a couple blocks and catch the D train at 167th Street. The trains is getting kinda crowded 'cause all the kids is outta school now, but we find two seats together in the last car. I gotta say, I'm feeling real good, not only 'bout the party, but 'bout Jasmine too. The way she was with all them kids, talking me up and making the party sound so good, man, it was just cool being with her and spending time with her away from Bennett.

All the way uptown, Jasmine talking nonstop. "I hope Hector doesn't come. He was the guy that was wearing the black jacket with the red trim, remember him? If he comes, and if Miguel is there too, there's gonna be trouble because I was going out with Hector first, and he was a nice guy for, like, two months, then that *maricon* started to disrespect me, so Emiliano made me break up with him, but I didn't really do it. Not all the way. But I started going out with Miguel so Emil wouldn't think I was still with Hector. You understand?"

"Yeah." Man, my head is spinning.

"So I was going out with Hector and Miguel at the same time, and Emiliano found out and he wouldn't let me leave the house. He kept telling me I was gonna come out pregnant, but I wasn't doing nothing with Miguel. Just Hector."

"Why you ain't stop messing with the dude that was treating you bad?"

"You seen how hot he was, right?"

I give her a look, like, do she really think I'm checking out other dudes? "So what happened?" I'm just trying to get to the end of this story already.

"Emiliano started driving me to school and back on the bread truck again, that's what happened."

I start laughing. "So who you like better now? Hector or Miguel?"

"None of them. I like you."

"You all talk, girl. Last night you dogged me."

She put her arms 'round me and kiss me on the cheek. "Try again tonight," she tell me.

"Nah. I don't like being rejected." I kiss her lips. "Am I gonna get rejected again?"

She smile, all sexy and shit. "Wait and see."

Damn. She playing games again. I don't know why I'm putting up with this, but, really, what else I got to do?

THIRTY

Emiliano live on Grand Concourse, not too far from Mosholu Parkway. The area up there is kinda alright, and most of them buildings is still nice too. Jasmine got a key to get in the lobby, but Emiliano changed the apartment locks on them, so when we get upstairs she gotta ring the buzzer.

I hear a man call out something in Spanish, and Jasmine say her name.

"You sure you don't want me to wait downstairs?" I ask her. "'Cause I ain't looking to cause no trouble or nothing."

The door open and Emiliano is standing there in sweatpants and a T-shirt. He ain't what I pictured neither. Emiliano gotta be forty at least. He kinda on the short side for a guy, and he thick like one of them dudes that be lifting weights everyday. He kinda diesel.

Emiliano give Jasmine a quick hug, then he talk to her in Spanish and I hear him say "Reyna."

Jasmine say something, and the funny thing is, I can tell she lying, even in Spanish, 'cause her voice get a little higher and she move her hands a lot more. She ain't as good at lying as Novisha is.

Then, finally, Jasmine introduce me to Emiliano, still in Spanish. Me and him shake hands, then we all go in the apartment, and, man, all I gotta say is, Jasmine was living good before Bennett.

Emiliano got his crib hooked up. Leather furniture, home theater with a flat-screen TV, audio system with surround sound speakers. And on the walls he got big pictures of him and Reyna, the kind you get done at Sears, and one of Jasmine in a white cap and gown, probably from her middle school graduation. And the whole apartment is real neat and clean. Shit. No wonder Jasmine want her sister to get back with this dude.

"Tyrell," Emiliano say in a thick accent. "Sit down." He look like he struggling to think how to say something else. Then he just give up and turn to Jasmine and ask her something in Spanish.

"He wants to know if you want something to eat or drink," Jasmine say. "He only knows a little English, and sometimes he gets embarrassed if he pronounces a word wrong, especially when he's around people he doesn't know yet."

"Um, you can tell him that I'm a'ight." I give Emiliano a little thank-you nod. Then I sit down on the leather couch, and it's so soft I could just chill here all night. The TV is on, but it's on some Spanish news channel. Not that I care. I don't need nobody to tell me how fucked up this city is.

Jasmine and Emiliano go to the kitchen and sit down at the table. I can hear "Reyna" over and over, and Jasmine is lying and lying, talking so much junk. I gotta say, it look like Emiliano real worried 'bout getting his woman back.

After a while I can't figure out what they talking 'bout no more 'cause I ain't learn shit in ninth-grade Spanish, that's for damn sure. I only understand one word here and there. I hear Jasmine say something 'bout *restaurante*, so I guess she telling him 'bout the waitress job she trying to get. Emiliano don't seem all that into it though. He telling her something 'bout *escuela*, like he don't want her getting no job if she ain't gonna have no time for her schoolwork. He trying to look out for her, like he her father for real. He do care 'bout her.

When Jasmine go to her room to get her dance outfit, Emiliano come over to me and hand me a small bottle of Malta. I seen Malta forever in them bodegas, but I ain't never tasted it before. And, to be honest, I don't really wanna taste it now. But when I try to turn it down, Emiliano just smile and say, "No. Try."

The bottle cap is off already, so I drink some and, man, it taste like cold piss. Damn, that's some nasty-ass shit. I try to smile so he don't think I'm being rude or nothing, but my smile probably make me look like a mental patient, 'cause all I really wanna do is gag.

Emiliano laugh and say, "Drink and you get, uh, you get use to it."

"Nah, I ain't never gonna get used to that." I'm kinda laughing too, but I still can't get the taste out my mouth. "You got water? *Agua?*"

He nod and I follow him to the kitchen. He hand me a bottle of water, and I'm, like, shit, tap woulda been good enough for me. I drink the whole bottle in one shot, and he stand there still laughing at me. "You funny," he say. "You keeping drink Malta. You like it."

I shake my head.

"You wanting coffee cakes?" He open one of the cabinets and he got all kinds of little donuts and cakes and shit in plastic wrappers.

Jasmine come back with a small duffel bag. "Don't let him give you no bread or coffee cakes," she say. "He's always trying to give away all the bread and cakes he brings home from work." She turn to Emiliano and probably tell him the same thing in Spanish, and they start laughing.

But he don't listen neither. Next thing I know, he packing up a loaf of bread and a whole bunch of cakes in a plastic shopping bag. "Take this," he say to me. "Sweet and very good. You like."

"*Gracias*," I say. I ain't never heard of the brand of bread he got, but it's a Spanish name, so that's probably why. And them cakes do look kinda good too. I know my moms is gonna like them. She love her some donuts.

Before we leave, Emiliano pull out his big calendar and remind Jasmine 'bout her appointments coming up. Whatever he say to her, Jasmine act real surprised. She even give him a big hug. Then he ask her something and the only word I understand is *Sabado*. Saturday. Jasmine tell him *sí*, and then we walk to the door. Me and Emiliano shake hands and, I gotta say, from what I see, he alright.

Emiliano reach in his pocket and hand Jasmine three twenties. Nice. They hug again and we leave, her with sixty dollars and a duffel bag. Me with a plastic bag of bread and cake. I ain't complaining.

"Why you ain't ask him if you could move back?" I ask Jasmine when we down in the lobby.

"I know him," she say. "He's not gonna let me stay there

217

without Reyna. It's not gonna look right, him there alone with a teenage girl."

"What he say 'bout Saturday?"

"He's off on Saturdays, and he asked me to go to lunch with him at this diner all three of us used to go to every Saturday."

"You gonna go?"

"Yeah. I think he wants to talk and make sure I'm okay. And you know what, he's still gonna pay for the dermatologist and orthodontist. I only have six more months 'til these braces come off." She smile.

"He a nice guy," I tell her. "Why Reyna don't wanna be with him no more?"

"She thinks he's too controlling because he doesn't let her go to no parties or clubs. And my sister likes to wear short skirts and low-cut tops, but he doesn't like that. He wants her to be a classy lady. Like me."

"Yeah, right."

She start laughing. "You don't think I'm classy?"

Before I can say anything, my phone ring and I know without even looking that it's Novisha. I tell Jasmine to hold on for a minute and answer the phone. "Hello."

"Ty, it's me."

I look at my watch. "It's practically four thirty. You now getting home?"

"Yeah. I stopped by my mom's job and she put me to work. She had me sweeping and dusting like I don't work hard at school all day. What did you do today?"

"I worked. I'm on my way back to Bennett now."

"I wish you were here right now."

"Your moms ain't there?"

"No, she went shopping. Wait until you see how much she's cooking for you guys. We're gonna have fun tomorrow."

"Yeah," I tell her, even though I forgot all 'bout that dinner thing.

"Is everything okay, Ty? You're hardly saying anything."

"Nah, I'm a'ight. I'm just 'bout to get on the train though."

"Okay. I love you."

Damn. Why she gotta say that when I standing here with Jasmine? But there ain't no getting outta it. "I love you too," I whisper. Jasmine cover her mouth so Novisha can't hear her laughing. "See you tomorrow."

When we hang up, Jasmine put her arm 'round my waist. "You in love?"

I don't say nothing.

"What's happening tomorrow?"

"Novisha moms invited my family to dinner." I shake my head 'cause I know my moms, and she don't know how to act sometimes. I mean, there ain't no doubt in my mind that this dinner is gonna be bad. Real bad. A fuckin' nightmare.

THIRTY-ONE

"What's wrong?" I ask my moms the second I get back to the room and see the look on her face. She sitting on the end of the bed looking mad as hell, like she heated 'bout something. And her face is tight. She, like, the opposite of how she was yesterday.

"I went to see your father today and he talking crazy, saying when he get out, he only gonna play at weddings and birthday parties and shit."

I can't stand when she curse in front of Troy, who sitting on the other bed playing with his new Game Boy. He in his own little video game world and probably ain't even heard what she said, but still. That ain't the point. I sit down next to him. "You finish your homework, man?"

"Yeah." He don't look at me once. He just keep on playing his game.

And my moms just keep on talking. "Ty, he crazy if he think he gonna come out that prison and start playing at weddings, working his ass off for no money. What he need to do that for?"

"You the crazy one," I tell her. "He trying to stay outta jail and be with us. That ain't crazy. That's smart. What, you like when he locked up? You like being here at Bennett?"

"He just gotta be more careful next time. I'm always telling him that, but he don't never listen, your father. But if he start playing weddings, we never gonna afford to live nowhere nice again. We gonna be back in the projects, and I ain't having that."

I stare at her for a long time, and she actually look like she believe what she saying. She dead serious. She really want her man to risk his freedom just so she won't hafta go back to the projects. Like things was so bad when we was there. "You know, I don't get you," I say after a while. "You always talking 'bout how much you love the man, but you don't never do nothing to support him. You just keep wanting stuff even when he don't got nothing to give you. You s'posed to want him to do the right thing."

"No. He s'posed to take care of us."

Damn. It's like that?

I don't even know what to say or do no more. I mean, the man trying to do what he shoulda did a long time ago, but she don't understand that. Now I know why he always taking chances and winding up behind bars. Like what Yolanda was saying, men do some stupid shit for women. And she wasn't lying. But do my pops gotta keep getting locked up just to keep my moms happy?

I take a deep breath and try again. "You make it sound like that's all a man is for. Supporting you. Taking care of you."

"I need your father," she say, and she look kinda lost too. "I can't do it by myself no more. I need him."

We just sit there quiet for a few minutes. The only sound is

Troy playing his video game. Then, just 'cause I feel bad, I tell her not to worry 'bout nothing, that we gonna be alright. I hand her the bag Emiliano gave me and, just like I thought, she see them donuts and smile.

Since I'm just sitting there, I open Troy notebook and check over his homework. Then, later, after I get him to turn off the game and write some of them vocabulary words neater, I get my basketball out the garbage bag, and me and him go outside to shoot some hoops in the cold.

Being at Bennett is messed up for me, but if I was a little kid, I woulda probably lost my mind by now. Kids his age need to run 'round and burn off all they energy. They don't need to be locked up in a little room from the time they get home from school 'til the next morning. It ain't right.

Only thing is, there ain't no basketball hoop on the block where Bennett is at, so me and Troy walk down the block to Hunts Point Avenue, to where there always be kids outside playing. Not that I wanna get in no real game, not with Troy with me. I just wanna show him some moves, let him know that even though our pops ain't there, he still got somebody to teach him how to play.

When my pops was out, me and him used to play ball all the time, and that's the only time we got to really talk. I mean, yeah, most of it was trash talk, but least we was doing something together. My pops used to be like, "You keep playing like that and I'm gonna buy you a dress."

And I would tell him, "Talk to me tonight when you got your knee wrapped and you whining like a bitch."

That would make him laugh, but then he would bump into me to take a shot. Like he ain't know he was fouling me. And every time he made a basket, he was like, "You gonna let a forty-year-old man kick your ass?"

"You ain't beating nobody," I would tell him, 'cause, truth is, we both knew I coulda beat him from jump. I just ain't wanna embarrass the man.

When me and him wasn't talking trash, we used to talk 'bout all kinds of shit, everything from music to females. And we used to make plans too. Like, he was gonna show me how to drive, so I would be ready to get my permit the minute I turned sixteen. Matter of fact, every time he rented a van to take the equipment to one of his parties, he would let me drive 'round the parking lot and on the side streets for a while, just for practice. Course here I am now, 'bout to turn sixteen, and where he at?

But that ain't the point. The point is, me and him had fun and we got to hang and shit. And I don't want Troy to grow up and miss all that 'cause, to be honest, he need a man to teach him what a man do. My moms can't do that.

Now me, I know I can't take my pops place or nothing, but Troy need somebody for now. So that's what I'ma try to do. Be there.

In bed with Jasmine that night, me and her do a whole lot of kissing in the dark, but she still don't give me none. The girl got me so worked up though, I gotta get up outta bed and go to the bathroom to take care of my situation. On the other side of the door, I hear her saying, "*Mira, asqueroso*, I hope you not doing what I think you doing."

I'm too busy to say anything to her, and I don't know what she talking 'bout anyhow. She probably just trying to make me feel bad 'bout something every guy do.

When I'm back in bed with her, she whisper to me, "You a bad boy."

"Just come kiss me," I say, and she do. Me and her is under the covers and our legs is wrapped 'round each others the way we always got them. And I'm feeling good, 'specially now that some of the pressure ain't there no more.

After a while we stop kissing and she talk 'bout her old schools and how she felt going back there today. "I'm a different girl now," she say. "And seeing all those boys again, *ay, dios mio*! It was so embarrassing."

"Just 'cause you used to be a ho, don't mean you gotta be 'shamed 'bout it. Everybody make mistakes."

"I know," she say. "What's your biggest mistake?"

"Damn. I got so many." But I ain't gotta think too hard 'cause my pops been on my mind from when me and Troy played basketball. "My mistake is pro'ly looking up to my pops so much," I tell her. "'Cause, yeah, he cool and everything, but he be messing up so much that sometimes I wish I ain't even care 'bout the man, you know. I mean, he knew he was gonna get hisself locked up again, but he ain't did nothin' to make sure we was gonna be a'ight while he gone. And now, 'cause of him, I gotta be the man. I gotta make the money to take care of my moms and brother. I gotta put my freedom on the line." I'm getting mad just talkin' 'bout this. "And what's s'posed to happen when he get out in August? I'm s'posed to go back to being a kid again? 'Cause I don't think I could go back, you know what I mean?"

Jasmine stroke the side of my face. "Don't worry about that now. You just getting yourself stressed."

Her hands feel mad good, warm. "Yeah," I tell her. "You right."

I close my eyes and try to stop thinking 'bout all that. All I gotta think 'bout now is the party. 'Cause in 48 hours, the party is gonna be on. And I gotta be ready.

THIRTY-TWO

After I leave Jasmine in the morning, I go wake my moms up and tell her she gotta take Troy to school. I'ma need to make as much cash as I can today and make sure everything is in place for the party tomorrow. Besides, my moms got a meeting with the caseworker from the EAU today at 10:00, so she gotta get up anyway.

But that don't stop her from arguing with me though, 'cause she ain't used to getting up so early. But after 'bout twenty minutes, she do drag her ass outta bed and into the bathroom.

"Why you can't take me to school?" Troy ask me.

"'Cause I gotta work." I reach in the plastic container and give him a handful of them orange peanut butter cheese crackers. "Here. Eat." I sit on the bed and eat some of them with him 'cause I know I ain't getting no kinda breakfast today.

"We ever gonna get out of here?" he ask, opening the crackers and licking the peanut butter off.

"Yeah, on Monday."

"Then we going back home?"

"Nah. They gonna put us in a real shelter."

"Oh." Troy keep on eating. I can tell he got more questions, but he don't ask none of them, like he probably don't wanna hear the answers. So I tell him we gonna be alright no matter where they send us 'cause we all gonna be together, and that seem to make him feel a little better.

My moms come out the bathroom all dressed and ready to go, but she still complaining 'cause she don't wanna go see that caseworker. "All I need is a shelter so my kids don't gotta be at Bennett. What she gotta talk to me for?"

"She pro'ly wanna talk 'bout the fraud case, what else?"

"That don't make no sense. Your father was paying back that money. The only reason we ain't paying no more is 'cause they locked the man up."

"Then all you gotta do is show that caseworker that you trying to do the right thing now," I tell her.

She nod her head. "I am doing the right thing. I'm holding it down while my husband is away, right? It ain't easy, but I'm doing it." She grab some of them crackers out the container. "C'mon, Troy. We gonna be late."

They walk out the door, and I can see Troy take off down the hall at top speed. I laugh. It look like he used to them boots already. My moms is gonna have a hard time keeping up with him today.

After I'm dressed, I book over to the subway station and hustle them working people for they dollar bills. Then I get to my old school by 7:45 and start promoting. I know just 'bout everybody, but I don't want all of them at my party, so I ain't telling everyone.

Just all the girls and the dudes I ain't never had beef with. But standing out there trying to get people to come to my party ain't easy. Not like when Jasmine was with me.

I only stay there 'bout a half hour 'cause school start and most of the kids go inside the building. Not all of them though. A lot of kids just come to school to sit on cars and hang out all day, no matter how cold it is out there. I mean, I ain't never wanted to go to school neither, but why get up out your bed just to freeze your ass off?

Still, I don't gotta understand them to promote to them. Only one thing I want from them. For all I care, they could pay they money and go sit inside a school bus all night if that's what they into.

"Ty, where you been at?" this guy Keshawn ask me. He leaning up against a SUV with one arm 'round his girlfriend.

"Working."

"I hear that."

I tell him 'bout the party and how much I'm charging.

"Fifteen dollars?" he ask. "You asking a lot."

"If you don't got that kinda money —"

"I got the money, man. I'm just saying."

"A'ight, then," I tell him. "I'ma see you there." I walk away 'cause I ain't in the mood to deal with some of the people from this school. There's just something 'bout them. Ain't no way I could come back to this school.

I put in a couple more hours at the subway station before heading uptown to Bronxwood. I ain't talk to Cal for a couple days now, and I still gotta work out the last-minute details with him and his brothers. When I get to the apartment, the only one there is Greg who ain't doing nothing, as usual. "Where Cal at?" I ask him.

"He with Andre. They coming back in a minute. You wanna get high?"

"Nah, I'm good." I can't be getting high when I got work to do. And shit, man, it's, like, 10:30 in the morning. I mean, if you getting high in the morning, you might got a problem or something.

I sit on the couch and watch Greg play his PlayStation game. "What y'all been up to?" I ask him.

"We makin' money," he say. "You ready to come work with us, man? 'Cause we really need a couple guys to work our new spots."

"Nah, man."

"Y'all still in that shelter?"

"We ain't even got to the shelter yet. We just in a motel 'til some space open up for us at a shelter."

"That's fucked up."

"Yeah, but if I make some decent cash on Saturday I'ma try to get us a apartment. 'Cause them shelters ain't hardly no better than Bennett."

Greg make some noise that tell me he ain't hardly paying attention to what I'm saying no more. He lost in the game, getting the man on the screen to kill as many people as he can. The TV is turned up so loud, I feel like I'm in the middle of that gun battle.

So I go in the kitchen, sit at the table, and call Regg on my cell. He still in Atlanta, but he tell me he gonna get to the depot no later than 8:00. I give him the directions. "What you decide to do about the beer?" he ask.

"I ain't really decide nothing yet," I tell him. Truth is, I don't got enough money to lay out for no beer. And I don't wanna give up my last dollar when I don't know what kinda shit could come up last minute.

"You know, I ain't trying to take no money out your pocket, Ty, but if you definitely ain't gonna do it, I'm gonna do it."

"A'ight."

"You sure?"

"Yeah, man," I say. I know Regg was trying to help me out by not charging me his twenty-five percent, but things is better now that he bringing the beer. Least this way he could get something outta this party, too. It's all good.

Cal and Andre come back after a while, carrying greasy brown paper bags. They sit down at the kitchen table and pull out three aluminum platters of eggs, bacon, grits, and home fries from the place 'round the corner. "You want some of this?" Cal ask me.

"Hell, yeah."

Cal get up from the table to go get a plate for me. He good that way.

All four of us eat breakfast and I go over the details of the party with them.

"We been telling everybody about it," Andre tell me.

Greg nod. "Yeah. Everybody."

"You gonna have half of Bronxwood up in there," Andre say. "You better know what you doing."

"You gonna be there?" I ask him.

"No, only Cal gonna be there."

"And I'm gonna be working here, taking Cal place downstairs," Greg say.

To be honest, that got me surprised 'cause I don't never see Greg outside working. Every time I see him, he inside either sitting on his ass, eating, or getting high. I still don't know what the fuck he do.

After we finish eating, I chill with them for a while at the kitchen table. Cal lean forward in his seat and ask me if I followed his advice 'bout Novisha.

"Yeah," I say, but don't get into no details with him. It ain't none of his business no how. But still, I can't help smiling when I think 'bout how far I got with Novisha. Man, I ain't never gonna forget seeing her all hot and worked up like that.

Cal start laughing. "See, I told you, man. All females is the same. They want they man to —"

I crumple up a napkin and hit him upside the head with it before he could finish saying whatever he was gonna say. Nigga talking garbage anyway. "Stop talking 'bout my girl," I tell him. "She ain't like all them other females 'round here. She different."

That get Cal and them going, calling me names and telling me I'm getting soft and shit, but that's alright. I can take it. I know who I am.

From Cal apartment, I go upstairs to Patrick, to get some more practice on the CD deck. I gotta get real good at it before tomorrow. And it got so many buttons and shit, it's gonna take a while to learn what they all do.

But, I gotta say, that thing got some real hot features. You put two CDs in there and, after you get the feel for the controls, it's like you working two turntables. You can fade, mix, sample, and even scratch, which is wild, you ask me. And it sound nice too. I mean, I know my pops wouldn't be all that into this new technology and shit, but for me, it's alright.

I stay with Patrick 'til my fingers know them buttons without even thinking 'bout it. 'Til my hands can make the sounds I wanna make without even looking. 'Til shit sound smooth, like I been doing this my whole life.

And that's all I gotta do, play the music. Keep people dancing and having fun. And keep Cal making money, so him and his brothers will get something outta this too.

Personally, I don't know how my pops do it, keep everybody at his parties happy all the time, but he do. I know that 'cause them same people be paying they money to come to all his parties, and them same people be working for him too. So he must be doing something right.

And 'cause I don't know what the fuck that is, I'ma hafta figure it out for myself.

THIRTY-THREE

When I get back to Bennett, Jasmine in the lobby on the pay phone. I try to get past her so I can get dressed for the dinner at Novisha house, but she hold her hand up to tell me to wait. Then she go on talking for another couple minutes like she don't got me waiting. But she do look real happy, and all she keep saying to the person on the phone is, "*Gracias, gracias.*"

She hang up the phone, run over to me, and throw her arms 'round me. Then she start jumping up and down and her body is rubbing up against mines. It's like she trying to work me up or something. I mean, I hafta move away from her before she get my body going.

"What? What's up?"

"I got the job!" She smiling, all that metal shining and shit.

"That's cool," I tell her.

"Now I'm gonna have my own money and everything."

"What 'bout Emiliano? He don't want you working, right?"

"No, not really, but what else can I do? Reyna left me here, and I don't know if she's gonna come back for me. And I can't keep getting money from Emil if Reyna and him aren't together no more. It's not fair to him."

Me and Jasmine walk up the stairs to the second floor. When I get to her room, I tell her I'ma come by later.

"Where you going?"

"Remember, we going to dinner at Novisha house."

"Oh, yeah." Her face fall a little, and all of a sudden she don't look as happy as she was, like, a minute ago.

"We ain't gonna be there too long." Now she got me feeling bad for leaving her alone.

"That's okay. You don't have to rush back here for me. I have to study anyway."

"On a Friday?"

"There's nothing else to do. And I'm gonna be working now, so, you know, I need to study when I get the chance."

"When you start the job?"

"Tomorrow at two for training."

"You still gonna be at the party, right?"

"Yeah. I get off at eight, so I'll come straight from work."

"Okay, good. See you later."

I get to my room in just enough time to get in the shower and change, but my moms is looking mad again. I don't know what for this time, and I don't really wanna ask neither. So I don't. I just start going through the garbage bag with the clean clothes to find something nice to wear.

But that don't stop my moms from talking to me. "You not gonna wanna hear what that bitch at the EAU told me today," she say.

I look over at Troy, but he ain't listening to her curse. He watching cartoons on TV. And he already dressed too.

"What?" I ask her.

"She said they ain't gonna send us to no Tier II shelter 'cause of my conviction. They still making me pay for something that happened years ago."

"What they gonna do? Put us out in the streets or something?"

"No, they gonna transfer us to some kind of program that do job training for single mothers."

"Where we s'posed to live at?"

"We gonna live there for eight weeks 'til I finish the program. Then they s'posed to find us a apartment, and I'm gonna have to pay the rent myself."

Man. What she telling me got me bugging. I ain't never thought they was really gonna throw us out the shelter system. I mean, the city put up with anybody that's homeless. All kinds of criminals and addicts and shit. Why they getting rid of us?

"And you ain't gonna believe the jobs they trying to train me for," she say. "Shit like home health aide and hospital food service, like I'm gonna do any of that. Working like a fuckin' slave for minimum wage when I got a man that take care of me."

For a second, I ain't sure who she talking 'bout. My pops or me.

"I got me a husband," she say. "I ain't no single mother."

"You are for now," I say. "'Til August."

"Well, I ain't going to no program to learn how to wipe shit off old people asses. That ain't gonna happen." Then she look at me again like she did the first day we got here. "You ain't gonna let your family go to no program like that, right?"

I don't wanna get in no argument with her again, not now when we s'posed to be at Novisha house by 7:00. So I just go,

"Nah. I'ma make enough money tomorrow to get us outta here, a'ight?"

"Yeah, okay. But even if you don't, you could always work with Cal and his brothers. Just 'til your father get home."

I ain't even gonna get into that with her now 'cause she know I ain't lookin' to sell no weed. If I wanted to do that, I woulda been doing it by now. "You get the caseworker to fill out that form so Troy can go to the after-school program for free?"

"Yeah," she say, but I can tell she still don't want him outta special ed. She too used to getting them SSI checks every month. 'Cept for what I make at the subway station, that's all the money we get every month and she scared to give it up.

I get in the shower, and all I'm thinking 'bout is this new program they wanna put her in. I gotta admit, working as a home health aide don't sound too good but, at the same time, it's 'bout time she learned how to take care of herself when my pops ain't 'round. 'Cause the way things is going, he probably gonna get locked up again in a couple years. So it ain't gonna kill her to learn how to do something to pay the rent. She need to have a backup plan so we don't end up here. Next time.

THIRTY-FOUR

On the train all the way to Novisha house, I'm telling my moms how to act when we get there. "You gotta tell Ms. Jenkins thank you for inviting us," I say. I mean, yeah, most people would know this, but I ain't taking no chances. I don't want Ms. Jenkins thinking my moms is so ghetto she don't got no manners or nothing. "And tell her that her apartment look nice, 'cause you know she always keep her place clean."

She suck her teeth. "I know, Ty."

"And thank her for all the food she been sending for us."

My moms don't say nothin', but I can tell I'm getting on her nerves. She turn her body away from mines and start staring out the window. We on the 5 train, up past West Farms, and out the window the buildings is flying by. But in a way the train ain't going fast enough 'cause I ain't seen Novisha since Wednesday, and I just wanna make sure me and her is cool.

"Watch me, Mommy," Troy yell. He been swinging 'round the metal pole in the middle of the car since we got on the train, but my moms ain't told him to stop yet. I mean, no, there ain't nobody sitting near him or nothing, so he ain't bothering no one, but still, the boy do need some home training.

"Troy," I tell him, "don't get your clothes dirty."

"Okay," he say, but he don't stop or slow down or nothing.

"Troy, I ain't gonna say it again."

That get him to stop, but he mad at me now. He sit down on the other side of the car with his arms folded in front of him, and every couple seconds he give me his mean look, like that's s'posed to make me change my mind and let him act a fool. But that ain't gonna happen.

In the elevator of Novisha building, Troy point to the puddle of pee in the corner. "Look, Mommy."

She look but don't hardly react.

"It's pee," Troy say.

"And?"

For me and my moms, pee in the elevator ain't nothin' but a thing. But Troy don't remember when we used to live here in the projects. He a Pelham Parkway kid.

We get out on the seventh floor and knock on 7C. When Ms. Jenkins open her door, she smiling real big. Real big and real fake. I mean, she probably ain't got nothing against my moms, but they ain't friends or nothing. When we lived here at Bronxwood, they was just the kinda neighbors that be going hi and bye when they pass in the streets or at the store. That's it. I don't even know why Ms. Jenkins invited us for dinner when she ain't had to.

"Lisa," Ms. Jenkins say to my moms, "I'm so glad you all could make it."

She open the door wider so we could walk through, and when she ain't looking, I give my moms the head signal to remind her what she s'posed to say. "Thank you for inviting us, Bonelle," she say. "It's about time we got together."

The whole house feel real warm from the oven and, even from the front door, I can smell the food. My mouth start watering right away. Man, I can't wait to eat.

"Ty!" Novisha come over and give me the good girl hug. But even that is alright with me right 'bout now. It's hard to explain, but she just fit so good against my body. Me and her is perfect together.

Troy run past us into the living room and go straight for the computer. "Can I play a game, Novisha?" he ask, sitting down in the chair.

Novisha let go of me and walk over to him. "I don't have any games on here," she say, turning the computer on. "But we can go online and try to find something." She kneel down on the floor next to him.

Meanwhile, my moms and Ms. Jenkins sit down on the couch, and I just stand there watching them. 'Cause, to be honest, I can't really relax in this situation. I know my moms is gonna say something stupid and the whole dinner is gonna get fucked up. There ain't no doubt in my mind.

She start right away. "Bonelle, I can't believe you still got that big ol' console TV," she say, laughing a little. "And them same ol' Jesus and Mary paintings and all this religious stuff all over the place. Girl, you need to change this living room already."

Ms. Jenkins look 'round. "I don't know," she say. "I like

everything the way it is. It's my home." But I can tell my moms got her thinking. She looking at her own place like she seeing it for the first time.

"Your apartment is real nice, Ms. Jenkins," I tell her. "You don't gotta change nothing. I like them paintings too. They real nice."

She smile. "See how wonderful your son is to me?" she say to my moms. "He's always welcome in this home."

"Well, if he has his way, you gonna be his mother-in-law in a couple years," my moms tell her. "Because my boy is serious about your daughter, let me tell you."

"Oh, our kids are too young to be all that serious," Ms. Jenkins say, but she look a little worried. "Right?"

"Well, with the way they been messing around, we better hope they do get married before Novisha end up pregnant."

My moms start laughing, but she the only one. Novisha look at me scared, and I look at my moms mad, and Ms. Jenkins put her hand to her mouth and say, "Oh, Mother Mary!"

"Mom, that's not gonna happen!" Novisha say, standing up. "Tyrell isn't like that. We're not doing anything."

Ms. Jenkins look at me and her eyes is like fire trying to burn the truth outta me or something. "Ms. Jenkins," I say, "I respect your daughter, and me and her never did nothing but kiss. Honest. Don't listen to my moms. She don't understand that me and Novisha is in love and we gonna wait 'til we get married." Ms. Jenkins is still looking at me with them eyes, so I say real fast, "Married in the Catholic Church, of course."

It take a while, but them eyes start to go back to the way they used to look, and Ms. Jenkins even start breathing regular again. "I know my daughter very well," she tell my moms, and she smile like she trying to keep the mood friendly. "She's a good girl who doesn't keep secrets from her mother."

Ms. Jenkins don't believe none of what she saying and we all know it. My moms look up to the ceiling like she think Ms. Jenkins is a fool or something for thinking Novisha tell her moms everything. And me and Novisha know her moms don't really trust her 'cause, if she did, she wouldn't be reading her diary all the time.

Novisha give me one last look, like, that was close, then she go back to the computer and Troy. I hear the computer dialing up to go online. "So how's school, Troy?" she ask, trying way too hard to get the conversation off me and her.

"Good. I'm gonna move to a new class on Monday. And I'm gonna stay in my old class too."

"That sounds interesting."

While Novisha and Troy talk and search online for a game, Ms. Jenkins try to talk to my moms, but they don't really got nothing to talk 'bout. They don't got shit in common. So they start gossiping 'bout some of the other people who live here in Bronxwood, like who husband left her, who man got locked up, all that kinda stuff. They don't got one good thing to say 'bout no man. But that keep them busy for a while, and I get to relax a little bit 'cause least they ain't talking 'bout me and Novisha no more.

"Go set the table," Ms. Jenkins tell Novisha after a while. "And set a place for your father."

Novisha roll her eyes, but her moms don't see her.

"I'll help you," I say, and me and her go in the kitchen.

Novisha look pissed. She whisper to me, "God, why does she always have to include him in everything? I'm getting tired of this already."

"Chill," I say, then I tell her the same thing my moms told me yesterday. "Maybe she need him. You know, she don't wanna be alone no more."

"She's not alone. I'm with her." She get the plates out the cabinet and hand them to me. Six plates at a table that's only really big enough for four. "She's pathetic. He's making her look like a fool."

We set the table, but Ms. Jenkins and my moms stay in the living room. I can tell Ms. Jenkins is trying to wait for her ex-husband to show up 'cause she keep looking up at the clock every couple minutes. But finally at 8:00 she say, "Well, we'd better get started. Let's eat."

I go grab the computer chair while Novisha get the chair from her room. Me and her sit together while Ms. Jenkins start serving the food: fried chicken, baked macaroni and cheese, black-eyed peas and rice, collard greens, and corn bread. Man. Novisha wasn't lying when she said her moms was going all out for us. The woman threw down.

When Ms. Jenkins finally sit down with us, she make us pray before we can eat. She thank God for getting us all together and ask God to find us a new place to live at. She real nice that way.

"I don't know where my husband is," Ms. Jenkins say after she finish praying. The empty chair is right next to her. "He said he'd get here by seven thirty, but he probably got stuck in traffic."

My moms suck her teeth. "If you want a man to eat dinner with every night, Bonelle, why you divorce him?"

Next to me, Novisha smile, but I wanna smack a muzzle over my moms mouth. She embarrassing the hell outta me.

And she don't stop talking neither. "Now I know your husband was doing his thing out there, but girl, you know how them mens is. It's up to us to do what we gotta do to hold our family together, not get divorced the first chance we get."

For the first time since I knew her, Ms. Jenkins look mad. And kinda shocked too. But she don't raise her voice or nothing. She just say real calm, "Well, Lisa, it's easy to put up with a man when he spends more time in prison than at home."

Damn. Ms. Jenkins went there.

"I'm just saying, Bonelle, that I was surprised when you and Jimmy got divorced, being all Catholic and whatnot. I thought y'all wasn't even allowed to get divorced." My moms shove a huge forkful of macaroni and cheese in her mouth like she trying to eat as much as she can before Ms. Jenkins throw us out or something.

I decide to stop this before there be collard greens and chicken flying 'cross the table. "Everything taste delicious, Ms. Jenkins. You should open up your own restaurant, right, Troy?"

"Uh-huh." He bite into a chicken leg with his mouth all greasy and shit.

"Well, thank you, boys. But make sure y'all save some room for the sweet potato pie. I made three of them."

I look at my moms and she just acting like nothing happened. And me, I just wanna kill her for disrespecting Ms. Jenkins when all the woman do is help us. There ain't no excuse for it.

Through the rest of the dinner my moms and Ms. Jenkins don't hardly talk, and I'm glad. Then Novisha so-called father show up with a hundred excuses for why he late. Ms. Jenkins feed him and she don't even act upset with him. It's like she just glad he decided to show up at all.

When we finish eating, my moms lean back in her chair, all

full and shit, and light up a Newport right there at the table. I mean, I can't hardly believe what I'm looking at. She actin' like she in her own house, and she don't care that everybody looking at her like she out her mind or something.

"Um, Lisa," Ms. Jenkins say. "We don't allow smoking in our home. I'm sorry."

"Oh, shit," my moms say. "I didn't know that." She take the cigarette, get up, and leave the apartment with it.

All of us look at each other, but nobody know what to say. I know if me and Troy wasn't there they woulda all talked bad 'bout my moms, but now they don't say nothing for a while.

Then Ms. Jenkins stand up and start picking up our plates. "Who's ready for dessert?"

"Me!" Troy say real loud. He even raise his hand like he at school. That get Ms. Jenkins to laugh and then we all start to laugh a little. By the time my moms come back inside, we all eating pie and talking like nothing happened.

After dessert, I thank Ms. Jenkins for everything. Then me, Novisha, and Troy go back in the living room while the three of them sit there drinking coffee. Course I'm trying to hear what my moms is saying. See how much she embarrassing herself. And me. But I can't hear nothing.

Novisha find some website with games that teach kids shit with cartoon animals and talking letters. Troy don't need no more help. He just take the mouse and get to work by his own self. So me and Novisha sit on the couch close, but not too close, and when nobody looking, I kiss her on the lips. "Ty," she whisper. "My mom and dad are gonna see us."

"Shh." I kiss her again. I'm trying to get some tongue action going, but she don't let me. Man, I wish there was some way to get her alone, but that ain't gonna happen today.

Novisha rub my head, trying to relax me the best she can with her parents right there. "I need to do some of these braids over."

"Let's go to your room then."

She look in the kitchen real quick and nobody look like they paying us no mind. So she go, "Okay." We get up and head for her bedroom.

"Where y'all think you're going?" Mr. Jenkins ask us. Damn, we cold busted. And by her pops. "What, y'all trying to sneak away from us?"

"I wanna fix Ty's hair, that's all. We're gonna keep the door open, okay?"

Novisha don't wait for no answer. She just keep walking, but just as I'm 'bout to go in her room, Ms. Jenkins say, "Tyrell, come get this chair. I don't want y'all to get on that bed."

I go grab the desk chair from the kitchen and take it back to Novisha room. Then I sit and wait while she get the comb and the grease from the bathroom. This time I don't even look for the real journal on her desk 'cause I know it's only gonna fuck with my head. And I ain't even get a chance to talk to her yet 'bout that shit she wrote the other day.

While Novisha doing my hair, she ask me, "So, is there anything new? What have you been up to?"

"Nothing," I say. Ain't no way I'ma tell her 'bout the party 'cause she gonna get all worried that I'ma get locked up and, truth is, that could happen. So, I'm like this: Why tell her something she don't need to know?

"Nothing?" She act like she surprised or something.

"Nah, same ol' same ol'. What 'bout you?"

"Just school. Nothing special."

I know she gonna get mad, but I gotta ask her, "You get any more of them letters from that dude?"

Her hands stop in the middle of a braid. "C'mon, Ty. Don't start."

"What that mean, that he still writing you or what?"

She start braiding again, but hard and tight now. "Ow." That shit hurt. I try to move my head, but she got my hair in a grip and I can't go nowhere.

"Stop moving," she say. "Or this braid is gonna be crooked."

I sit back. "I'm just saying, I don't want nothing bad to happen to you, you know? I'm trying to do my job as your man."

She lean over and kiss the side of my face. "I'm fine."

She make everything sound so easy, when it ain't. When she finally finish the last braid, she say, "There's more food. Are you ready for seconds?"

"Nah, I ain't all that hungry, but I could go for some more of that pie. I swear, your moms gonna make me fat."

She laugh. "One big piece of pie coming right up." She leave the room and, without even hardly thinking 'bout what I'm doing, I grab her schoolbag off the floor and start searching it for letters. If she ain't gonna tell me what's going on at that school, I'ma find out my damn self.

Novisha bag got all kinds of sections and pockets with zippers and shit. I start with the big section, taking out her notebooks and shaking them out. Then I go through the small pockets and find a letter right away, folded up real small. I open it, and all it say is, "You know you want it." Damn. This nigga getting raw now. How he gonna talk to my girl like this?

When I get to the last pocket, I pull out some kinda small notebook that got **ASSIGNMENTS** on it. I flip through to see if she got any more letters stuck in there, but there ain't none. But then I see what she be writing in that notebook. Damn. It's another goddamn diary.

I open to the last page:

I don't know what to do about Jamal anymore.

That's all I get to see before Novisha rip the diary out my hands. "What are you doing? I can't believe you're going through my stuff!" She drop the plate of sweet potato pie on the floor, she that mad.

"How many diaries you got?" I ask her. I ain't screaming or nothing, but I'm talking kinda loud. "What you need that one for?"

"Shh." She roll her eyes at me. "You have no right going through my bag."

I lower my voice 'cause I don't want her moms or pops to hear us, but she ain't the only one that's heated. "Answer my question. What you need another diary for?"

"For privacy, what do you think?" She holding the little diary real close to her body now, like it's a football or something. "I need a diary that nobody else is gonna read."

"Nobody else, like me?"

She nod. "Yeah."

"Let me see it," I say. "We not s'posed to have no secrets from each other. Ain't that what we said?"

"Well, what about the party you're throwing tomorrow night? You didn't tell me about that."

Fuck.

"I live right here. In Bronxwood. You think everyone is gonna know about a big party and I'm not gonna find out?"

I can't believe this shit. "Who told you?"

"Everyone. But the first person was Patrick. He talked to me about it like I already knew. And Cal and his brothers have been telling everyone. I heard two girls talking about it yesterday at the laundromat."

"Why you ain't say nothing?"

"Because I wanted to see if you would tell me yourself. And you didn't. So, if you can keep things to yourself, why can't I?"

She got me. I don't know what to say to that one. "I ain't tell you 'cause I know all you gonna do is worry 'bout me. I was gonna tell you after the party was over."

"Well, don't think about calling me from jail. I'm not your mother. I won't go through that with you."

She take her little diary and leave the room. A second later I hear her talking to Troy all nice and friendly. I don't know how she do that. Just flip like that. 'Cause me, I'm pissed. Pissed that she keeping that diary from me. Pissed that she know 'bout the party. I mean, I ain't saying it's right, but sometimes a brotha gotta keep shit to hisself. But what a female need to keep secrets for? There ain't no reason for that. Never.

It take me 'bout ten minutes to cool myself down a little. I sit on the chair for a while just telling myself to relax, but inside I'm boiling. I don't get what's going on between me and Novisha. Things is definitely changing, and I just want everything to go back to how they was before.

When I come out the room, Troy say, "Look, Ty." He still at the computer. "I'm doing Spanish."

Novisha is kneeling next to him, but she don't look up at me. She just stare at the screen like she don't wanna face me.

"That's good," I tell Troy. I stand over him and watch him for a couple minutes. The voice on the computer is calling out colors in Spanish, and Troy gotta click on the picture that match the color. *Verde*, turtle. *Amarillo*, sun.

"You're learning so fast," Novisha say. The diary is right there on the floor by the desk. Man, she really protecting that shit.

"I wanna learn really, *really* fast," Troy say. "My girlfriend can talk good Spanish."

Novisha laugh. "Oh, you have a girlfriend, huh? That's so cute."

"And when I grow up, I'm gonna marry her."

"Wow. Is she pretty, your girlfriend?"

"Uh-huh. Pretty *and* beautiful. I never saw any girl as pretty as her."

Oh, shit. I'm now getting who Troy talking 'bout. "Finish playing the game," I tell him real fast. "'Cause we gonna hafta leave soon."

"But I want the church girl to hear me talk Spanish."

Novisha look at me, hard, like she 'bout to accuse me of something, but she ain't sure yet. "The church girl?" she ask Troy, still looking at me. "The girl you and your brother went to church with on Sunday?"

"Yeah, her."

"And she's very pretty?"

"Yeah," Troy say. "When she smiling, she is *real* pretty. But she cry when she get scared. That's why Ty has to sleep in her room, so she won't get scared all by herself."

Novisha look at me with the widest eyes I ever seen. It's like she don't know what to think or do. Finally she grab her diary, stand up, and run to her room.

I follow after her. "It ain't what you thinking," I tell her when I get in her room. I say it real low 'cause the door still open.

"You lied to me, Ty. You said she was ugly, and now I find out she's pretty and you're *sleeping* with her!" Novisha is whispering, but she screaming at the same time. I don't know how she do it, but she good at it.

"I ain't sleeping with her. I'm just sleeping in her room 'cause she all alone. She got two separate beds and I don't be touching her or nothing. And she a religious girl. A church girl." Novisha still looking real mad, so I keep going. "The girl was scared to be alone, so I'm just, like, her guard dog or something, you know. And I don't even got a bed in my room. They only got two beds in there, so where I'm s'posed to sleep? On the floor? With the roaches?" There still ain't no change in her face. Man, I'm screwed. Then I start talking faster, and can't stop myself no matter what. "And she is ugly. She fat and she got acne all over her face, and she got braces. And she Puerto Rican. You know I'm only into sistahs. I mean, you. You the only sistah I'm into. You, with your fine self. I don't want nobody but you. Nobody."

"Ty, I wanna be alone. Can you just leave me alone?"

"A'ight. That's a'ight. But you gotta believe me 'cause I ain't lying. There ain't nothing going on between me and that ugly girl. Honest. I'm innocent."

Novisha put her hands on her hips. "Are you wrongfully accused?" She trying to be smart now. "Just like your father?"

"Nah," I say. "That nigga guilty. I ain't."

She sit on her bed and she look like she ain't even hearing me. She tuning me out.

I don't know what to do, stay or go. But I ain't gonna just stand there like some punk, so I just say, "I'ma call you tomorrow, a'ight?"

She still don't say nothing, so I walk out the room. If she think I'ma beg her to talk to me, she could forget that shit. I'm out. The good thing is my moms is ready to leave too. She thanking Ms. Jenkins for dinner and getting Troy to do the same thing. All of a sudden she know how to act.

And my moms is holding a whole sweet potato pie wrapped up in foil. Man, we gonna have pie for days. If them roaches don't get at it first. And I don't know how, but Ms. Jenkins got her ex-husband to drive us all the way back to Bennett, so least we ain't gonna hafta get on the train.

In the car, Troy is 'sleep before we even get to the Bruckner. Me and him is in the backseat and he got his head on my shoulder. While my moms and Mr. Jenkins talk 'bout how much Bronxwood changed and all that, I'm just thinking 'bout the way Novisha looked right before I left. She looked like she was through with me. And that look hurt.

And I'm thinking 'bout that little diary she got. Who the fuck is Jamal? He the guy that be writing them letters to her? And if the fake diary is for her moms to read, and this new diary is for her own privacy, then who she writing that diary on her desk for? The one that was s'posed to be her real diary? She just been writing all that shit for me to read? 'Cause that would be fucked up.

THIRTY-FIVE

By the time I get back to Bennett, I ain't in no mood to mess 'round with Jasmine. To be honest, I ain't even in no mood to be with her. But I go to her room anyway 'cause I don't know what she gonna end up doing if I ain't there. I know how she feel 'bout being alone. And I don't want her ending up with none of them other dudes just 'cause I ain't feel like being with her.

The thing 'bout Jasmine is that she don't even see how upset I am. From the second I get to her room, she busy runnin' her mouth, like she been waiting for somebody to talk to. "I called Reyna today," she tell me, climbing on the bed, "and I asked her if she's ever gonna come back for me or is she just gonna abandon me like I'm nothing? And you know what she said? She said to me, 'I'm not abandoning you. I want you here, but I'm not gonna force you to be with me. And I'm not gonna let you force me to leave my new boyfriend.' Can you believe that? She said, 'He's a really nice guy, and I like him.'" Jasmine shake her head. "She just met that guy. How does she know he's a really nice guy?"

I take off my jacket and throw it on the chair. Then I sit on the bed and take off my sneakers.

"I mean, you should of seen the way he looked at me, Ty. Real nasty. But the only thing Reyna said was, 'I'll protect you, Jasmine. I'll make sure he doesn't do nothing to you.' Does that make any sense to you? I have to live there with a guy she has to protect me from?"

"What 'bout Emiliano? When you gonna ask to move back in with him?" Really, I don't know why I'm asking her questions when I know that's only gonna get her talking all night. But at the same time, I can't just sit there and not say nothing. No matter how mad I am.

"I'm gonna ask him tomorrow," she say. "I have to. You know what, Ty? Today, after I got off the phone with Reyna, Mr. Mendoza comes up to me and says, 'I know you here alone. All I have to do is pick up the phone and call ACS and they're gonna put you in foster care.' And you know what I said to him? I said, 'If you trying to get me to disrespect myself again, forget it. I got money now and I got a job, so go —' I don't know how to say it in English, but it's like, go screw yourself. And he just walked away and that was it. You think he's gonna call ACS on me?"

"He just trying to scare you so you give him some."

"I know, but that's not gonna happen. I hope he has a good memory, because that's the last time he's gonna see me naked."

"Good."

"You think Emil's gonna let me stay with him? I'm kinda scared to ask him. Why would he put up with me when he's not even gonna get Reyna back?"

"It looked like he really care 'bout you," I tell her. "He ain't gonna want you in the system, and he ain't gonna want you living with no guy that pro'ly wanna get with you."

"I know. I was hoping Reyna would figure out this new guy is a jerk by now, so we could go back home. But she still thinks he's a good guy. So Emiliano's gonna have to know she got somebody else. He's gonna be so sad. But I'm gonna talk to him tomorrow at lunch and see what he says. The only thing is, my time is running out. They're moving us out of here on Monday, right?"

"Yeah." Damn. Why she had to remind me 'bout that fuckin' job-training program they sending us to?

"If Emil doesn't want me, I'm gonna be forced to move in with Reyna. Because as soon as those EAU people see that I'm here alone, they gonna stick me in foster care anyway."

"Me and Troy was in the system and you don't want that."

"Were you in a group home or a regular home?"

"A regular home with a lady that made a living off her foster kids. She had, like, six of us. All the kids was little 'cept for me. I was eleven, then the next kid down was, like, five. She ain't want me there, but the city try not to split up brothers. Being there was hard, know what I mean? So if you got a choice, go stay with Reyna, and just sleep with a baseball bat under your bed or something."

"Or a gun."

"Word." I take off my pants, throw them on the chair, then slip under the covers. Jasmine say she gonna stay up for a while reading in bed. She laying on her stomach, on top of the blanket, showing off that nice, big ass in them sexy black panties. Yeah, she got my attention, but at the same time, I'm too tired to deal with females right now. Novisha wore me out today. I ain't got nothing left for Jasmine.

So I just pull the blanket over my head and turn away from her. I'm trying not to think 'bout nothing, but it ain't easy. I'm still pissed that Novisha feel she gotta keep shit from me. Like, she got some guy stalking her, but she doing everything she can to keep me outta it. But that shit ain't gonna work no more. Monday afternoon I'ma be waiting outside that school, asking everybody who the fuck Jamal is. And when I find that nigga, I'ma kick his ass and tell him if he even look Novisha way again I'ma be back. It's time to put a end to this already. Then maybe me and Novisha can go back to the way we was before all this started.

"Was it really that bad in foster care?" Jasmine ask, like that's all she been thinking 'bout all this time.

I take the blanket off my head and turn over to look at her. The book she reading is closed, and she just staring at the wall in front of her. "Yeah," I tell her. "It was bad. I mean, living with people that don't really want you 'round. And me and Troy, we had other problems you ain't gonna have. Like, when we was s'posed to have supervised visits with my moms at the agency, she used to hardly ever come, and Troy would be crying and everything. And when she did come, she was depressed all the time."

"That's terrible."

"I know. She was just outta it, you know. And she ain't get it together 'til my pops got outta prison. He the one that got her to show up to the visits every week. And he got her to take them parenting classes and go to counseling like the court told her to. And my pops even took a legit job, installing floors and carpets, just so the court would see he had a job and let him get me and Troy outta the system. We was in there for a year and a half, and my moms never did what she had to do to get us back. But five months after my pops got out, we was home. Just like that."

255

"Why can't your mother do anything by herself?"

"She don't know how," I say. Then I tell Jasmine how my moms and pops started going out together when she was fifteen and he was twenty-one, and how they got married a week after she turned eighteen, just 'cause she wanted to get away from her mother. And I could understand why too. I mean, my grandmother was alright to me and Troy when she lived with us, but she was real hard on my moms, always criticizing her and calling her stupid and shit. My moms said that when she was growing up, all she wanted was to get away as fast as she could. "Before they got married, my pops promised to take care of her," I tell Jasmine. "And he did, 'cept for when he was locked up. But she never learned how to take care of herself. Or us."

"And your father's been in prison three times?"

"Yeah. The first time he got locked up, my grandmother was there to help us out. The second time, my grandmother wasn't there no more, so we lost our apartment and ended up in a shelter. Then me and Troy got put in foster care 'cause my moms used to leave us alone at night. And now I'm trying to make sure that don't happen again. I'm trying to keep my moms together, 'cause this time, they ain't gonna find no lady that's gonna put up with no fifteen-year-old foster kid in they house. 'Specially no boy. Me and Troy definitely gonna get split up. Now he pro'ly be a'ight, but me, I'ma be in some group home having to kick ass everyday. And I ain't going down like that. I'ma be gone."

Jasmine get up off the bed to turn the light out. Then, when she get under the covers, she start kissing on me, trying to get something going. But I'm through. Only way I'ma feel better is to be out cold. Sleep.

"What's the matter, Papi?" Jasmine ask. "You go visit your girlfriend and now you don't like me?"

"It's nothing to do with you, Jasmine. I'm just tired, that's all." I'm kinda mumbling now.

"You and Novisha still fighting?"

"Something like that."

"You wanna talk?"

"Nah." I turn back over and cover my head with the blanket again. Talking ain't gonna do nothing. I gotta figure this out for myself.

Only thing that keep me going is I know, if everything work out the way I want, this the last week things is gonna be this fucked up. By next week my family could be in our own apartment again, and me and Novisha could be back where we was before. Tight.

THIRTY-SIX

In the morning, me and Jasmine just lay in bed as long as we can. I ain't trying to get up early 'cause I know that party gonna go on all night, and Jasmine don't gotta meet Emiliano for lunch 'til 11:30. Jasmine take out that book again, and she read while I try to go back to sleep. But she don't let me. She keep rubbing her feet against mines, trying to get me to laugh.

"Stop, girl," I tell her. "A brotha need his rest."

"I'm not doing nothing," she say, but when I look at her, she got a smile on her face. "*Nada.*" She start laughing.

"Yeah, well, you keep doing *nada*, and I'ma jump on top of you and tickle you for a half hour straight."

"If you tickle me, I'm gonna pee on the bed. I always do that."

"A'ight. You win. I ain't gonna tickle you. Not in a bed I'ma be sleeping in."

She laugh again. I fall back to sleep and don't wake up 'til I hear the shower running. The girl taking the longest shower I ever seen. When she come out, all she got wrapped 'round her is a towel. And 'cause she think I'm sleeping, she take that towel off and I can't believe I'm finally seeing her naked. And it's better than I thought it was gonna be. Way better. Course, I don't move or nothing on the bed. I just watch her get dressed, looking at herself in the mirror the whole time. And I'm enjoying the show she putting on.

By the time Jasmine leave for her lunch with Emiliano, part of my body is awake, even if I ain't. So I decide to get up and go back to my room to check up on Troy. In the hall, I see Rafael walking with his moms. They carrying Burger King bags and shit. "Tyrell, what time you need me for?" he ask.

"Meet me in the lobby at four," I say. "And tell Wayne too. And make sure y'all ain't late."

He salute me like we in the goddamn Army. "Yes, sir."

Then his moms, who look a little drunk, salute me too. I ain't lying.

I shake my head and keep going down the hall. In my room, after me and Troy scarf down the rest of them peanut butter crackers, I take him outside for a little while. We don't really got nothing to do, but tonight is the party and I know after I leave, Troy and my moms is gonna stay stuck in that nasty room all night. So I just wanna air him out a little.

We walk 'round for a while, watch some Puerto Rican dudes play basketball, then stop by the store for some sandwiches, chips, and soda for Troy and my moms to eat tonight. Then, when we get back, I get on my cell and call Dante, who try to tell me all 'bout the party he threw last night. "Ty, it was wild, man. The music was —"

"Dante, I got like eight minutes left on my cell. I just wanna know if the equipment is a'ight and tell you where you gotta bring it." He tell me everything working, and I give him the address. "Can you leave me the van so I can bring the equipment back to the storage place?" I ask him.

"No way, Tyrell. I rented that van, and you don't got no license."

Asshole. All of a sudden a nigga like him got rules? "Bring the equipment by between five thirty and six," I say, and hang up before he can say anything else. Then I'm sitting there, like, fuck. What I'm s'posed to do with the equipment after the party? Carry it back on the train?

I call Patrick quick and tell him the problem.

"My uncle got a van," he say. "He probably let me borrow it for, like, fifty. Let me call him, and I'll call you back."

Five minutes later, my cell ring. "He work 'til five. So he gonna come by here after he get off. Then I'm gonna have to drop him back home."

"Where he live at?"

"Queens."

"Shit."

"I'll take the bridge. It ain't gonna take long."

"How much he want?"

"A hundred."

Damn. What happened to fifty? But I don't got no choice. "Tell him a'ight." I flip the cell closed. Man, I got so many hands in my pocket right 'bout now, it ain't even funny no more. I owe everybody, and I ain't made a dime yet.

Before I leave outta there, I ask my moms what her and Troy gonna do the rest of the afternoon and night. If I had money, I would give her some so they could go to the movies or something, but I don't got nothing. Not yet.

"What you care what we do?" My moms got a attitude again. "You gonna be gone all night."

I put on my jacket and try with everything I got not to get in no fight with her. But I can't do it. I can't let her act like I'm doing something wrong when I'm doing all this shit for her. "Why you gotta start?" I ask her. "You know the whole reason I'm doing this party is for us, our family. You the one that told me I'm s'posed to take care of everybody, remember? Well, that's what I'm doing. And you don't gotta do jack. All you gotta do is sit there and wait for me to come back with the money. That too hard for you to do?"

She don't say nothing and, truth is, I'm kinda glad she don't. 'Cause no matter what, anything that come out of her mouth gonna piss me off. And I don't need that right 'bout now. Not when I'm 'bout to throw a party and try to get people to have fun.

I meet up with Wayne and Rafael in the lobby at 4:00 and they look like they ready to get to work. Or least they ready to get paid. It don't really matter.

We take the train uptown, then, 'cause the bus depot is out in the middle of nowhere, we gotta catch a bus from the train. The bus let us out by the shopping center, and that's as close as it's gonna get. From there we gotta hike 'bout three blocks north. I don't know why I ain't think 'bout this location before. How them kids gonna find this place all the way out here? Are they gonna wanna come this far just to party?

The only good thing is it ain't all that cold out. It's kinda windy though. We walk by the fence they got all the way 'round the depot, following signs that say EMPLOYEE ENTRANCE. And inside the fence, there's more than a hundred buses and, like, twenty-something of them trailers they use at overcrowded schools for extra classrooms. Lights is shining on the buses from extra-tall poles, but by the time we get to the back, where they got the employee parking lot, it's dark. And there ain't no cars back there.

Only one there is Leon. He outside by the back fence, right where he said he was gonna be at. He standing there smoking a cigarette and just chillin'. Still looking as shady as he gonna get.

"We all set," he tell us as we walk up to the back door. "The whole place is empty and the security system is off. And you don't gotta worry about nobody coming back, not 'til around eight o'clock in the morning."

"How you know that?" I ask him. There's something real strange 'bout this dude. Straight up.

"You think I'm gonna set y'all up in a place that got good security?" That's all he say. Wayne look at me and I just shake my head a little. I still don't know nothing 'bout Leon, and something tell me I ain't never gonna know what he really up to.

We all go inside and I get a look 'round the place. The first thing I think is, man, it's a school bus depot. For real. I mean, what the fuck was I thinking when I thought we could turn this place into a club for one night? There ain't nothing but rows of buses inside there. Yeah, there's a lot of floor space, but the buses is taking up half of it.

"There any way we could move them buses?" I ask Leon.

"We can't put them outside 'cause I don't got no keys to open the garage doors, but I do got keys for the buses. Some of them is broke down, that's why they inside, but the others, we could push them tight together and free up some room that way."

"That sound good," I say. "Wayne and Rafael could help you. I gotta go back outside and wait for Dante."

"I don't know how to drive no bus," Wayne say. "I don't even got my permit or nothing."

"Two hundred dollars," I remind him. "You getting paid to work, not stand 'round doing nothing."

I go outside and, 'cause I'm kinda nervous, light up a cigarette. I wanna smoke only half, but I end up smoking the whole thing. My mind is full of shit that could go wrong tonight. I don't know how my pops do this. It's too much pressure.

A couple minutes later, a white U-Haul van pull up to the gate. It's just like the kind my pops rent for his parties. Dante right on time.

I stand by the fence while Dante get out the van, slow, like he ain't gonna rush for no one, 'specially me. I don't say nothing to him 'cause I ain't got nothing to say, so I just wait for him to open the back door of the van. I ain't seen the man since before my pops got locked up, but he still the same. He still a slick-looking, cheap-suit-and-leather-coat-wearing asshole that think he some kinda old G from back in the day or something. He ain't never gonna change.

Out there in the cold, me and Dante get to work without really talking, 'cept when it got something to do with the equipment. "Grab one of them dollies first," he tell me. I climb in the van and hand him a dolly, then me and him unload one of the speakers. Shit weigh a ton too.

While he go inside with the speaker, I start unloading the crates of records and stacking them on the street. Dante come back, and me and him work together 'til the whole van is empty.

And I'm watching him too. I wanna see how he treat my pops equipment when he don't think I'm looking. 'Cause my pops don't be letting just anybody handle his shit. I gotta admit, Dante is careful, but that's probably just 'cause he trying to get all my pops equipment for his own self.

By the time I get back inside, Wayne and Rafael is now bus drivers. They moving them buses back and forth and pushing them close together in the back of the room. Wayne lean out one of the windows and yell, "Yo, Tyrell. Check me out."

"Least you know what you gonna be when you grow up," I tell him.

"Fuck you. I'm grown now."

Rafael start beeping his horn nonstop, trying to make a beat.

I start laughing. "Hurry up, assholes. Y'all got more work to do." No matter how loud I yell, I don't think they hear me though. I can't believe I picked them two niggas, outta all the people I know, to help me with this party. I musta been out my mind.

Me and Dante open up the three folding tables and set them up the way my pops do, in a U shape with the opening in the back. One table is just for the equipment, and one is for the crates of records. The other one is where my pops put drinks and shit, anything he don't want near the equipment 'cause, like I said, my pops don't be playing when it come to his shit.

My cell ring. It's Patrick. "I'm outside. Come help me."

Patrick driving the van he borrowed from his uncle. It's old, brown, and got IEB PLUMBING on the side of it. Patrick is outside unloading crates of CDs and DVDs that he gonna try to sell and all the digital equipment and music I'ma use for the party. We carry everything inside.

Then for the next hour all me and Patrick do is set up my DJ tables. Dante help out too. He put the speakers where we want them, and he use duct tape to keep the speaker wires taped down to the floor. He even tape the speaker wire to the back of the amp just in case someone bump the table and shit get knocked out. Just like my pops do.

"Alright, Ty," he say, when he done helping out. "You got it from here, right?"

"Yeah," I say. I know he want me to thank him, but what I'ma thank him for? He wasn't s'posed to have my pops equipment in the first place. I ain't thanking him for giving back shit that ain't even his.

He stand there for a couple seconds then just walk out. Me and Patrick look at each other. "What's his problem?" Patrick ask.

"He one of my pops friends from back in the day," I tell him. "But he the kinda friend I'ma hafta watch 'round my moms, know what I'm saying?"

"Do your mom like him?"

"Nah, but he helping her and shit, giving her money to get her hair did and, like, buying my little brother new boots. Got her thinking he a good man."

"Your father would kill that guy if he found out what he was trying."

"Word." I kneel down and duct tape all the power cords to the floor. I don't want nothing to go wrong that's gonna make all the music stop and kill the whole party. I seen that happen a couple times at my pops parties, and I ain't taking no chances.

While Patrick set up the digital equipment, I can't help but hook up the two turntables next to the CD deck. My pops use the Technics 1200s, and he always tell me that he bought his 1200s the same year I was born and, no matter what they been through, they still work as good as when they was new. Then he usually go on and on 'bout how all the new shit the DJs use now, all that digital shit, ain't nothing but garbage that's made to break after a couple years.

Now, I don't know why I'm really setting up the turntables when everything the kids is gonna wanna hear is on CD, but the DJ table ain't gonna look right without them. That's just me.

While me and Patrick is plugging in cables and making sure everything is working right, I'm calling out orders for Wayne and Rafael. First I got them sweeping 'cause there's all kinds of little screws and other metal shit on the floor, 'specially over by the work area where the broke-down buses was getting fixed. Then I got them helping to set up the lights over the DJ table.

When all the equipment is hooked up, I put on a Tupac CD and the shit sound real nice with my pops speakers. I mean, I'm really feeling the music.

Patrick feeling it too. He start setting up his little selling area on the third table with a smile on his face. Nigga came prepared too. He got empty cases of all the new CDs and DVDs, and he go to work displaying them so kids can see what he got. Then he put the crates on the other side of the U, near the wall so nobody can't take nothing.

"How much you selling them for?" I ask him.

"CDs is one for five, five for twenty. DVDs is one for ten, three for twenty-five. How many you need?" He start laughing.

"You make good money with that?"

"Hell, yeah. I go to all the city office buildings in the Bronx when the workers get paid. Man, them folks love to spend they money. They payday is *my* payday."

"Nice," I say. When my pops got locked up, I probably woulda went into the bootleg CD business myself if it ain't cost so much to get started. I mean, there wasn't no way I could afford all the computers and shit you need to make all them copies. Meanwhile, the MetroCard business only cost me $125 a month.

Course now, if this party go okay, I'ma be in a whole new business, and I'ma hafta save up to buy my own DJ equipment. 'Cause when my pops get out, I know he ain't even gonna let me use all his stuff no more. He gonna be, like, "You grown now? You wanna play parties and make your own money? Then get your own equipment and leave my shit alone."

"Who ready for some warm beer?" The voice is deep, strong.

I look up and see Regg standing in the door. Man, I ain't seen him in a while, and to me it look like he even bigger now. If that's possible. He not only tall, he wide, and none of it is fat neither. He, like, the size of one of them defensive linemen or something. Ain't nobody gonna get past him in this party 'less he let them. "Damn, man," I say, "where you been?"

Regg laugh. "Hot-lanta, man, where all the money is at."

I go over to him, and he grab me in a guy hug that kinda hurt. "Look at you," he say. "You look more and more like your pops every time I see you. Shit."

I don't really know what to say to that, so I just go, "My pops wasn't never this fine."

"Oh, I'm gonna tell him you said that." Regg laugh again. The funny thing 'bout Regg is his personality don't match the way he look. I mean, yeah, he know how to use his size to put fear in a person, but when he ain't trying to be threatening, he the most laid-back dude out there. That's why my pops like him so much. He can go from kicking ass to kicking back in, like, a minute.

Me and Regg go outside to his SUV and carry in the cooler, then go back for the cases of beer and ice. The cooler so big, it's only a little smaller than the size of a fuckin' coffin. Practically all the cans fit at one time. Even with the ice. We set everything up by the door where Regg is gonna be getting the money from the kids. Then Regg take Wayne and Rafael to work on the lights in the room and show them what he gonna need them to do while the party going on. I'm real glad Regg is there, 'cause he know what he doing. Even when I don't.

THIRTY-SEVEN

By 9:00, the room is set up. It's dark, but not totally black. I got lights set up over the DJ table, and Regg kept the lights on in one of the offices in the back of the room. So, people can see each other, but it still kinda feel like a club.

Cal the first to get there, and Regg almost don't let him in without paying. I gotta go over to Regg to tell him Cal is working the party too. "But he s'posed to be outside," I say so Cal can hear me.

"I'm just trying to warm up," he tell me.

"Why you can stand out in fronta your building in the middle of a blizzard, but you can't keep your ass outside now, when it ain't even all that cold out there?"

"You know, man, you getting uptight. What happened to the Ty I used to hang with?"

"Just stay outside, Cal. Bad enough we ain't s'posed to be in here, but I ain't looking to go down for selling no drugs when I ain't even doing that shit."

"Dude, have a beer or something. Chill."

I walk away from them, back to my table, but a minute later Cal do go back outside. I throw my pops headphones over one ear, smack another CD in the deck, and turn the music up loud enough so I can feel the vibrations in my whole body. The beat is nice, but I don't know what the fuck the rapper talking 'bout. It don't matter though. It's all 'bout the music. That's what gonna keep people dancing. If anybody ever come.

So in the meantime while we waiting, I just stand up there frontin' like I'ma real DJ. I'm playing one rap song after the other, and the music coming out the speakers is filling the huge space. Everyone standing 'round watching me, waiting for somebody to show up.

At 'bout 9:30, they start coming. First a group of 'bout twelve kids. Then, right behind them, another group of, like, ten. Course they mostly females, which ain't helping me make no money, but least they coming. I just hope I don't get, like, 75% females up in here 'cause that ain't gonna do shit for me.

Patrick stand next to me handing me CDs when I ask for them. All of a sudden, he like my assistant or something. And I'm working that CD deck too. Slowing down and speeding up songs, trying to mix like I know what I'm doing. Funny thing is, after a couple of real fucked up mixes, I start doing alright.

A hour later, I'm up to 'bout a hundred fifty people. Some of them is dancing, some is drinking beer, and some is just standing there. I get on the mic for the first time, and to be honest, I don't know what to say. But I don't want people paying they money to be bored and shit. I want them to have fun. So I just go, "How the fuck y'all doing?" My voice come out mad loud, louder than the music. "Y'all a'ight out there?"

Some of the girls yell something I can't really hear, but they smiling and looking happy, so I guess they having fun.

"Well, if y'all ready to party, I wanna see some asses shaking. And I ain't talkin' 'bout you dudes neither." I start laughing on the mic.

I throw on another song that got a nice break, and when it get to that spot, I loop it over and over. Then, so it don't get boring, I blend in the line from that other song I heard at Patrick house — "I like it when the honeys shake it, shake it"— and together it sound hot. Like my own remix or something. To keep all that going at one time, my hands gotta work the deck, but it's worth it. I gotta do something to make them new rap songs sound better. 'Cause after a while, they all sound the same. Not like back in the day.

I look over to the door and see eight hot females coming in like they a pack or something. They don't even look like they in high school. They probably more like nineteen or twenty. Them girls go straight to the floor, and they pick guys and start dancing with them. And they kinda freaky too. If they ain't had no clothes on, they woulda been screwing right there. Me and Patrick look at each other. We don't know where them girls came from, but they turning the place out. With them dancing like that, the floor start to fill up, and I can tell people is starting to loosen up and have fun. For real.

Patrick hand me a beer, like he know how thirsty I am. Me and him smile 'cause we working good together. Then, just when I think shit is going alright, I see Leon standing near the door, over by Regg. I lean close to Patrick so he can hear me, and ask, "Why the fuck he still here? I thought that nigga woulda been gone by now."

271

Patrick shrug. If people wasn't dancing and having fun, I probably woulda left the DJ table and let Patrick take over so I could go up to Leon and tell him he don't gotta stay or nothing. But nah, not now. He probably just waiting to collect the $200 I still owe him. Like I'ma leave town or something without paying his ass.

Patrick tap me on the shoulder and point behind me, to where them buses is parked. One of them freaky girls is getting in a bus with some guy. I smile, 'cause least somebody getting some. I sure ain't.

The thing is, one by one, them girls get on the buses with guys. As one girl pass by the table, I know I seen her somewhere before 'cause she look mad familiar.

But before I can even think 'bout it, out the corner of my eye I see a small group of people coming through the door, and I'm, like, damn. It's Novisha and her Catholic school friends — Shanice, Ana, and them same three guys they was with on Tuesday. I can't believe what the fuck I'm seeing. Why she gonna come here? What that girl thinking?

THIRTY-EIGHT

"Take over," I yell to Patrick, and rip off my headphones. In a minute I'm on the other side of the room over by Novisha. "What you doing here?" I ask, leaning over so she can hear me.

"Ana and I are sleeping over at Shanice's house. And the boys were there studying with us. Then we just decided to come to your party to see you DJ." She talking like things is alright between us. I look them dudes over real quick. I hope, for they sake, one of them ain't trying nothing with Novisha. That's all I gotta say.

Novisha look cute in her short red jacket and them black jeans I don't hardly get to see her in. I take her hand and move her away from her friends. "You talkin' to me now?"

She smile a little bit. "Yeah."

"'Cause after last night, I ain't think we was together no more."

"We are. If *you* still wanna be."

"Yeah," I say. "I do. I mean, we still gotta talk though."

"I know, but let's talk tomorrow." She put her arms 'round my waist. "You wanna dance?" She tilt her head to the side when she ask, actin' all cute and everything.

I look over to Patrick. He got my pops headphones on, and he flipping through his CD collection like a madman. But he look like he holding things down. For now. "A'ight," I tell Novisha.

We walk over to where everybody else is at and dance for two, three songs. The music is fast, so we don't get to slow dance or nothing, but we having a good time. Then I see Cal coming 'cross the floor in my direction. Why he don't understand what the word "outside" mean?

He come over to me and put his arm 'round my back. He lean over and tell me, "I got the call. Tina in labor."

"Damn, man," I say. "You lying."

"Nah, it's going down right now." Cal start laughing. "Her moms told me if I don't bring my narrow Black ass over to Lincoln Hospital right now, she gonna come over my apartment tomorrow and go upside my head. And she gonna bring her own frying pan too."

"Your mother-in-law gonna keep you in line," I tell him.

"Shit, she ain't my mother-in-law. But the woman do scare the shit outta me. I better go." And he gone, just like that. Me, I'm standing there thinking, Cal 'bout to be a father. Damn, that just mess with my mind.

Me and Novisha dance a little more, then I gotta go back to the table. Patrick starting to sweat a little, and he playing some real crap now. One of the dudes Novisha came with start dancing with her, but he keeping his hands to hisself, so I'm cool with that.

Since Patrick don't look like he doing no business, I get on the mic and tell everybody that, if they liking the music, my new assistant, Patrick, selling CDs. A minute later, he getting some customers. Folks came with money.

Then Jasmine show up, all late. She carrying her little duffel bag and come straight over to the table. When she try to give me a hug, I move away from her. "What?" she say.

I get close to her ear. "My girl here."

"Novisha? Can I meet her?"

"Nah," I say. "No way." I'ma hafta keep them two females apart.

I expect Jasmine to give me more of a attitude 'bout this, but she don't. She just leave from behind the table and go over to some of the kids from her old schools. She hugging girls and guys, but there's something different 'bout her. She don't look as happy as she was when me and her was promoting to them same kids. I don't know, maybe she just tired from working all day. But I can tell it's something else too. Damn, Emiliano probably told her she can't move in with him.

Two songs later Jasmine come up to me again. "When you want us girls to dance?"

I look out on the floor. Most people is dancing now, not counting the people hooking up on the buses. I don't wanna stop the music right now, but when I get a good look at her friends, I tell them to go get changed in they outfits. Them girls is pretty hot. Jasmine hand me a CD and tell me to play track three when I'm ready for them.

"Y'all got a name?"

"Yeah. We're called Caliente."

"I hear that."

275

Five minutes after they go to the bathroom to change, two girls from my old school get in a fight on the dance floor. They pulling at hair weaves and shit, and the dude they fighting over act like he trying to break it up, but he loving it. Smile so big it look like his face 'bout to break. And everybody else who was dancing is now cheering the girls on like they watching a fight at the Garden.

It take Wayne and Rafael to break them females up. And even when they being dragged away from each other, they screaming and cursing and shit. One girl sweater is tore up and she showing her bra to everybody. Every dude in the place is into what's going on. Females fighting always turn a nigga on.

I try playing music through the fight, but by the time the girls is off the floor, nobody is dancing, so I throw that CD Jasmine gave me in the deck.

"A'ight," I say on the mic. "Round one is over. Now we gonna have some entertainment. Come on out, Caliente."

The salsa music blast through the speakers, and Jasmine and her friends come out the bathroom in the shortest shorts and what look like bikini tops. And the way they dancin'— man, they working they bodies like the females in them Spanish videos. I mean, no, they ain't doing nothing dirty, but they moves is killing me. Jasmine was right too. Them girls know how to get the crowd going. Even other females is watching them shake they asses. And when they through, everybody clap for them.

I mix from salsa to a rap song, which ain't easy, and Jasmine and all her friends go into the crowd and dance with some of the guys.

Wayne come over to the table. "You need anything, man?"

"Yeah, another beer," I tell him. That's what I like to see. A dude that's working hard for his money.

Then, after I get my beer, I look over to see if Leon is still there, and he is. He still with his back against the wall. And right then, one of the freaky girls come off the bus with some guy, and I see her hand Leon some money. The girl turn 'round and now I know where I seen her before. She the girl from McDonald's. The one that was serving Leon. The one he said looked too good to be working there. And I musta been the stupidest brotha on the planet, 'cause all this time I ain't know what Leon was up to. But now I finally get it. Leon a pimp. Straight up.

That's why he wanted me to have the party here. He was eyeing them buses and knew he was gonna use them to make some money. It's so fucking obvious now. He wasn't helping me for no $350. He was helping me so he could really get paid.

I'm just 'bout to go up to him and throw his ass out, but I see Novisha friends on the dance floor surround her, and they screaming at some guy, trying to get him away from her. And I can tell by how mad her friends look and how scared she look, that the guy they yelling at is Jamal. The stalker.

THIRTY-NINE

It don't take me a second to run up on that nigga. He ain't even looking my way when I bum-rush him and knock him down on the floor. Then, before he even know what hit him I'm on top of him punching him over and over in his face. Blood shoot out his nose, and my fists is covered in it, but that don't stop me none. I ain't thinking 'bout nothing 'cept killing that dude.

And I am yelling at him too. "You put your fuckin' hands on my girl? And now you following her?"

Jamal ain't get one punch off me. He looking up at me in shock. "Who the fuck is you?" he ask me.

"Her man, what you think?"

He turn his head to block my next punch, so my fist connect with his ear. But that don't stop me. It's like I ain't even there no more, like I'm somebody else. Or a animal protecting what's his.

And just like my last fight, Wayne is there trying to get me to stop. "Ty, you gonna kill him, yo." I feel Wayne grabbing me from behind, trying to lift me up off the dude. But he can't move me. "C'mon, man."

"Fuck you," I tell Wayne.

It take Regg to get me off Jamal. By then, all the boys is 'round me, Wayne, Rafael, and even Patrick. The music been stopped, and everybody at the party is watching us fight, cheering us on.

Jamal get up and wipe the blood from his nose. Shit is thick and nasty. He take that same bloody hand and point to Novisha who crying while all her friends is hugging her. "That bitch is your girl?" he ask me.

I try to get away from Regg, but he holding me back with one hand on my arm. No matter what I do, ain't no way I'ma get outta his grip. "You calling my girl a bitch?" I yell.

He laugh at me. "Nigga, she got you believing all that virgin bullshit, man? 'Cause I hit that so many times. Busted her out."

That's it. I get away from Regg and I'm back on Jamal, punching him dead in the eye. I feel the pain in my own hand, the punch is so hard. But Regg is back, dragging me away, and Wayne and Rafael is pushing Jamal over to the door. Throwing him outta there.

Everybody eyes is on me, and my heart is pumping. I'm outta my mind. I break through Novisha little circle of friends, grab her wrist and pull her outta the room, down the hall to one of them empty offices. She crying the whole time, saying, "You're hurting me, Tyrell. Ow, you're hurting me." But I don't give a fuck.

I turn the lights on and kick the door closed. Then I take Novisha and slam her up against the wall. Hard. For a second she don't say nothing, and I know I probably knocked the wind outta her. I get up in her face. "Is it true?"

279

She cover her face with her hands and cry.

"Is it true?" I ask again.

This time, she nod. "Yes."

And man, it's like the wind is knocked outta me now. That pain hit my stomach like a fist. It take me a couple seconds to catch my breath, and when it come back, I'm breathing hard.

When I look at Novisha, she still up against the wall with tears rolling down her face. I grab both her shoulders and hold her there in place. "I can't believe you played me like this," I say, pressing her against the wall real hard. "I can't believe this."

And I know I could hurt her. I could beat the shit outta her right here. And I'm so fucking pissed at her right now, it's like my body is revving me up to do something to her. Make her feel some pain. The only thing that stop me is the look on her face. She scared. Scared of me. She look the way my moms did right before my pops beat her. Like she waiting for what she know gonna happen.

Damn.

"I didn't play you," Novisha say. She look me in the eyes for a second, then down at the floor.

"You let that guy —" I can't even say them words. But in my mind, I see the whole thing, him on top of my girl, and that thought hurt. It kill me.

I take my hands off of her, and she move away from me fast. Then she start rubbing her shoulders like she in pain. And I just look at her standing there crying, but I don't even know what to think or feel.

From the other room I hear the music start up again. Patrick even on the mic saying something, probably trying to get the party going again. He picking up my slack.

"Let me explain it to you, Ty," Novisha say after a while. She crying like a child now. "It happened before you and I started going out. At that stupid Bible camp my mother made me go to." She stop talking so she can cry some more.

Meanwhile, I'm just watching her, waiting to hear the rest of the bullshit. Bible camp was a year and a half ago. She was only thirteen years old. She really expect me to believe all this went on back then, and it ain't happened again?

"You remember how I was back then, after my father left? I didn't even wanna go to that camp. Six weeks away from home. Jamal was there. He was a little bit older than me, and he acted like he understood me and cared about me." She look up at me. "I'm sorry, Ty. I made a mistake."

"Just one mistake?"

She shake her head.

Damn.

"I didn't think I would ever see that jerk again," she say. "Then he transferred to my school after Christmas break."

"Then why you ain't tell me 'bout it? You coulda told me what happened. I'm s'posed to be your man."

"You *are* my man."

"Fuck you," I tell her. It's probably the first time she ever heard me curse, but I don't give a shit. "I mean, I'm here thinking you waiting for the right guy, and when me and you get married, I'ma be the only guy you was ever with, but now, come to find out you was lying from day one. So what I'm s'posed to think? That you can give it up to some asshole like that in a couple weeks at camp, but me, the guy you say you love and all that, you put on hold for a fuckin' year and a half? What up with that?"

"I changed after camp, Ty. I wanted to forget all about what happened. And I didn't wanna make the same mistake with you. So what I did was recommit myself to God and reclaim my virginity."

The shit coming out her mouth is so stupid, all I can do is look at her and shake my head. "It don't work that way," I tell her. "You only get to lose it one time, baby. You lying to me and yourself if you think you could keep on being a virgin over and over."

Novisha sit down on a metal folding chair and for a long time she just cry and tell me that she sorry, she sorry.

But sorry ain't cutting it this time. 'Cause, the truth is, I don't even know who she is no more, this fucked up girl crying like she got no sense. This ain't the same person I thought I was going out with. She fake.

Someone knock on the door. "Yo, Ty, we need you, man." It's Wayne. He open the door a crack and stick his head in. "Something about to jump off out there."

What the fuck else could happen tonight? "A'ight. I'ma be there in a second."

I turn back to Novisha. "Stay here." That's all I tell her. Then I just leave her there.

Novisha friends is in the hallway looking all worried and shit. I tell them to get in the office and don't leave 'til I tell them it's safe. Then I go over to the door where Regg is at 'cause I see something going on over there.

Regg is standing there blocking four thugs from coming in. And the way they looking at him, I can tell they musta got into something with Regg before I got there. Them four dudes is

282

trying to look hardcore too, but Regg ain't blinking. If they think Regg is gonna back down and let them in, they out they mind.

I come up behind Regg. When the dude standing in the front see me, he say, "We lookin' for Cal. Where he at?" Nigga got a gold tooth right in the front.

"I don't know no Cal," I tell him.

"You gonna be like that?" he ask me. "We know Cal here. We was just over at his building and seen his brother out there. And everybody know if he ain't there, he here."

"So what y'all want then?"

"We just wanna give Cal a message. Tell him and his brothers to keep they business in Bronxwood. That's all."

"Then why you ain't tell that to Greg if you seen him out there? Why you only wanna see Cal? 'Cause he the youngest and your pussy-ass is scared of Andre and Greg?"

The guys behind him start saying shit like "He ain't scared of nobody." Assholes.

"Okay," Regg say. "Y'all little niggas through. Get up outta here now."

Right before they turn 'round to leave, the guy with the gold tooth open his jacket a little so we could see that he packin'. Like he the man or something.

After they gone, I know if Cal was here, that shit woulda got outta control 'cause them guys was looking to hurt him. I go down the hall, back to the office where Novisha and her friends is at. All of them is still surrounding her and taking care of her like she the victim or something. Like she ain't do nothing wrong.

I take out my cell phone and call Cal, but it go straight to voicemail. "Cal, watch your back, man. Some dudes with guns and shit was looking for you, and —" I'm just 'bout to give him the message they left for him and his brothers when my fuckin' cell die on me. I'm outta minutes.

I leave the office and I'm 'bout to go back over to where Patrick is DJing, but I see Leon still standing there and figure I might as well throw his ass out first.

I get close to him and say, "Get your two hundred dollars from Regg and get the fuck outta here."

Leon fold his arms in front of him. "What your problem, Little Tyrone?"

"I ain't Tyrone. I'm Tyrell. And I know what you doing, and I don't want that at my party."

"Shit. I'm just doing what your pops used to do. How you think he made so much money at his parties?"

"He wasn't no pimp," I say.

"That what he tell you?"

"Get your money and get out."

"I ain't going nowhere," he say. "You think I set this whole thing up for you? I'm a businessman, Tyrell. I ain't leaving 'til I make my money. You understand that, right? You look like a smart boy."

I stare at him for a while, but I know he ain't gonna leave. And Regg ain't gonna make him neither. Regg knew what Leon was up to. That's why he told me to call him. I was the only one in the fuckin' dark.

So, alright, I ain't gonna sweat it. I leave Leon standing there and walk 'cross the dance floor. Patrick doing a okay job at the DJ table. The music sound good, and a lot of kids is dancing. But he doing my job.

So I do what I gotta do. I put everything that just happened out my mind. 'Cause thinking 'bout Novisha and Leon and them drug dealers ain't gonna help me make this party off the hook. And yeah, people is dancing and everything now, but the music me and Patrick been playing ain't me. And ain't this s'posed to be my party?

FORTY

I get back to the table, lean over, and ask Patrick if he can drive Novisha and her friends over to Shanice house. He don't ask no questions. He just grab his jacket and he gone just like that. Man, me and Patrick wasn't never real friends before, but he my boy now.

I flip through my pops vinyl records and find the one I want. Then I put the headphones back on, lower the music volume, and get on the mic. "A'ight. A'ight. I'm back, and I ain't got a scratch on me." Everybody cheer when I say that. Ain't nothing like kicking a nigga ass to get people to like you. "Now I'ma hafta change shit up on y'all. 'Cause, me, I'm kinda old skool, ya know what I mean? So, I'ma turn this shit out now and make this a real DJ Ty party. Y'all ready?"

People start clapping a little, like they kinda into it, but ain't so sure yet. So it's gonna be up to me to school them, make them understand this music. I fade out the rap song that's playing, and bring up the volume on "The Message."

The music fill the room and some of the kids keep dancing like ain't nothing changed, but some of them is looking 'round like, what the fuck is this? But 'bout a minute into the song, more people start dancing and kinda getting into it. And even the ones that ain't dancing is listening and moving to the beat. Man, ain't no way you could listen to this song and not see where the man coming from. Them lyrics is deep.

Don't push me 'cause I'm close to the edge,
I'm trying not to lose my head.
It's like a jungle sometimes,
It makes me wonder how I keep from going under.

And the way Melly Mel say them words, man, you know he feeling them. He talking 'bout life on the streets and how you don't hardly get to have no kinda childhood when you grow up in the hood. The song is mad real.

From there I start playing all kinds of old-skool rap. Whodini, Sugarhill Gang, Run-D.M.C., 2 Live Crew, Public Enemy. I mean, how somebody not gonna feel a song as raw as "Rebel Without a Pause"?

Meanwhile I'm working both turntables, pulling my own records, and trying to put them back in the order my pops had them in. 'Cause if something outta place, he gonna know it. The thing is, though, no matter how cool Patrick CD deck is, man, it ain't nothing like my pops 1200s. Them turntables is smooth, and it's nice moving them records back and forth with my hand, trying to find the right beat before I let them play. You ask me, scratching with vinyl is the only way to do it.

Another good thing is, after the first couple songs, the dance floor is packed. Only the people screwing on the buses ain't dancing. I mean, yeah, I know it could just be that these kids paid they money and they looking to have fun no matter what I play, but it do look like they into the music.

Jasmine out there too. She still dancing with her friends, both guys and girls. She smiling a little more now, but I can tell she ain't all that into it. It's like she forcing herself to have a good time tonight.

Patrick come back and give me a nod, like everything okay. Novisha and them is safe. Right away he start helping me out with the records 'til we working together like we been doing this forever. We having fun too. It's like we both high or something even though I only had two beers. That's how good I feel.

The party go on and on, and I'm playing every song I like from the seventies, eighties, and the early nineties, everything from Afrika Bambaattaa to Curtis Blow to Notorious B.I.G. And more people is still coming in too. It's like 1:30 in the morning and folks is now getting here. This girl come up to the table while I'm playing Digital Underground. She lean over to me so I can hear her.

"You play private parties?" she ask.

"Yeah."

"Good, because in March I'm gonna have a big sweet-sixteen birthday party at a community center in Mount Vernon. You think you gonna be available?"

"You got the date? 'Cause March is tight." Yeah, I'm frontin' like I be playing parties all the time, but sometimes a brotha gotta play the game.

She tell me the date and, course, I tell her I'm free that night.

I get some paper from Patrick and she give me her name and phone number, and I give her mines.

"And you can play some of this old stuff if you want," she say, folding up the paper. "Because my parents and their friends are gonna be there too, and they gonna love what you playing!"

When she leave, Patrick like, "You going legit on me?"

"You like playing at bus depots?" I ask him. "I mean, yeah, we pro'ly the first people that ever had a party in a place like this, but ain't nothing wrong with a community center party, you know, with people parents and aunts and grandmothers and shit. I mean, every now and then."

Patrick reach in his pocket and throw his lighter at me, and it hit me in the chest. "Shut the fuck up."

I laugh and put my headphones back on. I mix into "Wild, Wild West" by Kool Moe Dee real smooth. Then I look out and see Jasmine dancing with some guy, but she ain't even looking at him or nothing. She just going through the motions. So when that song end, I get on the mic and tell everybody I'ma slow things down a little bit. I put on "Fire and Desire" by Rick James and Teena Marie and take off my headphones. Then I go out on the floor and just take Jasmine away from the dude she dancing with.

Man, slow dancing with Jasmine feel good, but I ain't danced like this with nobody besides Novisha in a while. We got our arms wrapped 'round each other real tight, and we into the music.

You turned on my fire
And you burn me up within your flame
Fire and desire
And we're both to blame, both to blame

The weird thing is that, yeah, I'm feeling bad 'bout what happened with Novisha and how ain't no way we can be together no more the way we was. Still, I'm feeling mad comfortable with Jasmine.

"You okay?" I whisper in her ear.

She shake her head. "Not really. You?"

"Not really," I say.

Then I look at her face and there's something different 'bout the way she look. She look like a little child, lost and helpless and beautiful. I can't explain it, but I wanna kiss her, and not like the way we was kissing all week. I'm talkin' 'bout a real kiss. One that mean something.

So I just go for it and kiss them soft, pretty lips. And me and her keep on kissing for a good while. All through the whole rest of the song. It's like we in our own world or something. She kissing me like she really need me, and right 'bout now, I know I need her. 'Cause really, she all I got.

The party don't end 'til 'bout five in the morning. That's when I finally get too tired to play no more and the last group of kids finally leave. Regg give Leon his money so he can take his hos and get outta there, then Regg sit on the cooler so he can count out all the money.

Meanwhile, me and Patrick unplug all the cables and wires while Wayne and Rafael load the speakers and crates in Patrick uncle truck. Patrick all happy 'cause he made some good money, and he already talkin' 'bout the next party. Jasmine all quiet, trying to pack up Patrick leftover CDs and DVDs, but really she ain't doing much of nothing. And she still look a little sad.

Regg come over to me and hand me a thick wad of cash. Man, I can feel the pressure leave my body just holding that kinda money. "You still need to pay Rafael and Wayne," Regg tell me. "And you gotta give Patrick the money for the truck. But after that, you still made a little more than eighteen hundred dollars. And I'm gonna give you the two twenty I made from the beer. Y'all kids be walking 'round with too much money these days — I kept raising the price of the beer all night, and they kept buying it. I was up to five dollars a can by three o'clock." He laugh. "Now, with all that money, y'all should have enough to get out that shelter and get a small apartment or something."

"Regg, you don't gotta do that."

"Walk me to the door," he say, and I drop what I'm doing and walk with him. "You a good DJ," he tell me. "I had a good time watching you tonight. And you kick ass too." He laugh again. "Call me when you having another party." We get to the door and he grab me in another one of his guy hugs. "And tell your pops I'm watching out for y'all, okay?"

"A'ight. Good lookin' out, Regg."

And he gone. Man, that's a good dude.

It's still dark outside while we put the rest of the stuff in the van. When everything loaded up, I go back in the depot to turn the lights off so it ain't so obvious people was in there all night.

The place is fucked. Right before I decided to end the party, some drunk dude went 'round breaking windows on the buses for no reason, so there's glass all over the floor, not to mention all the cigarette butts and beer cans. And a lot of kids musta threw up 'cause there's all kinds of vomit puddles on the floor. The bathroom is a whole 'notha story. It's just plain nasty.

But we ain't get caught, everybody had fun, and I got rent money. Far as I'm concerned, that's all that count.

Patrick drive the van, and Rafael sit up front with him. Me, Jasmine, and Wayne sit on the floor surrounded by all the equipment, and all the plumbing shit his uncle got back there. We go straight to the mini-storage place and drive 'round to the side where our room is at. I jump out first and unlock our gate, then I get everybody working. I don't even pay Wayne and Rafael they $200 each 'til all my pops stuff is unloaded.

Man, every time I come to this storage room, I get mad depressed 'cause all the stuff that used to be in our apartment is here. Everything. Our living room furniture and beds, the TV that was in my room, all Troy toys and books, and my moms shoes and clothes. When we got evicted from our apartment, the marshals padlocked our door so we couldn't get in. Not that anything was still in there. The landlord already took everything out our apartment and brung it here. We had to pay the first month storage fee just to get in here and grab what we thought we was gonna need for a couple days at the EAU. We ain't know we was gonna be going from motel to motel for two weeks, then get stuck at Bennett for another. We thought we was gonna be in a real shelter by now.

I cover all the equipment with a blue tarp just in case there's a leak. Then, just as I'm 'bout to leave and get back in the van with the guys, I look over at Jasmine who standing next to me doing nothing. She been all up under me since we got there, and it look like she wanna talk.

"I'ma be right back," I tell her, and go out to the van. "Y'all can go," I tell them guys. "Me and Jasmine, we gonna get back to Bennett by ourself."

Course that just get them going, talkin' all nasty like me and Jasmine wanna be alone so we could screw or something. I don't tell them no different. Let them dudes think what they wanna.

I go back inside, and Jasmine is sitting on the dirty floor crying her fucking eyes out. She turned to a mess in, like, thirty seconds.

I get down on the floor with her, put my arm 'round her, and let her cry. She need to get it all out. Meanwhile, I'm just saying shit like "It's gonna be a'ight" when I don't even know what's wrong yet.

Finally she wipe her eyes and say, "I feel so stupid, Ty. Why did I have to ask him?"

"You ain't the only one feeling stupid right 'bout now, know what I mean?" My mind start to go to Novisha, but I don't let it. I need to keep my mind on Jasmine and find out what happened with Emiliano.

"Yeah, but I was —" She shake her head and them tears start coming again. "I thought I knew him. I thought he cared about me, like I was his own daughter."

"What he say when you asked him?"

"You know what he said? He said yes, I can live with him."

Now I'm confused. I mean, I know I been up all night and I'm starting to bug out 'cause I'm so sleepy, but if he said yes, what she so upset for? "Why you crying then?" I ask her.

"Because. You know what he told me? He said, 'You can move back in, but I gotta tell you something first.' He was acting all strange, Ty. He said, 'I've been in love with you since the first time I seen you, and I'm always gonna love you and wanna be with you.'" Jasmine start shaking now. "He said if I move back in, he wants me to be with him, like his *novia*. His girlfriend."

Damn. Every guy this girl meet just wanna get with her, use her. It's messed up. "I'ma kick his ass," I tell her, trying to remember the address where Emiliano live at. I'm pissed and he gonna hafta know it.

"Don't do nothing, Ty."

"Look, he try to touch you?"

"No, he's not like that. He told me he's not gonna pressure me to do nothing with him, not 'til I'm ready, but I don't know what to do. I thought he was . . . different. I wanted him to be, like, the one man who cared for me because of me, not for nothing else. Just because I'm me. And now I feel so stupid because he's not the man I thought he was."

"You don't hafta go live with him," I say, even though me and her both know she don't really got no other choice. Where else she gonna go? "What Reyna say 'bout all this?"

"She doesn't know yet."

"Well, ain't she, like, your legal guardian or something? She ain't allowed to just dump you somewhere and forget 'bout you. You her responsibility."

"But it's not fair to her, Ty. She's been taking care of me for, like, her whole life. She was only eighteen when our father died and she's been stuck with me since then. But what about her?

When does she get to have fun without some kid to worry about? If I go live with Emiliano, she's probably gonna feel relieved that I'm not her responsibility no more. She's only my sister, not my mother."

"Yeah, I know, but she ain't gonna want you with no old dude like that."

"Emiliano will take good care of me. You seen how he was with me the other day. He will do anything to make me happy."

It sound like she already made up her mind or something. I could try to talk her outta this, but what I'ma say? She gotta look out for herself now.

While I'm locking up the storage room, Jasmine change the subject and talk on and on 'bout her first day at work and all the mistakes she was making. "I know the lady was getting mad at me because she told me she was only gonna let me help another waitress for a few days, until I learn what I'm doing. Can you believe it, Ty? I'm an *assistant* waitress now. How pathetic is that?" She try to laugh a little.

I smile. "Yeah, that's crazy."

"Ay, *dios mio!*" Jasmine say, all of a sudden. "I almost forgot. I promised to help the lady at the church today. Remember where I took you last week? She's cooking for the homeless people again and I'm s'posed to meet her there at seven thirty. You wanna come back to the church? We can go get Troy first."

"Nah," I say. Sitting through two hours of Spanish church ain't something a brotha gonna do twice. Even for the food.

Me and Jasmine walk 'cross the parking lot to the street, and I grab ahold of her hand. I feel real bad for her, having to deal with all this. I mean, I know Emiliano gonna take care of her, make her go to school and the doctor and dentist and all that, but she gonna hafta give up a lot for that. And it ain't right.

We catch the train, and Jasmine get off at the stop before me 'cause it's closer to the church. It's only 7:00, but it don't make no sense for her to go back to Bennett then hafta walk all the way back to the church. When I get off the train I stop at a bodega and get me a $25 card for my cell. Then I buy orange juice, some rolls, cheese, and donuts. I want me, my moms, and Troy to eat a good breakfast 'cause I'm hoping we could go out today and start looking for a apartment. 'Cause if we don't find nothing, we gonna hafta go to the job-training-program place tomorrow, and yeah, Bennett is bad, but who know how bad that place gonna be? Probably gonna be worse.

I walk out that store with the food and still can't believe I got $2000 in my pocket. It's wild. One night work and I don't gotta worry 'bout nothing for a while. That ain't bad.

I walk in the lobby of Bennett kinda feeling good, 'til I see Mr. Mendoza behind the desk. I'm glad Jasmine ain't with me 'cause I don't want him looking at her the way he do. "Tyrell," he say as I'm trying to walk past him. "Wait a minute. I got something for you."

I stop walking. "What?"

He holding out a envelope. "Here. This is really for your mother. The ACS people left it for her."

"ACS?" I ask him. "Why was they here?"

Mr. Mendoza smile a little. "I called them."

I go over and snatch the letter out his hand. I try to read it, but it's like some kinda legal shit. Only thing I see that make sense right now is where somebody wrote TROY GREEN on the line that say CHILD'S NAME. Then it go, "The above-named

296

minor child will be placed in the custody of the New York City Administration for Children's Services pending a family court hearing."

And I'm standing there like, fuck, I can't believe this shit. Troy gone.

FORTY-ONE

A hour later, I'm in my room sitting on my bed feeling as bad as I'ma get. Sick. My moms fucked up again. She left Troy alone. One of the guards told me that Troy woke up, ain't know where his moms was, so he left the room and came down the hall to Jasmine room to find me. But when nobody was there, the kid just lost it, started crying and shit. Them guards had to come and get him. They waited for my moms to come back, and Troy even remembered my cell number, but course I ain't had no minutes left. Three hours later, when my moms still ain't get back, they ended up calling ACS 'cause they ain't know what else to do with him.

And I'm like this, what the fuck I do all this work for? It's like the party was a waste of my time or something. I mean, I did everything I could to keep me and Troy outta foster care, and my moms ain't had to do nothing but watch the boy. So, yeah, I got money now, but how that gonna help us? The cash in my pocket ain't gonna do shit for us.

And now, I'm so fucking tired and I can't even sleep 'cause I'm waiting. Waiting for my moms to come back so she can see what she did, see how she screwed up our whole family. Again.

I open that letter again and read it for like the fifth time. The front just talk 'bout how the city took custody of Troy because he was being neglected. Then on the back it say my moms gotta go to family court tomorrow morning, probably so they can tell her what she gonna hafta do to get Troy back. Not that she gonna do none of it. She never do. And I hope they don't think they gonna try and put me in no foster care too, 'cause I'm too old for that now. I can take care of my own self.

Sitting there thinking 'bout Troy start to get to me. I'm seeing his face in my mind and I just want him back. Here. And, to be honest, I get some tears in my eyes. I mean, Troy was probably scared out his mind when he woke up and nobody was here. Then to have some strangers come in the middle of the night and take him away. That probably scared him even more. Least me and Troy was together the last time ACS removed us. Now he gonna hafta go through this by hisself, and he don't deserve that. Nobody do.

My moms get back 'round 8:30 and she walk in real quiet like she expect Troy to be still 'sleep or something. And when she see me, she act all surprised. "You back already? How was the party?"

"You see anybody missing?" I ask her. My voice is flat and cold.

"Where your brother?"

I don't say nothing. I just hand her the letter from ACS. She open it but don't even hafta read the whole thing 'cause she been through this before. "Oh, no," she say. "What happened?"

I feel like I'ma explode. For real. "What you think? You left him here by hisself again. How many fuckin' times I told you not to do that? What the fuck is your problem?"

"Watch your mouth," she say. "You still a child. Don't think you grown enough to talk to me any way you like."

I get up off the bed. "Oh, it's like that? I ain't grown enough to curse, but I'm grown enough to work my ass off to support you, right?"

"When they take him?"

"How I'm s'posed to know? What time you left here?"

"Around midnight, but I was trying to get back before he woke up."

"Where you go?"

She don't say nothing. She just start taking her jacket off like I ain't even ask nothing. But she look mad guilty though, and that look say it all. She was with Dante. All night.

She sit on her bed and read the letter. Meanwhile I dump all the clean clothes outta the garbage bag, shake any roaches out the stuff that's mines, then put it back in the bag. The rest of the clothes stay right there on the bed. Then I go through the room and pack all my shit in that bag. I still got the keys to the storage room, so I don't gotta worry 'bout that.

"I gotta be at the court by nine thirty tomorrow," she say, "and I want you to come. You can tell the judge that I left you to babysit Troy, and you was the one that left him alone. Then they can't blame me, and we can get Troy back."

No matter how many times it happen, she still surprise me sometimes. 'Cause I can't believe what she saying to me. She want me to take the blame and cover her ass again. But if I did that, what's gonna happen the next time she fuck up? How I know the next time she do something like this, Troy ain't gonna end up hurt, or kidnapped, or killed? Fact is, she ain't in no condition to take care of a child by herself. She can't do it. Simple as that.

"I ain't going to court," I tell her.

"What you mean? You want me to walk up in there alone? Don't you care 'bout getting your brother back?"

"I can't go," I say. "Monday I got a appointment with a lady at ten." I pick up my garbage bag and open the door.

"Where you think you going?" she ask me. "And where's the money from the party? Dante landlord said we can have that apartment as long as we give him two months' rent and the security deposit tomorrow morning."

"Go be with Dante," I tell her. "I'm out."

I slam the door behind me when I leave.

FORTY-TWO

I really look homeless walking through the streets carrying the garbage bag with practically everything I own inside. I'm tired and beat down and miserable, but I still get to Iglesia de Dios del Bronx by 9:00, a hour late. I ain't think they gonna let me in that late, but they do, no problem. I sit in the back again with the rest of them homeless people and can't believe it was only last week that I was here before. With Troy.

I close my eyes and sleep, and the pastor gotta wake me up when the service is over. He say some shit to me in Spanish and point to the basement door. I grab my garbage bag and stumble to the door, so tired I can't hardly see straight. I just wanna see Jasmine and talk to her, let her know I'm leaving Bennett now.

Downstairs I find a empty table in the back. Ain't no way I'm sitting with none of them other folks down here. They the nasty kinda homeless, not like my family or Jasmine. 'Cause we been holding it together. We ain't just give up and stop caring 'bout how we look or smell. And that's the difference. Some people just don't care no more.

Jasmine is helping the lady serve the folks in line. She smiling when she give people the food, and I don't know how she do it, but she don't even look all that tired. The pastor come up to me and try to get me to line up for some food, but I shake my head. "*No hambre*," I say. I ain't sure I'm saying it right, but it look like he kinda understand me.

Jasmine don't see me there 'til after a lot of them folks is gone. She run over to my table. "Ty!" She sit next to me and give me a hug right there. "I thought you weren't gonna come." She see the garbage bag on the floor next to me. Then she look 'round the room. "Where's Troy?"

"ACS snatched him up." Saying them words feel like somebody stabbing me in my chest.

"She left him alone *again*?"

I nod my head.

"*Ay, dios mio!*" She cover her mouth with her hands. "That poor little baby." Then she start crying herself.

I put my arms 'round her and try to tell her everything gonna be alright. The pastor come over again. He starting to get on my nerves, you ask me. Him and Jasmine talk in that Spanish, and I know she telling him what happened to my brother. He pat me on the back and say in a thick accent, "You brother, he okay."

I try to smile a little.

Then the lady from the restaurant, Jasmine boss, come over to me with a plate. She made all them same things she had last week, and some kinda sandwich too. "Eat," she say. "Very good."

I can tell she don't hardly know no English neither. She seem like a real nice lady though, always helping feed people that don't got nothing. "*Gracias*," I say.

While Jasmine go back to help the lady clean up, I sit there and try to eat some of the eggs. But it's hard 'cause I feel sick to my stomach 'bout Troy. I'm thinking 'bout everything, like where Troy at right now, what he doing, what he feeling. I hope they find him a good foster home with somebody that's gonna treat him nice, and I hope he ain't gonna hafta go to a different school, not now when they was just 'bout to put him in some of them regular classes.

But no matter where Troy at, I'ma find him and see him. Ain't nothing or nobody gonna stop me. 'Cause I know the second he get the chance he gonna call my cell, and when he do I'ma let him know that I still love him. And I'ma tell him that, even if we ain't together everyday, we still brothers, and no ACS is gonna change that.

Jasmine come back over to the table when she through cleaning up. "What's the matter, Papi? You not hungry?"

"Nah," I say. "What kinda sandwich is that anyway?"

"You never had a Cuban sandwich? It got roasted pork, ham, and cheese, and it's so good. You want me to wrap it up for you to take back?"

"Nah. And I ain't going back there." I tell Jasmine 'bout the fight me and my moms had and how she wanted me to take the blame for her in court. "I can't take it no more, Jasmine. My moms need to grow up, and she need to do that by herself." Then I think of her and Dante, and that make me even sicker. "She gonna hafta work out her own problems while I work out mines."

"C'mon, Ty. Eat a little bit," Jasmine say, like she talking to a child or something. "You need to stay healthy."

"A'ight." It's nice, her trying to take care of me instead of the other way 'round. "I'ma eat."

"Good. I'll be right back. I wanna use the pay phone." She kiss me on the cheek before she go.

I sit there and take a couple bites outta the sandwich, trying not to think of nothing. Not my moms, not Novisha, not Troy. Not nobody. Then my cell ring.

I flip it open and all I hear is, "I got me a son, yo!" It's Cal. "He just got here, like twenty minutes ago. He twenty minutes old."

"A son. Congrats, man."

"Ty, the whole thing, the birth, that shit ain't no joke. I don't know how them girls be doing it. Man, it's crazy."

I start laughing.

"But you gotta come to the hospital and see him. He all wrinkled and shit. I hope he grow up and look like me though."

"What you gonna name him?"

"Calvin, man, what you think?"

"Little Cal?" I ask.

"Nah. C. J. Cal Junior. You like that?"

"Yeah, that's cool. You get my message?"

"Yeah, but I ain't worried 'bout them dudes. Andre and Greg is gonna handle them." He putting on his act again, like ain't nothing can touch him. "How the party go after I left?" he ask. "You make money?"

"Yeah," I say. Then I tell him 'bout everything else that happened at the party and what happened when I got back to Bennett.

"That's fucked up, man," he say. "But Little Man gonna be a'ight. He a smart kid."

"Yeah, I know. Look, y'all got a extra bed or something over there?"

"Extra bed? Man, I still got the bunk bed." Cal start laughing. "Remember from back in the day?"

"Damn, man." The bunk bed. When I used to spend the night over there, when we was in fourth and fifth grade, me and Cal used to do some stupid shit, like jumping and flipping from the top bunk, trying to be Power Rangers or something. Most of the time we just busted our ass, but we had fun though.

"Why?" Cal ask. "You gonna come stay with us?"

"Yeah," I say. Jasmine come back over to the table and sit down. "But I ain't sleeping on the top bunk no more, man." Cal and I both start laughing 'cause he was forever making me sleep up there. I look at Jasmine, and she got that sad look in her eyes again. "And Cal, I'ma have somebody with me, a'ight?"

Jasmine look up and smile at me.

"Cool," Cal say. "Greg over there now. I'm gonna call him and let him know you coming."

"A'ight."

When I hang up from Cal, Jasmine ask me, "Where are we going?"

"Over to Cal apartment. C'mon."

Outside on the street, Jasmine tell me she gotta go back to Bennett to get her clothes and schoolbooks. I throw the garbage bag over my back like I'm fuckin' Santa Claus, and me and her hold hands as we walk.

A block later, my cell ring. I let go of Jasmine and reach in my pocket, but when I see who calling, I just put it right back.

"Novisha?" Jasmine ask.

"Yeah. But I'm too tired to deal with her today." I grab ahold of Jasmine hand again.

"You still love her?"

"Course. I got mad love for her, but I gotta trust the girl I'm with. How I'm s'posed to trust her now?"

"You lucky you got somebody who loves you."

"I know."

"And you love her. Why don't you just start again with her? Try again."

"I wish it was that easy. I mean, my whole life was built 'round hers. I had everything all figured out, know what I mean? I thought she was —" I'm trying to find the right word to describe what I thought I had with Novisha.

"Perfect?"

Damn.

"Nobody's perfect, Ty. Not even you."

"A'ight," I say. "You got it. You right." But I ain't really think Novisha was perfect. I just thought she was perfect for me.

We cross the street and start walking down Barretto Street. "What you gonna do 'bout Emiliano?"

"I just called Reyna and told her I'm gonna move back in with him."

"She gonna let you?"

"I didn't tell her that Emil has feelings for me or nothing like that."

"What you tell her then?"

"That he still loves her."

I stop walking 'cause I wanna say something to her serious. I drop the garbage bag on the sidewalk, then turn to her. "You know, you don't hafta do nothing with him. Not if you don't wanna. Don't let him put no pressure on you."

"I'm not. Don't worry."

But I am worried 'bout her. And I don't even wanna say what I think 'bout a guy that would put a girl like Jasmine in a position like this. I mean, why she hafta go through all this just to get somebody to take care of her?

"This week was a test for me, Ty," she say. "Sleeping with you every night and not doing nothing. Now I know I can hold out with a guy 'til I'm ready. Even with Emiliano."

"Great," I say, and start laughing. "You tortured me every night, teasing me and everything, but I'm glad you got something outta it."

Jasmine laugh and wrap her arms 'round my waist. "I wasn't teasing you," she say, giggling in my ear. "I was teaching you how to be patient."

Man, she so sexy it ain't even real. I kiss her. "Patient for what?"

"For me," she say. We kiss again, and I wanna keep on kissing, but she stop me before I can hardly get my mouth open. "C'mon." She grab my hand again. I pick up the garbage bag and let her pull me down the street.

When we get to Hunts Point Avenue, I tell her I'ma wait for her on the corner 'cause, straight up, I'm through with Bennett. I don't even wanna see that place no more. While I'm standing there, I see some dudes playing basketball at the hoop I brung Troy to the other day and, man, it hurt that Troy ain't with me no more.

But at the same time, I do kinda feel free. I mean, I know I ain't s'posed to feel this way, but it's like what Jasmine was saying before, that her sister deserve her freedom. And I need that too. I need time where I don't gotta worry 'bout nobody but myself. I mean, it ain't my job to be no father at fifteen. I ain't Cal.

When Jasmine get back with all her duffel bags and shit, I decide to catch a cab uptown. I got money now. The second we in the cab, I throw my arms 'round her and start tonguing her. Deep. And she into it too. The cab driver probably watching us in the rearview mirror 'cause a couple times, the cab swerve and he go, "Sorry."

After the third time he try to kill us, we stop kissing so he can pay attention to what he doing. Me and Jasmine rest our heads together and both of us practically fall 'sleep. I'm dead tired. "Do we have to sleep on the top bunk?" Jasmine ask, half 'sleep.

"Yeah."

"Does Cal have to be there?"

"He ain't there now. Only his brother, but he gonna be in the living room playing video games. That's all he ever do. You wanna sleep right now?"

"Okay," she say. "Then when we get up, I wanna go out somewhere and have fun. This is gonna be my last night of freedom."

This gonna be my first night of freedom, far as I'm concerned. "I'ma take you wherever you wanna go. Your decision."

Jasmine smile.

"And don't think that after you move in with that guy, that me and you ain't gonna see each other no more," I tell her. "We gonna always be friends, no matter what. I ain't 'bout to let no Emiliano keep you away from me."

"Well, I'm gonna see you everyday at school, right?" She ask the question like she already know the answer, so there ain't no reason for me to say nothing. "How long are you gonna stay with Cal?" she ask me.

"I don't know. A couple months, pro'ly. Or 'til my pops get out."

The cab driver pull into Bronxwood and ask me what building I'm going to. "Building A," I say, pointing to the first building on the right.

He pull up in front, and I take the roll of bills out my pocket and pay the man. Before I can open the door, Jasmine stop me. "Promise me you not gonna start working for Cal and his brothers." She look all worried 'bout me all of a sudden. "Promise me."

"Nah, I ain't working for them." I start smiling, thinking 'bout the party. Yeah, there was some wild shit that happened, but it was all good. My next one gonna be even better. "I'm a DJ," I tell her. "C'mon, you seen me up there working them turntables. Girl, I got mad skills!"

Jasmine shake her head and start to laugh. Then I open the door and we get outta the cab. I stand out there for a couple seconds looking 'round at them eight buildings and, man, I gotta say, it feel good coming back home to the projects. Where I belong.

ABOUT THE AUTHOR

Coe Booth started writing "novels" in second grade, then digressed, working with teens and families in crisis in the Bronx and as a writing consultant for the New York City Housing Department. After receiving an MFA in creative writing from The New School, she finished *Tyrell*. She was born in the Bronx, and she still lives there.

For more, check out *www.coebooth.com* and *www.thisispush.com*.